THE HUNT IS ON

"Ready?" LaChoy asked.

I nodded, not trusting my alkaline vocal cords. My hands were sweaty on the rifle between my knees. I caught myself leaning forward, tight. Today was it. I wasn't in a pleasure bubble or virtual place anymore. No mind-expanding technicolored clouds, no blood-heating alcohol. No phony talk or phonier sex. I had got away from civilization, all right. All the way away. I had asked for it, and here it was.

BLOODSPORT

BLOODSPORT

WILLIAM R. BURKETT, JR.

HarperPrism
A Division of HarperCollinsPublishers

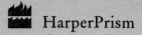

HarperPrism
A Division of HarperCollins*Publishers*
10 East 53rd Street, New York, N.Y. 10022-5299

ISBN 0-06-105822-X

Cover illustration © 1998 by Donato Giancola

First printing: January 1998

Printed in the United States of America

Visit HarperPrism on the World Wide Web at
http://www.harperprism.com

❖ 10 9 8 7 6 5 4 3 2 1

ACKNOWLEDGMENTS

Jesse H. Coleman, the first friend I made when my family moved to Florida over forty years ago, gave me the idea for Ball the year the first Sputnik flew.

Years later, Richard Baron roared into my weekly newspaper office to bitch about a typographical error which created an implication U.S. fliers were after Ho Chi Minh's buried treasure (hoard for horde) and stayed to become a friend. He introduced me to Python, taught the greer to sing, and inspired me not to give up writing science fiction.

Shirrel Rhoades, with whom I broke into the Sunday magazine business over thirty years ago, never gave up on me as a writer. Ultimately, on a recent visit out here to the Northwest, he hauled this manuscript back to New York City in his carry-on to find me an agent.

Wanda has co-existed with me in the thirty-year-long black hole between publication of my first science-fiction novel and this one. Which has to serve as some kind of record of forbearance in dealing with writer's block.

THE WAY IT STARTED ON PONDORO WAS ORDINARY ENOUGH. IF YOU CAN
call any of my life ordinary since Ball came into it.
We went aplanet without a hitch. Ball got passenger
Instead of baggage status due to the fact the ship's
crew were more like betentacled Balls and less like
octopod humans. I never did get straight what star-
cluster they called home. When the Pondoro Health
Authority robots had pretty thoroughly impressed us
with their fastidiousness, we finally were allowed
as far as the Customs Shed via floater. Ball balanced
his weight on a bench seat meant for three more or
less human types and made little feedback noises
about the sanitizing process. I had been around him
just long enough to know the muttering meant trouble.

We were last off the floater and went into the last
unoccupied Customs cubicle. As soon as the balding
Cervantes caricature behind the counter did a double
take on Ball, I knew how the trouble was going to
start. Pondoro thinking is that experimental men
should be made in man's image. Ball's thinking of
course is just contrariwise.

The Customs agent of the sad countenance looked
from Ball to me and shook his head.

"It seemed like a good idea at the time." I passed
my passport, ID chip, and media rep carte across his
counter.

"How does it seem now?" Sad asked.

"Not as good," I admitted. "But I was drunk on good free whiskey, and things looked brighter then."

"I trust your host's cabinet justified the error in judgment."

Pretty good for a petty bureaucrat on a back-planet. Ball, of course, didn't think so.

"The only mistake here apparent," came the sullen rejoinder from somewhere in the neutral sphere of his manbuilt exoskeleton, "is that your mother's rapists were spermatically effective."

I cringed, but the agent hardly batted an eye. Customs work on the gates of Pondoro could harden one, I suppose.

"It's a pity, isn't it?" Sad asked me, ignoring Ball.

"What? Ball?"

"A pity robot designers no longer revere Asimovian ideals," he said. "The nonstandard shapes are part of it, too, mark my words. Decay, that's what it is. Just decay."

Ball applied power and bounced sharply up onto the counter, scattering the news flimsy the agent had been reading. The voice he chose was sweet reason.

"How can simple vocalization of a glaringly evident fact be considered at variance to those venerable duties of robots—if I were one, which I'm not?"

The sphere-shoving act startled the agent, but he stood his ground manfully.

"Your classification, InterGalactic Cybernetics TS-T-210 (Experimental Cyborg), is, under Pondoro statutes, closer to *machine* than *citizen*," he said. "On Pondoro, injury to a human, per *Asimov*, has been defined by our highest courts to include oral abuse."

"Oh," said Ball in a small voice.

The Customs man started to relax, having trotted out the law.

"Oh," said Ball again, "are *you* what passes hereabouts for human?"

The Customs man vibrated like a strummed guy wire and came out of it rigid and with his shape-prejudice showing.

"I think that's enough, *machine*," he said, deadly calm.

"Not a bit of it, *citizen*," Ball breezed. "*Enough* is yet to come. . . ."

As the Customs man had completely forgotten my existence, and since Ball has never been entirely sure of it to start with, I walked on through the turnstile. Out on the crowded movewalks I skipped walks until I found a bar. By the time Ball had reduced the Customs man to legal action or a straitjacket, I had time for at least one quick one. I wasn't sure whether the Pondoro jails served cocktails or not, but the frontier nature of the planet argued against it. I figured to have a head start on them.

The bar was crowded with hunters and guides, and there was a ratty insect-chewed hide sprawled the breadth of one wall, with golden small-lights moving on its purple-black sheen. I've seen better pelts after the wolves back on Acme, up in the North Continent highlands, got through with a winter-weak *fragle*. Still, it was the last temporal remains of a Pondoro wolverine, and some of the obvious tourists were staring at it fixedly. Others glanced at it from time to time with a look of impossible superiority on their faces. Those would be the successful hunters, waiting to space out, back to the fat central planets and whatever empires they were building.

A couple of the faces were easy to pick out as

regulars on newscasts. Others bore the stamp of idle millions. I had come to know that particular look pretty well in the jungle of never-ending partygoing and gaming and the rest of it that followed as naturally as royalty payments when I finally got the good parts and the bad of Acme out of my system and down onto words that could be sold. The jungle those faces were carved in was rougher than the big woods of Acme, and probably rougher than the wilds of Pondoro, the Pondoro wolverine notwithstanding.

I looked at the hide again and sipped my drink. When the writing finally went stale and I knew nothing else was going to come out clean, I lost all of it but the journalism. I was living in the pocket of ones like those whose faces I saw here, and they enjoyed me, and used me for whatever satisfaction they got from it. The women especially had been bad, though some weren't too bad. Some of the men never did understand that when you're born and shaped in a place like those old Acme highlands, some things just won't work.

By the time I understood it again, and got ready to break it off, nothing really seemed to have any point anymore, not even getting away from that pack and into real air again. I tried to go home to Acme but it was no good. To be the way I had remembered and then wrote it, it had to be grown up in. I could not have written it if I had stayed there always, but after I wrote it I couldn't go back and be that way again.

The you-can't-go-home-again theme has been pretty well mined out over the ages, and there was nothing for me to write about my life since Acme, except a deepening and complete self-disgust. Enough of that has survived the various civilizations and their collapses that got mankind to here. Too much.

I was ripe for any new thing when I came across the old drunk at a weeklong party where it was over with the cybernetics heiress for the final time and I couldn't see anywhere left to go but under.

A full-body mount of a Pondoro wolverine in the host's trophy room caught my eye. The old man noticed and came over. "They named 'em *wolverine* from some animal of Old Earth," he told me. "One of its most ruthless hunters. On Pondoro, they call 'em greers. Bigger than a *soponik*, smaller than a kodiak. This was my best one, so I spent enough to support a poor planet for a fiscal year to have this done by the robot who did my Earthtrout and tiger. My worst took my right leg and I had hell's own time getting a proper new one that grew just right and everything."

"I've never read anything about it, though," I said. "I've never even heard of Pondoro."

"Nobody's ever written the greer," the old man said. "I can tell you about how it is to hunt greer, but there's no way I can make you see it. Haro was better at it than me, but last season his best greer of all was faster. There wasn't enough left to build a new body on, and that was the end of Haro. He kept going back and going back, until he was dead. These"— with a disdainful wave at his guests—"just don't understand that kind of thing at all.

"But nobody has ever written the greer. Nobody ever could, until you. You could write the greer and make us all remember and maybe some others really see. You could write him and make them taste the fear. I went to Acme once because of what you wrote about the *fragle*. I never did get a decent trophy. But a man who grew up hunting *fragle* could hunt the greer and then write it. You could do it, but if you don't, I guess it may never get done."

Drunken sentimentality, but it got something going again in me way down deep, and I guarded it and never let anybody know it was there. I took an advance on Sirius III royalties and started outfitting. Right up until departure it seemed impossible I truly was leaving all that.

Some idiot cousin of the cybernetics heiress, who didn't know about how that had ended, or maybe who did and was extracting a subtle family vengeance, built a fantastic farewell party and in the middle of it unveiled Ball, the newest creation in his company's cybernetic/organic symbiotes. Designed as the ever-perfect secretary, Ball was the peerless prototype, the like of which would never be built again. The cousin said Ball was a spherical super-Friday for a stellar Crusoe, losing me as to which mythical heroes he referred, and offered me Ball at cost, a mere half of what I had left, which was still enough to buy a good-size fiefdom on a backward world.

In the midst of all those to whom I had become the house-trained hairy man in residence, I was too much of a social coward to refuse. Anyway, I was drunk enough to somehow get the idea Ball could do all my word-processing, take pictures of me and my trophy or my trophy and me, whichever came first, drive away autograph seekers and mix manhattans in a special compartment in his neuter globe. As I told the Customs agent, it seemed like a good idea at the time.

"Mr. Ramsey?"

I looked up. The Customs agent was at my elbow in the bar, post abandoned.

"You found me easy enough."

"Your credentials, sir." He handed them across. I noticed that Ball's disk was in order.

I looked at the man. He had a certain vague aspect about the eyes. "Are we free to go?" I asked.

"You are more than free," he said with sudden animation. "Listen: go anywhere you like. Pondoro is free. Also large, though with lots of ocean. But go. Please go. Please take your—your—"

"Ball Friday?" I suggested.

"Friday ball," he said. "Take your Friday ball and *get the hell away from me!*" He collapsed on a stool.

I caught the eye of the bartender. "Twice what he was going to drink. All doubles. Bill me at Hunter's Rest. Keith Ramsey."

The agent looked up at me. "Can't. Duty—"

"Screw duty," I said. "You've done yours for the week." I took the credentials from him and started for the door. He was ordering before I got out, and it looked as if he were going to take me seriously. To hell with it, it was only money.

Wondering how it was that I wasn't in jail already, my first day on Pondoro, I went to look for Ball before the broken man in the bar could let my liquor fire up the vengeful side of his nature.

2

SUNTO KILLED AND FED IN THE FALSE DAWN, BLOOD AND DEW ON HIS claws and neck fur. He quenched his thirst in a misting rivulet that bounded down a cliff from the loftier peaks of his hunting range, and evacuated his bowels healthily, before he made his way to the meadow of the council pool. By the time he reached that shrine, dayfire was on the crags, burnishing their stone to deep purple brilliance, and was hunting the lower ridges for the last of night.

He had hunted formally today, spurning the younger rams of the herd he kept in the breaks above the council pool. His lower belly had cried out in simple body hunger for the warm, strong flesh of the youngsters, but his higher belly knew more than mere food was needed for this pilgrimage. So he hunted the old herd ram, which had escaped him before this, determined to go hungry to the pool if he failed.

His belly, seat of all knowledge and hunting power, fashioned invisible nets of fear around his chosen quarry, unstrengthened by that flaring full-bellied force that could hold a bison herd in blizzard country against all its collective instinct to migrate to its winter home. Such force, brutally applied, would have melted the old ram's courage and forced it blind with terror to the shallow alluvial terrace where Sunto waited to break his fast.

But such brute force would leave nothing of the

ram's courage for its slayer to drink with its blood, so the ram moved to its fate at a natural pace, nervous but without suspicion. It was a hunt worthy of a hunt singer, to sing it down among the hahns that old Sunto of the Orange Claw still was best of them all.

Sunto somberly considered his spirit brother in the surface of the pool, and his brother faithfully studied him. A pebble dislodged into the pool could shatter his brother's visage as no natural blow, but the big-shouting fireclaw of a Two-Legs could shatter his own. But the waters of the pool would regain their calm, and the brother would return to mimic his dislodger scowl for scowl, as no hunter ever returned from the well-struck blow of a Two-Legs.

He considered the ancient puzzle of cubhood: where does the spirit brother hunt, when the flesh brother forever leaves the pool? But his stomach quickly provided another, grimmer question: where would all spirit brothers hunt if all hunters forever left the pool? And he was back in the grip of the awful dream that had awakened him in his mountain den, hackles lifting. The change in him had wakened his mate, a low rumble of half fear rising in her throat as she sensed the strangeness on him.

"Sunto, what *troubles* thou?" It was an accusation, as if the thing that drove him from his sleep was his own doing. But she was heavy with pregnancy, and irritable.

"I smell tomorrow." Shivering.

He heaved out of his sleeping crouch, regretting loss of body warmth in the tangled moss, but unable to lie quietly.

"I smell tomorrow, and it is full of peril! The hunt, the hahns, the very herds we live by—danger,

danger—don't thou *smell* it? The lesson of the Permanent Lairs, coming now to pass . . ."

The belligerence went out of her then, supplanted by an almost superstitious awe. "Speak not of the Permanent Lairs with the cublings so near birthing—would thou mark them with that old madness? Out, Sunto—out, old Orange Claw dreamer! Run the bare mountains, hunt, drink good hot blood—that's what thou need to wash away this fever!"

There was no point in arguing—Sunto went.

And now the pool, strange premonition uneased. The meadow's life moved nervously around the furry form crouched at its shrine. A small winged hunter stooped clumsily, half missed its mark. Its prey skittered off unevenly, leaving an erratic tracing of dark blood on the still-damp grass. A flock of bright-feathered fowl, which had frozen in a bright-leaved thicket when the winged hunter struck, now exploded in a wasted burst of fear sound and buzzed off down the falling ground. Came a snort and crash upwind as a hilldeer, coming to the water, suddenly sensed the neural leakage from Sunto's troubled belly and fled with no scent to guide it.

The Permanent Lairs. Always, those had been the danger, humping stubbornly above the ground where the large glacier river flowed out onto the plains. There had the Orange Claw hahn of his fathers ranged, and in its pride turned aside from the natural order of things. Fullest-bellied of all hunters, finest trackers ever known, invincible in the brutal hahn wars of those bygone times, their blind pride had sown the seed of Orange Claw ruin. They alone defied the rhythm of the seasons and stayed in their sheltered valley while all other things great and small followed the dayfire's migration to its winter home.

For survival of their winter-born cubs, they raised Permanent Lairs of river stone, muscled into place with the fear-driven labor of the huge, slow-footed eaters of tree trunks, and cemented firm by the big-toothed, flat-tail river dam-builders, working in a near coma of dread. For their winter diet the hahn marshaled a well-mixed herd of fat plains game in the valley. Young hunters sharpened their stomachs by holding the herd against its mindless drive to migrate. The Permanent Lairs had seemed the finest thing a stomach could digest, much envied by the hahns, before the Lesson fell upon the Orange Claw.

It was a Lesson then, as now, beyond misreading.

Those of the Orange Claw who survived its learning hunted the mountains far from those accursed Lairs from that point forward. Hunted far, and sickened and died—or changed—beneath the poison winds the Lesson spawned. All hahns knew fear when the Lairs would not fall back of themselves into the mother water, but none would risk marshaling the builder-beasts again, to undo the mischief, for fear of calling down another Lesson.

Sunto shifted uneasily.

Now, visions of those slowly eroding structures haunted his belly when he woke and when he slept. His recurring dream was of the dayfire come down from heaven, coalesced into a burning ball of flame to hunt among the Permanent Lairs for the spoor of the builders. . . .

Such a vision was sheer madness. The hunting thing in the dream was kin, and yet not kin, to Two-Legs. It was spirit brother to the bright boulders light as thistle in which Two-Legs floated from hunt to hunt, and in its heart and in its hide the lurid dayfire burned.

Sunto's dreams had begun when that strange long Two-Legs without a fireclaw had denned these recent seasons in the Permanent Lairs. The long Two-Legs did not hunt, and would not be hunted, though full-bellied hunters tried their stomachs against him. He denned, he ate, he wandered the Orange Claw valley as on a quest. His belly called strongly and strangely, but he did not hunt.

Or did he?

The long Two-Legs held the hidden memory of the hunting dayfire ball deep within his own belly, that much was clear. It was a puzzle, but Sunto's belly told him it was so, reading things beyond the reach of eye and claw.

Reading of the puzzle was heavy work, too heavy for solitary brooding by the pool. Sunto raised his heavy head to study the innocent reflection of dayfire where it gathered in the council pool, then sent his silent summons flashing to the hahns.

3

IT WAS GOOD TO GET AWAY FROM THE CITY. THE SMALL HUNTING CAR dived smoothly into the evening sky and settled onto a course the dash compass called north. Cold night air breathed into the cockpit from pressure-vents.

"Mind?" the pilot asked.

"No," I said, and the Pondoro air flowed more freely.

The raw chill, after weeks of the spacer's rigidly controlled environment, was good on my skin. We were low enough for it to have a fresh dirt smell to it, and then the pungent odor of a salt sea, and that was good, too.

"Ramsey?" Ball loomed, incongruous, in the rear passenger seating.

"What?" I didn't want conversation now. Not with Ball, not with anybody.

The rejoinder was suspiciously gentle. "The empathometer is reading well into the creative zone. Do you wish to vocalize?"

For a moment I had forgotten what century we were in. Izaak Walton and Hemingway and all those back then were lucky; they never had their quill and inkwell fitted out with Ball's technology. They could loaf when they wanted to, without having to justify it to their writing machinery.

"No," I said. "Let it build. It's been a long time gone."

"Not in fact," said Ball. "Simply out of use. According to the readout—"

"Let it rest, Ball."

"Are you sure?"

"I'm very sure."

And they didn't get pep talks from their writing equipment, either. I was beginning to realize why Intergalactic Cybernetics had scrapped the design. There are certain points beyond which humans still won't be pushed. The meter must have wavered, because Ball shut up. The pilot concentrated on his driving. No automatics. I liked that, too.

I lay back in the right-hand seat and let the feel of the dark bulk of the world beneath us come up. The odors. Now I could distinguish faint, indefinable alienness. At first it had smelled like home. Like Acme. Like Old Earth, for that matter. Funny how you immediately catalog the familiar before you start on the strange. The world below was hospitable to terrestrials, so it was home immediately by contrast to the spaceship. Not for the first time I wondered what makes spacemen tick. But I really wasn't interested, no more than I was interested in what makes big-city cab drivers tick.

The guide was named Nail. Just that. Small, quick-moving man with lots of sun and weather on his face and arms, eyes that looked nervous until you saw they were looking at everything instead of away from anything. Hunter's eyes. And a bit of hunted, too. Enough hunted to increase my respect for the greer, sight unseen.

"Where're we headed?" I asked.

"Straight to camp. Unless you'd rather stop at the lodge." A sideward dip of his head indicated my shipboard informals.

"No. The camp it is. I'll change right there. I did want to sight my gun for Pondoro atmosphere, though. Will we be too close to the game?"

"LaChoy has some hushers. You got a beam gun or what?"

"I've got a rifle. I don't believe in beamers."

He looked at me full face for the first time since we had left the spaceport. "Greers are tough critters."

"That's what I hear."

"They are," said Nail. "They are tough, and they kill people who didn't think it would happen."

"I'm sure they do," I said. "So do germs and viruses and spaceships that phase into the lost dimension. So does old age, for all those billions who can't afford restoratives."

He nodded. "Like that, huh?"

"That's why I'm here."

"I think you'll like it here, Mr. Ramsey."

He turned back to the controls, laid the car over and pointed it at a warm yellow-red eye that centered in the forward windscreen and swelled rapidly. He pulled out of the swoop with a touch of his stick and planted us like a dropped feather in the peripheral glow of what turned out to be a big campfire.

"Atmosphere," I remarked.

"We do it straight here, Mr. Ramsey," Nail said. "Go on over to the fire, I'll unload you. You don't want to miss the snake."

"The snake?"

"More of our atmosphere, I guess you writers call it," he said. "Pondoro's only eight-foot-tall storyteller-in-residence."

"You're right," I said. "Who would want to miss a yarning boa constrictor?"

"Python," said Nail.

"What?"

"He calls himself Python."

"Okay, Python." I headed for the fire, with Ball drifting silently behind me.

Python. Twenty paces from the fire I saw it was apt. Of the maybe half-dozen figures around the blaze, there was no question who held center stage, reclined on one elbow at full length along the ground. His mellow baritone was almost tangible in the fire-glow. The audience would be captive sparrows, I thought, and that voice would be the weaving of the neck—or was that the method of the cobra? I am weak on Terran histecology; never mind: Ball could fill in the blanks.

"Ramsey . . . ?" Ball murmured.

"Yes," I said. "Yes, record it."

There were empty camp chairs. I dropped into one to listen. Ball eased up beside me.

"You hunters," the long man tolled in his bell of a voice. "You hunters of greer around your fires from night. Will you be brave when the toril spits you out into the sunlight to face the death you came to find?"

"Death!" The voice belled it sweetly. And again, "Death!"

Python's hooded gaze swept the assemblage, ignoring Ball. The eyes were deep-set, introspective. I met the gaze, and it moved on.

"Ball?" I asked softly.

"Toril?"

"Yes."

Python was speaking again.

". . . Plastic worlds in plastic orbit, on a plastic plane, and all the sharp ground down and coated plastic. Unprecedented lifespan, all the microscopic legions worse than tigers held at bay, wondrous argosies to ply the void in as peaceful commerce as homo sapience will ever know—what is there, then, to stir the blood and excite our glands awake to our after-all mortality?"

Dramatic pause.

"Why, here on poor Pondoro there is the greer, so here to poor Pondoro come captains of the universe to make their sport—or be made sport of, which? To seek a death, though not too close, lest the palate be glutted of plastic life and yearn too strongly for the one flesh finality, which the greer supplies full gladly."

"Ramsey," Ball said.

"What?"

"A toril is the gate through which fighting bulls enter the arena to confront their antagonist."

"That only?"

"The term is archaic. Very old. Used only on worlds where the mortal combat of man and bull is viewed as sport."

Python's voice tolled on.

". . . Do the captains care that the greer have other reasons to exist than for a kind of death dance they build themselves? Not one particle of matter, or of energy, or of time, is what the captains care, so long as the sport be hot and deadly, and their aim be true.

"But if the greer, who hunted these reaches undisputed for ages, should weary of the sport, what then, O Hunters brave by firelight, what then? For the greer is a mighty breed—how mighty, no one dead remembers, no one living knows—"

"Are you for real?" said a voice. Ball's.

The mood snapped, and shadows moved restively around the fireglow.

"Who's that?" one of the men said. Lean, big-mustached, leaving no question he considered an answer his due. That would be LaChoy, my principal outhunter.

"Ramsey," I said.

"And what is that?" He nodded chill disapproval at Ball.

"My fortune, what's left of it," I said.

Ball loomed forward into the firelight, the reflected glow flaming along his side. "What's it to you, hairlip?"

"Watch it, Ball."

"Ramsey, this has gone far enough," the man with the mustache said. "Your reputation has preceded you, but you left it at the spaceport, grab?"

"Don't be tough," I said. "I can't control him. I spent enough on Ball to buy your goddamn contract with change for enough goons to make you eat it, and I can't do a thing with him."

"I won't have it interrupting."

"Interrupting lies," Ball said coldly. The fire crawled and fluttered on his great impassive hide as he circled the storyteller. "Lies told as stories is story-telling, but lies told as phony mysticism is nothing but lies."

"That's you doing that," LaChoy said. "Quit it, Ramsey—that sounds just like you."

I shrugged. "Thanks for reading my stuff, but you're wrong."

"Customs wouldn't let an uncontrollable machine on this planet!"

Ball sniggered. Sure, they recorded it for him somewhere. Some black mass, maybe, or some vampire revel. But it sounded as if it gave him the most fiendish pleasure to introduce that sound into the growing tension.

"Customs will allow all *kinds* of unimagined things on this world," Ball said. "Especially in the way of machines."

I didn't get it, but LaChoy did; his face went stiff and his eyes got very, very watchful. He was looking at the cyborg in a way I did not like at all. This was getting serious fast. Except to Ball.

"Lies," Ball said contemptuously.

He circled the supine storyteller with a kind of wavering hop that was slow and hypnotic—and wholly a part of whatever Ball was up to, because Ball's usual method of locomotion is a dead steady drift, like a satellite in eternal orbit.

"Unreasonable lies at that. Baseless imaginings, told as precognition. The great galactic mousetrap, about to spring on mankind's neck right here on poor Pondoro; and well-deserved at that, humans being what they are."

Python rose without using his arms. His legs tucked themselves with a swift economy of motion I should have recognized then. His arms drifted out in front of him, moving like twin magnets tracking Ball, and the hands began to flex slowly with what seemed enormous power.

"Where's the foundation for it?" Ball said. "The planet talks to you, and whispers greers are more than men. Tell the planet for me that it is full of crap."

Someone was breathing like a sump pump on an Acme barge. Python. The arc of his arms gradually widened. The hand-flex continued. Ball continued his insolent promenade.

"Why don't you tell a true tale, storyteller born of woman and therefore man. You *were* born of woman?"

Ball always came back to that, even with bottle

birthing common as the womb between the stars. His harping on it was always tinged with that deep rancor of the formless cyborg encased in artifice, a womb's miscarriage, a bottle's spillage, cursed to live.

Python said nothing, but Ball had scored. Ball usually scores. He was birthed, if that's the word, maybe spawned is better, by a society where this kind of conversational savagery—all others being prohibited—is the planetary sport. The storyteller continued in his trance.

"Well?" Ball said. "Will you tell a true story to this gathering, you pathetic creature—or shall I?"

There was a slow movement in the outer darkness. Nail, gliding in a hunter's crouch, a short spring gun in his hand. Python's gyrations had fined and strengthened until it was incredible that bone and sinew could bear those tensions. Nail raised the gun and I saw it jerk. When the hyposliver bit, Python went straight up as if catapulted, arms flashing like scimitars. There was a sodden thud, and a nasty wet snapping sound, loud against the inhuman silence of that lunge.

In the middle of his gigantic leap, he buckled. Completely. With his feet high as my head, and the rest of him a whole lot higher, he just sagged in the middle and seemed to come all apart.

Ball hovered over the fallen storyteller. He made a small cryptic sound I have come to call his real laughter. I hoped nobody else caught on just then.

"You have a Medfac?" Ball's voice was neutral, but there was no question he was speaking to LaChoy.

"Yes."

"You might use it. He fractured his right forearm,

cracked two fingers and jammed his entire right hand trying to skewer me. With accompanying flesh, circulatory, and nervous system damage, of course."

LaChoy was very quiet. "Of course. Do you know what he could have done if Nail hadn't—?"

If Ball could have shrugged, that would have been the place for it. "Destroyed himself trying to use me for a volleyball," he said. "They made me to last longer than he was made to last. Any reasonable creature could tell that without coming to harm. Well? The Medfac?"

"I'll help carry him," I said.

"Not necessary," LaChoy said shortly. He spoke loudly then. "S-M!"

"Sah!"

A figure materialized at his elbow. It had been there all the time, just far enough away to be invisible except to Ball, because now his crack about illegal machines here made sense. The S-M was a Rongor battle robot, absolutely outlaw stuff.

"Take Python to the med-tent and plug him into the Medfac," LaChoy said to the Rongor. "Dial up whatever's needed to fix the damage, will you?"

"Sah!"

The gunport where a human face would be snicksnacked a salute. I couldn't see if the armament was in place. The robot glided smoothly around Ball, lifted the limp form of the storyteller, and was swallowed in the darkness.

LaChoy walked over and studied the dark smear where Python had lain. "I think this needs sleeping on. Your machine shouldn't have started it, Ramsey."

"Agreed."

"Cyborg," Ball said, and made the laughing sound.

"Ball!" I said.

He made the sound again.

"Ball, quit!"

His sphere actually seemed to contract and sulk, but he quit.

"Agreed," I said again. "You thinking about civil charges?"

LaChoy waved a hand. "Forget it. Python was the actual aggressor. Counter charges?"

"Skip it. On both counts: host and antagonist."

"Done and recorded."

"This was a bad way to start. We'll pull out tonight."

"No. Sleep tonight."

"We'll kick it around tomorrow. Now, me for bed. Your tent is ready."

The others—I figured them for a client, another full-time guide, a campy, and what would be two mechanics an outfit this size would carry—had stayed out of it, and now they rose and faded, making no move to introduce themselves.

Nail came up. "Your tent is this way."

"Sorry we ruined the act," I said.

"It's done. LaChoy will speak on it in the morning."

"Runs a tight camp, does he?"

"Tight. Good night, Mr. Ramsey."

"Good night," I said, but I didn't believe it.

4

IN THE ICED WANING OF THE NIGHT, PYTHON STIRRED IN THE MEDFAC
creche, caught between nightmare and awakening,
his unconscious mind haunted by the invading processional from another time, another place.

Always it began with the voice, imprinted on
some inner level of awareness all those weary kilometers ago. The voice had droned far above the
preparation rooms, above the neural breathing of
the coliseum crowd, which was like a large, soft,
hungry entity lurking above the arena. The coliseum
was never quiet, but in the dream there was no
sound except the voice. . . .

"*The ninety-fifth playing of the Twelve-System
Games has been one for the histories in Palikar, a discipline old before the Terran Service, which has
spread with its rule. . . .*

"*The Ursine Worlds and Aldebaran have domi-
nated for decades, but today, in one of the most
important events, the bets are going down that Old
Earth has found a champion in Baka Martin. Martin
is a heavy favorite, having defeated grim Na-
Saladin and Merry John French of the Terran Service. . . .*"

From the voice to the sybil-awareness—two tiny
pills beneath the tongue, fire and ice, ice and fire,
feeding the sybil virus hidden in his brain, speeding
the neural links. The lower jaw, the teeth, numb then

)fficials had to know, had to know, and yet ꜜonitor had tattled, and he was once more in the unmonitored prep rooms. The numbness and the tenderness dropped from him with a dizzying rush, his pulse fluttered out of its metronomic rhythm for one erratic heartbeat, and he was ready.

"*. . . Baka Martin, parentage unregistered, was accepted by the schools of Old Earth before his first birthday. A foundling, nothing is known of who brought him to the first home of mankind . . .*"

Palikar, the many-colored cloak of the scholars of Manhome, had been pushed beyond that pragmatic combat science the Terran Service had employed, as it had employed so many others, in the ordering of the known galaxy to proper civility and service—or civil service, went the hoary saw—to become a way-of-life, an art-of-living, a religion.

Shepherded by a School Mother who loved her wayward charges with all the tumultuous love of a gene tree with ages of motherhood in it, dried beyond repair by an unshielded flare of atomics on her homeworld, Baka Martin had learned the mantra of Old Earth. The homeless and the poor, the weary and the unwanted—Old Earth took them, for none was otherwise available for its purposes. It took them and taught them the ancient myth of Manhome as ultimate arbiter of truth and beauty and of mercy, armed them with Palikar against the sharp edges of a sprawling and occasionally bumptious civilization, and expected respect from the stars.

Not enough. The stars, if they respected anything, respected strength, respected winning. The rules of the games were specific but known to be ignored. G'hunu from Hot 'n' Heavy held the Palikar crown for five playings of the games across thirty years, and dropped in his home gym, massive heart imploded by toning work, the official death certificate said. Metabolic destabilization was the growl, triggered by the sybil parasite. Other, lesser champions dared less and escaped the final violent reaction with lesser prizes. Not completely. Never completely. The processional moved unrelentingly on. . . .

"The contestants are in the ring. Martin seems to be slowing since Roget-Fosse cracked his upper left rib with the foul that disqualified him only forty minutes ago. Can the rejuvenos build that bone back to the strength and flex of seven years' conditioning in less than twenty minutes? Fennec is starting his warmup. . . ."

Through the funnel focus of his sybil-awareness, Baka Martin saw Fennec clap his hands and start to twirl. Martin clapped his hands, and the arena began to revolve.

A growl from the waiting crowd.

"Look: Martin has stopped!"

In a sudden cold sweat, Martin tried to force the cone of his awareness away from his opponent. The unaltered part of him warred against the strength of the sybil-parasite—and lost.

I must not fight this man. He wants his medal too hard. There is death in me, his death. How do I know? How does the crowd?

For the crowd was growling steadily now, low and harsh, and it sounded—hungry.

Fennec charged. Martin moved against his will, in a leaping step that flexed his wiry body like a whip. Flex, reflex. Fennec coming with force and fury. The computer alarms shrilling, extrapolating too late what the crowd had known by instinct. Baka Martin's foot took Fennec in the chin and nearly tore his head off.

"Good God!"

The announcer's voice went into the upper register. The crowd gasped audibly—but in horror or delight? Computers howled for the medics. . . .

Python woke in the med tent and knew he had been injured. He was whole now, and undamaged, but trauma-residue clung to his nerves like dried sweat. Last night he had damaged bone and flesh in his attempt to destroy the cyborg for *knowing*. Just for knowing what, long unknown, had begun to be just a little bit untrue. The injuries must have opened that carefully suppressed processional of memories. Trauma recalls trauma, and all those years ago he had crushed his own bone and blood vessels with the force of the kick that destroyed Fennec.

He opened his eyes. The Medfac bulked like some alien shrine. Frigid air breathed in at the tent flap. Far off, he heard the musical ululation of a hunting falconet. The hour before dawn.

The dregs of his dream drained away. The games computers were irreversible, and faulted Fennec for overextending his charge. The growl went that the death Fennec had planned was not his own. The computers . . . missed . . . the sybil-residue in Martin's blood. Old Earth had its medal, and the rest of the games were anticlimatic.

Old Earth inherited a frisson of fear from the rest of the civilized galaxy. If a skinny castoff like Martin could be trained to fatally best the best the stars could offer, before even computers could intervene, what were they *teaching* in those bastard schools of theirs? And how ruthlessly might those lessons be carried out between the stars if Iron Fennec had been snuffed to prove a point?

Suspicion was rampant where powerful leaders

convened, but there was insufficient data to challenge the result. To do so would be to show weakness, and weakness above all things was to be avoided between the stars.

The administration of Old Earth and the bureaucracy of the Terran Service were equal to the windfall of fear and doubt that, in a scrambling interstellar society, equaled heightened respect.

Baka Martin was not. Had they used him? Could they? Or had it been something wholly out of the dark depths of Baka Martin, orphan from a lost planet, triggered by the sybil-parasite, exiled from its own homeworld, striking back?

Python shut it off. Just shut it off. It wasn't hard, after all these years. Next he cleansed the trauma-residue from the fresh wounds: equally simple, earliest and best of his Palikar training. And . . . sleep drug! He was surprised, and then realized Nail had not been present in the group beside the fire. The hunting guide was a native of this planet who earned his living jousting with the greer. He could move undetected when he chose. Nail had probably saved him further damage from a continued assault on the cyborg.

He brooded over the cyborg for a space as he cleaned out the sleep drug. There came the passing tread of the Rongor battle robot, on sentry go. Python felt a sudden surge of repugnance for man and all his creations—the polar opposite of the occasional yearning that drew him to the human campfires and companionship. He had an overwhelming urge to be off and moving. He owed nothing here, was owed nothing here.

He went, unremarked even by the Rongor.

5

TOWARD MORNING IT GOT COLD. I COULD SMELL IT, THOUGH THE TENTS OF
LaChoy's camp were set to keep us sleeping warmly
at a temperature decided as human optimum in an
election I don't recall.

There was frost whiskering the long safari grass
when I got outside. The Rongor, its blunt oxidized
snout projecting from the dome above its sensory battery, skewered me with a steel gaze. War surplus
from the Rongor system is getting around these days
despite the rules. Its chameleon paint looked as if it
had stassed about the time I earned my first *twon*
blind at the age of eleven. It glided toward me
smoothly enough. Its ancient ceramoglas legs flexed
as easily as the human infantrybone they had been
poured to emulate before I was born.

The Rongor presented its blast-snout for inspection,
not pointed at me. Suddenly I was back at the front
on Zion when the Orthodox offensive came through,
with an override on the media-immunity circuits. The
chammy coats of the Rongors in their order-of-battle
had been flaking off them, too, and some of the
heavy units creaked a bit when they caught the Federal cross fire at the gap. But they wheeled on line
like infantry moving at armor speeds, or maybe cavalry, like Genghis Kahn out of Jeb Stuart, or maybe
Guderian, and they drove through the Federal lines to
the Lebanon-Said locks before the suborbital air came

down and tore them. The Rongors retreated in good order, but they had never been programmed for Zion sub-orb jet jocks. The jetmen had a field day, and wrecked half of Lebanon-Said before the last Rongor stopped shooting back. It all made a good story for the newscasts.

"Sah!" the kill machine barked. Just like some regimental sergeant major on parade.

"Just a walk," I said, "to smell the air."

"The air smells of greer, sah! Wind quartering, south-southwest, one decimal five knots, scent positive, estimated range twelve kilometers. Hunting males."

The morning turned sour a little. "And does LaChoy use you to hunt and kill the greer?"

"Sah! No, sah! I am programmed to perimeter defense only, sah! Mr. LaChoy does not wish his hunters disturbed in their rest, sah!"

I hadn't really thought about that last night. My rifle was still in its travel case. Too much civilization had made me stupid.

"The greer attack the camps?"

"Sah, individual attacks by single males are on recent record. No attacks by hunting packs in this century, sah!"

"But you don't hunt the greer?"

"It is prohibited by the hunting regulations. I may not hunt for you, sah."

"It's just as well, considering I don't want you to, and would probably try to have your boss thrown in the slammer if you did."

"Yes, sah."

"May I walk outside your perimeter?"

"Unarmed? No, sah!"

"I'll get my rifle, then."

"Records show you have not been briefed, sah, on the greer."

"Now, look—"

"Orders, sah!"

"Ramsey?" Ball trundled into view.

"I was taking my constitutional," I said. "I didn't call you on."

"You were getting creative when you were interrupted by this outlandish pile of junk." He didn't approve of the Rongor. "My duty is to nurture your creativity. Shall I scrap this thing for you?"

The Rongor went by me so fast it seemed to blur. Ball made that whirtling, high-pitched sound he makes when he's playing with gravity or a planetary magnetic field, or both. As fast as the Rongor moved, Ball was gone when the robot got there. The Rongor upended and would have fallen, but Rongor engineering philosophy was that robot infantry can't advance if sudden shocks bowl it over. It pirouetted nicely, got one steel hand on Ball—and stuck as if glued. It was sucked into a silver dervish, spun with astonishing force, and launched across the grass. It demolished the stylish toilet tent in a thunderclap of sound.

While it was in the process of regrouping, a little more slowly this time, five watchful natives, armed with heavy flamers, materialized. LaChoy was in the lead. They weren't formally dressed, but they were ready. The other paying guest was only a little behind them.

Nail shouted a command that broke the Rongor's second attack. The killing machine took up its momentum in a kind of boxer's shuffle, and went quiet.

Pools of writhing reflections from the sun skittered across Ball's featureless exoskeleton. The whirtling sound had passed human hearing in a heartbeat, but whatever Ball was doing, the Rongor still was reading him, all right. There was an almost human quivering in the robot. It seemed to take me a long time to realize Ball was killing the killing machine.

"Stop it!" I said. "Right now!"

"This scrap metal attempted to do me violence," Ball replied calmly. His voice was completely unaffected by his exertions. The air hissed from the speed of his rotations, and the temperature seemed to have elevated slightly.

"Your fault, Ball," I said. "You threatened to scrap it. Rongor robots were built for war; it was taking defensive action."

"It *thought* it was defending itself," Ball corrected. "It was wrong on two counts; there was no danger, because you did not tell me to scrap it; and any defense it could offer itself against me is so pitiful as to constitute a programming myth."

The shudders of the robot were growing more pronounced. Its main armament—that miniblaster capable of wrecking an armored column with one full-strength squirt—snapped convulsively in and out of its head like a demented cuckoo.

"Don't kill it, Ball," I said. "That's an order. Don't even *damage* it. That's an order. And sit still!"

Ball's smooth rotation altered a bit, like a top beginning to wind down. I had been around him long enough to know it indicated reluctance.

"Ball, dammit!"

For a longish moment I thought he was past control and going to kill it anyway. Then he came down all at once, and the sound he made came back into hearing at about the intensity of a small jet engine, went through the octaves at an ear-hurting plunge, and cut off at about the fingernail-scraping range. He drifted silently to the grass, and the twinkling sunfire became motionless in the facets of his ornery hide.

There was another heavy impact, like the sky falling, and the Rongor measured its length in the ruins of the toilet tent.

"It's not seriously hurt," Ball said quickly. "Think I can't follow orders, Ramsey? I was just unscrewing its orientation a little. It'll screw back into place on its own. I didn't weaken its circuits—just road-tested them a bit. Pretty sound software, for it not to be Intergal Cybby stuff." It was a grudging admission.

"The Rongor experimenters were pretty sound engineers, all right," I said. "They meant business."

"Monkey business," said Blaise LaChoy. He grounded his big Colt-Vickers frontier pacifier and looked Ball over. "I'll buy it from you," he said.

"What? Ball?"

"Anything that can handle a Rongor S-M like that needs to be working for me."

"You have half the price of this planet in your account?"

"Pondoro isn't for sale."

"Neither is Ball." Sometimes I can't help myself.

"Why, Ramsey," said Ball, "I didn't know you cared."

"Go to hell!"

"Give me a star-map and an ETA," he countered serenely.

"I'll pay for the toilet tent," I told LaChoy. "Can I send another one out when I get to the spaceport?"

"Already on the way," LaChoy said. "Forget it. Insurance will take it. Pay hell's own premium for coverage of a camp in prime greer habitat. Can't get any coverage at all without the Sergeant Major there." He nodded at the Rongor as it got feebly to its feet.

"Sah!" The Rongor snapped to attention, teetering. It wasn't going to break attention if it had to topple over again.

"Permission to repair yourself. You are relieved of the duty."

"Sah!" The gunport clicked and the gun popped out of sight. The old machine wavered unsteadily across the clearing and behind the tents.

"Modesty?" I said.

"Atmosphere," LaChoy said. "The serene dawn of the hunting camp as the mighty greer-slayers drink their billy and prepare for the uncertainty of the day. You know the drill. Spoiled by a battered old war machine across the fire with its guts and an oil can in its lap."

"Not if it was the way you describe."

"You're the writer here. You were saying something about leaving?"

"I was, yes. After that business last night . . ."

"Forgotten. Python has. Gone before dawn, even the S-M didn't see him."

"I find that hard to believe. A Rongor Infantry Nine Command model doesn't miss much. The gunrunner who cleared that deal must be retired on Old Earth."

"Not exactly." LaChoy grinned for the first time, crookedly. "It's a bit of a story, actually. Remind me to tell you before you get collected by your greer. Or collect him. I notice the S-M's presence impressed you a sight more than your valet there. Yet Ball made child's play of him."

"Ball is a decadent test-tube experiment locked in a cybernetic girdle and totally insensitive to the entire cosmos outside his own programming. He can shoot sound-on-color news footage—or home holos, if you prefer—and whip his weight in barbarian robot infantry. Probably at the same time. I fail to be surprised by anything Ball does. But I was on Zion for the Federal suppression; I've seen Rongor stuff in action."

"No lie?" His eyebrows went up. "When?"

"I was in Joshua Sayeth when Rongor units went against the Fortress of the Word. I saw Model Nines like this one gang up on Federal siege tanks deployed at the Gates of David. Their S-M skipped along a line of those tanks with his blaster fined down tight like a kid running a stick down a picket fence. The line was over ten kilometers long! The rest of the Rongors opened the slits he'd cut in twenty-gauge Eterna with their hands. Just grabbed them and peeled them open, like field rations. Then they killed the crews. They didn't use firepower inside; might have destabilized the piles. They used their hands. It took them ten minutes. If it takes one of them to keep a greer out of my bedroll, you may inherit Ball."

"You know how prissy insurance companies are, surely?" LaChoy said. "The S-M calms any fears they may have to return any tiny fraction of the premium to the customer. Ball has screwed their statistics for this year, so I find myself fond of him already. But I won't feed you to the greer so I can have him. Not raw, anyway. Shall we just get some breakfast and then get on with shooting in your gun for local atmosphere?"

"We might as well. Ball has had *his* fun for the day."

6

THE TARGET SHOWED AT ABOUT 150 METERS, THROUGH A GAP IN THE thornbush. My seven gun settled naturally against my shoulder and recoiled almost at the same instant. There was no report. LaChoy's hushers were the best you can buy, and he didn't want gunshots to disturb the area around camp. The target flipped over with a spastic twitch, just like any other shooting gallery.

"Nice shot," LaChoy said. "May I?" He held the rifle the way a man raised with guns holds one. "Nice," he said again. "We don't get many primitive-weapons hunters here. I like this: a hunk of metal and wood with the old equals-and-opposites still in it. This is Terran walnut isn't it?" He snapped the gun to his shoulder. "It's all right to carry a two-pound elephant slayer if you want, with enough countercoil built in to brake a spaceship, but this is a fine sporting arm."

"You're just accustomed to those big Pacifier beam guns," I said. "You associate weight with stopping power."

"Have to use 'em," he said a trifle defensively. "Goes with the license. My own sporter is a custom two-barrel in a three-hundred-year-old smokeless powder number, 9x57. Got it off a robot 'smith in the port city for the price of a safari or two."

"This is a seven-millimeter, just as old as yours. Not the fifty-seven-mil case, though—one of the stretched cases with enough powder to drive these special enjeckosplode pills. The basic round is almost as ancient as muzzleloaders, as you ought to know with that 9x57. But the combinations I can load for this give me everything from a supervelocity armor-piercing pencil bomb to a superslow solid that'll dump things the size of a pachyderm in short order. The bomb is illegal, and useless except against hostile robots. The solid is useless against softskinned critters. I'm using target spitzers here."

"Have you got any of the stuff you plan to use on greer?" LaChoy asked.

"Yes."

"Let's try some of it. Nail has got to get a reading on stopping index. Hunting regs, you know. Let alone insurance premiums."

I loaded some medium heavy expansion points.

"The next set of popups are greer replicants; they're three dimensional and density matched. We know your gun shoots on, and you can hit with it; now we need to know if your hunting rounds can stop a greer."

"They'll stop a leopard," I said. "They'll stop an Old Earth kodiak."

"How do you know that?"

"Because one of the first things I bought with my royalties was a traditional Old Earth safari. I killed an elephant and a kodiak and a leopard, and some of the plains game."

"I've always wondered about those hunts," LaChoy said, somewhat wistfully. "Know it's foolish, but I just can't believe there's decent hunting that deep in the civilized sector. How was it?"

"It started okay, but ended badly. I went through the motions out of some stupid idea about getting my money's worth, but I wish I hadn't. You stayed in a hotel in Rome and flew out every morning to hunt. The game was all picked out for culling, and located, and all you did was make the shoot."

"Did you have to shoot from the air?" he asked with some distaste. "I heard the insurance companies require it."

"I might as well have. They turn you loose within a quarter mile, and if the game starts moving, they reposition you. It's a ranching operation, not hunting."

"Jesus!"

"I got the elephant early, before the novelty wore off, and so maybe I got a taste of what it must have been like all those centuries ago. I got the leopard clean, but it was small and came to the bait too easily. Then I went on to Alaska. The kodiak was worst. I slipped one in low, and it turned and came for me. The damned safety robot threw a hyposliver into it to slow it down. The drug knocked it completely out."

"What did you do then? Hit it in the head with a bloody rock?"

"No, I slipped one of those PBs I wasn't supposed to have into my gun and blew that robot all to hell. Then I finished the bear and made the camp robots bury it decently. I didn't take the hide, and I left Earth that night."

"Must have caught hell about using illegal ammo on that robot, though."

"Not really. The threat of adverse publicity is more fearsome than a sunbomb to most organizations, including Old Earth's tourist bureau. My book wasn't all that long off the lists, and the Zion dispatches were fresh then, so I was a pretty hot property. An exposé would have cost them plenty, so they just let me go.

"Might of the bloody media, hey? And now you're after greer?"

"Now I'm after greer."

"Sometimes," he said, looking off at the horizon, "I think it's the other way 'round."

"Meaning what?"

"I mean sometimes these beasts can be so cagey— and yet so stubborn. We hunt them hard and see them every day, one glimpse, seldom enough for a shot, and then usually a miss. They should break their pattern, move out of the hunt area. But they stay right in and keep coming around, until it's almost like the beggars are hunting you." He looked back at me. "There are no air platforms here, and no safety robots. There's me, and I hate to let a client get completely killed, even when they specify that in the contract. Don't look so amazed; there's lots worse ways to die."

"Lose many clients that way?"

"Enough to consider that remark tasteless. I generally try to bang them off you after they've ripped off an arm or a leg or torn out your jugular. We've got Battlefreeze on the fliers, the Medfac of course, and the Central Receiving here is quite efficient, of course. I'm told interns opposed philosophically to combat prefer it for emergency room experience like no other in this end of the cosmos. They can get you back even when you're pretty far gone. I've yet to have a client complain, come to think of it, even the ones who planned to die here. Those who thought they wanted to die seem to end up resenting the greer's single-minded attempt to accommodate them so much that they decide to go on living just to spite their trophy. A couple of them knew they were going home to death sentences, medical or political. It didn't matter anymore, once they bested a greer."

"When you get ready to write your memoirs, let me know," I said.

He smiled in his mustache. "Client confidentiality, I'm afraid. But an amusing thought nonetheless. I do get the odd types through here, no question. Sector administrators, Commonwealth politicians, movers and shakers, that lot. They come here as one kind of person and they leave . . . different. I don't just mean in body tubes or urns. They leave as different people. Sometimes better, sometimes with their pride completely broken. But enough yarning for today; on to the only thing that matters: the chase! I will now instruct you in the killing of the greer."

"Instruct away."

"All right. With a rifle such as yours, if you blow his brains out, he dies. If you shoot for the head of charging greer, you die, because you miss. If you bust his right foreshoulder, he pulps you with his left paw. And vice versa. If you are quick enough to bust both front shoulders good, you may slow him enough for a head shot. There's nothing too fancy about his plumbing. He's got what serves for a brain, heart, stomach, and so forth, about where you'd expect them to be, and he runs on hydraulic blood, even as you and I. He's got nothing particularly spectacular in the way of a nervous system, except that it appears immune to pain. A lung-shot greer will kill you and lope away to heal somewhere. Their recuperative powers are enormous. Whether he's whole or hurt, he comes at you dead silent, and until he's stone dead he doesn't even notice. Don't try to turn him; he won't turn. The spine shot is best, or the head if you must."

"That all sounds pretty basic," I said. "I don't have a prayer."

"Bloody right. Any man who hunts a greer is a fool. Or a hunter."

"There's a difference?"

"Not so's you'd— *Greer!*"

A trampling rush of underbrush, a hurtling shadow out of the corner of my eye—the seven gun slugged my shoulder with unnoticed recoil.

The apparition appeared to flinch, and my gun jumped again, all in eerie silence. I worked the bolt with speed I couldn't remember since my teen years. My balls, belly, and heart seemed squeezed into a pea-sized lump somewhere behind my breastbone.

The second shot rolled the thing over, but it rolled right back with a horrid, liquid vitality, and was coiling for the spring when I let drive into the bunching, rippling knot of shoulder muscles behind the nightmare eyes.

The muscles uncoiled, but in a spasm, not a lunge. The thing dropped like all the strings had been cut at once. Its massive skull flailed around loosely, jaws wide, and my fourth shot centered the brain pan.

I remembered to breathe.

My hands shook in reaction, before I remembered to look for LaChoy. He was unmoving, hands resting on his big Pacifier, grinning from ear to ear. I let my gun sag. There was a nervous tic in my cheek. I tried to control it and couldn't.

"What are you so goddamned happy about?" My voice sounded fluttery as my pulse.

"That's pretty good gun-handling for the first day," the hunter said. "Damn-near tops for close-in work. Also, you've got a sound killer's instinct: uncluttered by secondary worries about tearing up your trophy.

First you get it dead, and let the stuffers worry about the cosmetics. On Pondoro, that makes you a hunter." He wasn't even looking at the mangled beast.

"I mount my trophies in my head, remember?"

My voice steadied down. I could feel the exultation of having shot well before a critical audience. The best shooter there is can blow the shot when somebody's around to observe. I hadn't had time to think about that. There had just been the greer and me, and nothing else in the universe until that final shot.

Already I was beginning to regret the premature victory—another emotion every hunter learns, the other side of repeated failures—when suddenly I understood.

I looked back at my trophy. The seven gun had busted him up good. Smashed some ribwork, ripped large exit wounds, busted his spine and rent his skull. But there was no blood. A silvered edge of some gear wheel dangled drunkenly from one of its chest wounds. My trophy was part of LaChoy's shooting gallery.

"You son of a bitch," I said.

"Don't feel so put-upon," he said happily. "He would have been just as finished if he were the real thing. Nail's got positive readings on your loads; plenty of stoppo."

"I told you that!"

"So do most people. People who simply won't take the local expert's advice. Old Waldo saves all amount of bickering. Only thing he won't do for you is claw you, being a tame robot. Pretty fair imitation, though, otherwise. Lose some clients right here, I must say. Trouble with their nerves, sphincter, it takes different turns. I have to tell you that some of them like the game so well they head back to port and sign up at a fancy shooting gallery they have there, rack up a couple dozen of these and go home happy with a synthetic pelt. I'd be unhappier if I didn't own stock in the place."

My overriding reaction was one of intense relief that it wasn't over yet and the storied greer was still to come. "You mean they quit here?"

He nodded. "Better than losing them in the field. Better on the reputation of the company, too, if not the bank balance. Good deal better than letting someone start something I might have to finish. Tends to weed out the ones who don't deserve a greer. Got to see if they'll take the steel, so to speak, to get at the horse, if you follow the bullfights."

Something in his phrase roused old reportorial instinct, never too far away despite the action. "Bullfights? Python used a bullfight term last night."

He rubbed his chin. "Think maybe he introduced the concept during one of his yarnspinnings, now I recollect. I like it. A weeding process, so only the bravest of the bulls go out to face the sword."

I was coming down from my emotional orbit. I was glad it hadn't been a greer, glad I had measured up to LaChoy's oblique standard, particularly glad I had smashed his toy so badly and hadn't fouled my pants. And angry he had taken it upon himself, unasked, to test my mettle.

"There's something wrong with that image," I said. "We're not bred on farms to come and die to prove the courage of the greer."

LaChoy shrugged. "Whatever. I still like the idea, and it sells big with the paying customers." He peered at me closely. "Pissed off at me, aren't you?"

"Last trick like that?" I said, not wanting to admit it.

"Last trick like that. From here on in, it's as real as it gets."

I let it all out in one long exhalation. "All right."

"Good man." He pounded me on the back, and I knew the casual drubbing admitted me as a Pondoro initiate. Corny as it was, I felt fine.

Nail showed up from the flier where he had recorded the action. "Good bison herd about twenty klicks south," he said. "Some other grazing herds, too. A few Pondoro mammoths."

"Mammoths, for God's sake?"

"Big, dumb brutes, hairy as hell," LaChoy said. "No big teeth, like the original, and no fire like old *tembo*, though they have a trunk very like both of them. They chew the tops out of trees and usually stay in the forest. Sometimes a greer pack will push them out on the plains, but not for long. Not worth hunting, really. Shall we go get some fresh bison chops, and a bait or two for the greer? We'll hunt tomorrow."

"Real life this time?"

"I said: as real as it gets."

7

IN THE PALE DAWN, IN THE RUINS BESIDE THE RIVER, PYTHON FOUGHT
with phantoms. Lavender mists rose off the slow slid-
ing of the broad water. Off where the world was
piled up in jagged battlements against the sky, black
crags were touched with soft, deep orchid tints from
the autumn sun. The stone beneath his shuffling moccasins was cold and unyielding as Python executed
his morning ritual.

"Come—*out!*"

His mellow baritone boomed softly across the stillness. His body blurred into a shadow that repacked
into solidity three long strides away, behind a flashing foot that struck at nothing and recoiled, in venomous imitation of the name its owner carried.

"Come—*out!*"

Another blurring, interlocking series of moves, mur-
derous fist and leg strikes at nothing. Flood-deposited
rubble grated beneath his moccasins.

"*Wherever you are!*"

He whirled into a slower spin, arms out and droop-
ing like the weary rotors of ancient hovercraft. His
head was back, eyes closed, not looking at today. The
sweat ran freely and his breath puffed whitely. It
was the ritual of his daily dance and nursery chant,
more than anything else, that had persuaded hunt
authorities to leave him to his own devices here: a
harmless lunatic.

The peaks took on sharp edges in the brightening dawn; violet now, and a lacing of hard maroon. Sounds other than his shuffling moccasins obtruded. One of the little rodent diggers that sheltered in the ruins scrabbled nearby. An awakening sillyfowl grumbled bad-naturedly. On the river, a sharp wet *pop!* betrayed one of the beaverlike dam builders sounding reveille for his workmates. At the other end of what once had been a primitive thoroughfare, heavy claws clicked and dragged as the crippled greer that denned there moved down for morning water.

Python's eyes flickered open on the drab soulless ruins revolving past. Daylight spilled down and opened up all the distances in the elbow of the river, and revealed in full what had to be the remains of an ancient village. Almost shapeless blobs, fashioned out of graduated layers of river-smoothed rock—but they had been homes. Roofless; maybe they never had roofs, and maybe the roofs had fallen back to dust before humans left Manhome.

That the ruins remained at all argued against great antiquity. Yet on this whole plateau there was no other trace of the builders. Not one. The Federation survey had searched carefully; its records were open to anyone. Now Python searched also, in his own way.

The only builders he found were the never-still beaverlike beings, an interesting case of parallel evolution, and that was all.

Through no stretch of his quite flexible intellect could Python discern any atrophied ghost of the vanished village-builders in the dam-builders. They used the red-gold clay of the river floodplain for their stream-diverting dams. The village-builders had used the same clay for mortar in their stone shacks. But the

beavers—he called them that—flourished in their eco-
logical niche, and the villagers were gone without a
fossil or artifact to mark their going.

That was the first riddle of this place. The second
was more sinister: at some time before this world was
settled, furious beams of energy had played hotly
upon the town, blurring its symmetry, perhaps inciner-
ating what served for roofs. Molten stone had flowed
out in telltale fans and cooled. The weather and the
river's floods had worn down those traces of violence
for a long time now, but still they were unmistakable.

The blasts were too thinly spaced, and erratic, to
suggest a systematic massacre. They might have been
the accumulated target practice of generations of
greer hunters, were it not for their great age and the
fact their presence had been recorded on First Survey.

Public records showed that the exhaustive search
for indigent intelligence, required before Freehold
was granted, had been all the more intense because
of this solitary village, and particularly because of
these very energy scars. But there had not been one
other structure on the entire surface of the planet. Nor
below its seas, where the searchers had probed in
memory of Earth's own ancient millennia-huge rift of
fossils, which had taken hundreds of years to puzzle
out. The village-builders had not crawled back into
the sea. Finally the village was simply cataloged
among the thousands of things not fully understood
since men had spread among the stars, and Freehold
was granted.

To Python's sybil-altered awareness, the scent of
ancient trouble was almost palpable above the ruined
walls, an irresistible puzzle as surely as it seemed to
repel all other humans. He knew the difference: it was

the sybil. The insidious meshing of parasite with self at some complex depth of cellular integrity—total wedding of basic human stuff to inhuman substance—transmuted his perceptions of the *now* to a different plane.

Interstellar rumor said the original sybil-host walked the most terrifying of the Blocked Worlds unafraid, capable of coopting any monster through the agency of the sybil. How Survey pilots of the Terran Service had escaped those worlds with knowledge sufficient to rule the entire system off limits for all time probably was a yarn worth campfire spinning. But until Federal bureaucracy collapsed, the yarn would not be spun. Sybil would remain a modern bogeyman between the stars, kin with other superstitions of a determinedly scientific race.

Here in these ruins, the sybil awareness flushed more strongly through him than it ever had, triggered by some signal he had not recognized. Here, he could forget awareness of himself as a flawed and altered being. He became a unified awareness, unlike any other, and his symbiotic awareness quested with the intensity of a neural searchlight across uncharted seas.

He dropped abruptly into a position long ago called lotus, until preempted by the Palikar discipline.

Trouble. The air itself breathed trouble this bright fine morning.

His first actual memory of Pondoro was linked to the distant lure of that diffuse unease. He had come awake from a drifting sybil-dream in a cheap spacer's crib near this planet's only spaceport—and awareness of this lifeless ruin had come, impossible to ignore. He had hitched a ride on a fishing vessel, hauling nets for passage, and then walked unerringly right across this continent, through prime greer habitat, unmolested.

This scent of trouble is real—real! Have I fulfilled my Terran oath by spreading my rumors down among the hunting camps that all is not as it would seem on this dark and brooding continent? I know the Terran Service will hear; they will harvest the rumor on a dozen powerful worlds, to which the hunters of greer return, and they will come.

My Terran oath? Now there's a random thought! Do I attempt to keep it still, though I deserted the Service after Fennec? But the Service will come, because it does trust rumor better than a thousand spies. Best then for all concerned that I be far away, and soon. Already the skin of Python of Pondoro begins to itch for shedding.

But the riddle obsessed him.

Did man's presence here create the unease? Men were hunters on this continent, fishers of the teeming seafood in the world's vast shallow seas, or of some vital service to either, or to both. Too few, too uninclined to attempt to change the planet in any permanent way. Hunters and fishers, following the herds and the spawn, had no desire for the reshaping of things. Profitmakers, following both, cared only for enough wealth for a fat passage to the brighter worlds, where they could take their place in more important doings.

There were no alien citadels here to catch the eye of the crusader or reformer, no mineral riches to tempt the miner or the pirate. Vast forests and plains, rough-cut mountains and vaster seas—and this single small huddle of violated stone that once had sheltered sentient life. Nothing here to whet the appetites of men, and stir the particular nightmares of their greed or evangelism.

But the unease is real—real! The fear is real!

The crippled greer hunted clumsily along one of the river's feeder creeks. Once, there was a huge splash followed by explosive grunts and threshing. Had the beast fallen in, trying for one of the succulent dam-builders? The splashing stopped, and after a while the dragging tread was heard again. The greer had never had this much trouble getting breakfast. It shuffled and clicked, snorted and huffed, prowled and lay in wait.

As the sun climbed to where it could warm the roof-less angle of rock where Python kept his vigil, he realized he was beginning to be afraid. Afraid! The realization rocked his consciousness. It was a phenomenon worthy of study, and he studied it. Through all the interlocking mental disciplines of the Palikar, it had taken his primitive brain stem this long to force recognition of the fear-stimulus into the cortex.

Afraid. He examined the emotion, and found it unreal. He had no fear—could not remember ever having experienced natural, primitive fear—and yet he was afraid. The paradox was exquisite. He would have dwelled on it at length, but the antics of the crippled greer compelled his attention. They had shared this drab lair now for half this world's rotation around its star, and its habits were as familiar to him as his own. The crippled beast was long since done with hunting men; if this had not been so, it would have hunted him before this.

How incredible, then, to realize it was hunting him now.

Instantly, the sybil-change flooded along his nervous system, and he was ready.

However weak an imitation his parasite might be of its Blocked World rootstock, its lightning reaction

to any perceived jeopardy to its host was unequivo-
cal: supernatural strength and prowess fairly hummed
through his Palikar-trained body.

Curiously, the fear did not wane, but thickened
noticeably until it seemed to blur the sun with a
deadly miasma.

He remained motionless and self-aware at last:
master practitioner of Palikar, slayer of Iron Fennec,
infused with alien strength past reckoning on any
human scale—and numbingly afraid of a crippled
and clumsy old beast!

Python flowed into a tumbling somersault that took
him to his feet on open ground, poised and ready to
face the attack that should have been raving at his
throat.

The greer glanced at him briefly across the ancient
flow of molten rock, and ambled out of sight through
a breached doorway. The scrape and rattle of pebbles faded gradually, and was gone. The fear
washed away dizzily.

Python collapsed weakly against a sunny wall and
searched himself uneasily for a return of that sense-
fogging fear. The sybil industriously neutralized his
overload of adrenaline before he could become ill.
Time seemed to pass in a broken shuffle, in imitation
of the vanished beast. His sweat dried in the sun. The
greer stayed gone. Reluctantly, Python began to consider the uncanny notion that he had been toyed
with.

*LaChoy is mad. LaChoy is utterly mad to hunt these
beasts. And those other ones—the soft ones, from the
soft worlds—corporate heroes—are madder still. The
king-makers, the sun-turners. Does a hunting greer
care how many souls you hold in thrall? I was right to
tell it down around the campfires. That fear. That*

focused, specific fear is part of the riddle of this place, if I can only see it. . . .

He returned to the little lean-to he had fashioned and resumed his meditation. After some time, he dozed, comforted by the sun in a way artifice could not. But it was Pondoro autumn, and the rising chill off the river roused him too soon.

The greer was restless again, down at its end of the village, but no longer offered a threat. Python didn't question how he knew. No dam-builder barked, no sillyfowl crowed in the twilight stillness. The world seemed to hold its breath.

Something's going to happen. A storm? Something . . .

He shook off the sensation, impatient with himself, and reached inside to lift his water bucket and drink. Then he stepped to a wing of the crumbled wall that always caught first light and where noon sun had full play, and selected a supper from the hardy vegetables growing there. Terrafood, lab-toughened and mutated over the centuries to adapt and grow in minimal conditions at either end of the Terran ecoscale and at all points in between. They thrived on useful alien nutrients, and transmuted or rejected harmful ones. It was lifeboat equipment, appropriated during a stowaway hop between two back-world systems, with a blanked call from well away from the spaceport to advise the purser of the sloppily secured ship to check her lifeboat stores. The money for the untraceable call came from begging through the better part of the spaceport town. All in all, satisfactory.

He selected his meal and ate it cold, washed down with more water from the bucket, then resumed his doorway vigil. He could no longer hear the crippled greer.

The only motion anywhere was the constant flow of the river, and the high, lazy circling of a hunting falconet with sun still on its wings. When the temperature reached a certain point, Python moved inside and donned his lightweight explorer's sleeping robe. His knapsack was his pillow. The robe and bucket and knapsack, together with his stout walking stick, were all the luxury he had ever needed in his wanderings. He had been home wherever he found himself. Tonight, though, it was a good long while before sleep came.

8

THE WINGED HUNTER, DONE WITH HUNTING FOR THE DAY, FLEW IN AN expanding spiral, wide wings lazily cupping the updrafts off the river basin far below. To the eye below, it was at last a purple dot adrift in a darkening lavender sky. Its dominion widened and flattened as it soared, and betrayed the alien red-gold twinkle of human campfires against the purpling dusk. The crags that drew the hunter home still were afire with day, but shadows marched out of the gorges to meet the wider darkness as it sifted down upon the land.

Within that gathering darkness, more substantial shadows moved with purpose, giving the human fires a wide berth, making for the mountain passes.

They padded through virtually gameless climax forest that cloaked the lower foothills. They hurried beneath the thick double canopy of *coli*, burubi, and Pondoro oak, avoiding without effort the swift cold streams that lurked in time-sawn gorges for the unwary.

They moved with no sound to mark their passage. Instead: a swelling sense of dangerous urgency which froze to fearful stillness the nocturnal small-life of the subalpine transition zone, unaccustomed to the nearness of such fearsome power. No living creature dared move long after they had passed. . . .

Sunto, satisfied, released the bird of prey to its nest

and left the Permanent Lairs, to become another sound-less phantom, running in the dark like a youth. Because his was the shortest path, and because his old muscles were attuned to the mountains and not the plains, he outdistanced them all to the council pool.

His belly grew warm with pride as the Chosen of the hahns slipped out of darkness to take up station around the pool. It was his first summons in a long hunt of dayfires, and all of their bellies were full of new hunting feats to sing, both in their wardership of the lesser beings and in their hunts with Two-Legs. But they held their peace beneath his somber brood-ing. They crouched in silence, sharing only the voice-less communion of the belly, until the last leader was in place, coming all the way from the shore of the Great Wet which drinks the dayfire when it hunts the end of the day.

Full nightfire blazed misty and many-pointed from the canopy of illumination they called the Lake of Light, when Turso, Arnic leader, oldest of the hahn chiefs, broke the silence.

"Thou sent a calling, Eldest of the Orange Claw and Only. To keep the Way, we of the plains have dipped our paws in the river clay which gave thy van-ished hahn its naming, and come thus to the council."

"This one sees."

Sunto looked to Girta of the Hahn DiTenka. "DiTenka are most accurate singers of us all, their chieftain's song the sweetest. Sing us now how Two-Legs came."

Girta had expected the ritual. He flowed up, his bulk drinking a gap into the Lake of Light.

"Eight and eight full claws of snow have come, and rested on the land, and gone, and then a half-claw more, since Two-Legs returned at last to us."

His heavy croon was like mountain rivers swollen in the spring.

"Times are good since Two-Legs returned to join the hunt we have prepared for him. Yet times were hard those untold winters gone, when came the first Bright Boulder light as thistle to the Permanent Lairs of the Orange Claw. . . .

"For it is cubhood learning that all new knowledge makes hard lessons, from first breath to last. The Lesson that fell on the Permanent Lairs was hardest ever taught: that this strange new hunting breed loved and feared such dens beyond all else.

"Loved, for first of all things beneath the sky these Permanent Lairs drew them down to us from beyond the Lake of Light. And feared even more. For—having hunted, having killed, having carried Orange Claw hunters rendered senseless within their strange bright blind—they clawed down the Permanent Lairs with great claws of fire the like of which the dayfire cannot match.

"Then did the Orange Claw call them strongly to come out of their Bright Boulder to resume the hunt in proper fashion, but they heard or heeded not. They all died badly, when the hunters they had captured woke to their hahn-mates' call, and hunted hard within the Two-Legs blind itself.

"Last living of those first Two-Legs then flung their Bright Boulder light as thistle against the mountains in his terror. There was a thunder and a flash the like unheard since mountains cursed at history's dawn. . . ."

Girta paused, but no one broke the silence, while they studied their faint reflections in the pool.

"All this passed long, long ago, time past easy reckoning, but never to be forgotten. All hahns saw and heard the mountains curse. Full well all knew whose hunting marches lay beneath that storm of fire.

"When the mountains settled back to sleep, all smelled the poisoned wind which killed or changed living things in ways beyond our digestion. All hahns hunted wide of the Orange Claw valley, and that awful wind, until our ancestors heeded a calling not unlike the summons we have heeded now.

"The Permanent Lairs were full of death, and the Orange Claw remnants waited beneath the poisoned wind to sing its final hunt.

"The Lesson was clear: the Permanent Lairs drew this strange new hunting breed among us, and would again, in time. No hunter doubted the fallen Bright Boulder contained a hunting party which scouted out new ground, even as all hahns but Orange Claw always had moved to warmer lands ahead of winter. . . .

"All claws orange alike in the clay beside the ruined Lairs, the stomachs of our ancestors digested the Lesson: hahn war must give over to vast preparations to teach this strange new hunting breed to hunt and die with proper dignity. Nevermore must a Permanent Lair be raised by any hahn, to frighten and excite Two-Legs from proper hunting ritual, or risk the death of mountains in their fear. To Orange Claw, our elders assigned the keeping of the council pool."

"Listen!" said Korhu of the Doredonnen, rising in his turn. "Times are good since Two-Legs returned. It was a rich joke on this one's hahn when young hunting males hot on a fresh strange scent found the next Bright Boulder, and died. Nor in those days was Doredonnen alone in those first new days of hunting and of being hunted, both."

"Aye!" Turso. "There came in time a spill of Bright

Boulders light as thistle all across our marches. They
were little more than river stones, or they were of a
size and color of the Silver Mountains in frost time.
Such a hunting then there was as may never come
again. Then did the strongest bellies of my hahn hunt
the Permanent Lairs those first Two-Legs tried to raise
upon our marches, as those first Two-Legs hunted the
Orange Claw Lairs. We did not claw them down with
fire, but we did fill their days with hunting and their
nights with dreams of it, O my brothers!"

"Times were good when Two-Legs learned the
Lesson. Good times remain, to this one's digestion."
Korlu, from the shore of the Big Wet. "Yet Sunto,
eldest and only of the Orange Claw, called this council not to sing songs known among us all."

"Full true," Sunto acknowledged heavily. "The Permanent Lairs are the danger; that always has been
the Lesson."

"The Lairs are the danger!" The response was in
one voice, with liturgical fervor. Sparks out in the
Lake of Light reflected briefly in their upturned eyes.

"Then hear me now: for I have smelled tomorrow."

For a heartbeat only the steady courage they wore
like winter fat fled and revealed another thing
beneath. They had no confusion about his meaning,
and the thing that flared briefly was fear.

"Listen: since the proper hunt with Two-Legs began,
hunters have known a full, happy time. Blood feuds
between the hahns are bitter memories, and individual feuding on the hunt reduced to proper ritual. The
hunt with Two-Legs is the all. Against the Hot Claw of
the Two-Legs our fiercest hunters find full measure for
their fury. Those who prevail, and still seek out the
hunt with Two-Legs, find full measure of their final
worth, and their songs are the pride of their hahns."

A murmur of assent rumbled around the pool.

"But listen: good follows bad, and the bad the good, as dark follows the dayfire. When then again the time for evil? I have dreamed tomorrow, and this I tell for all the hahns to know: evil hunts among the bones of the Orange Claw Lairs to end our Way."

"Then call its name, and we will hunt it, too!" Voina, Aland hahn, inheritors of the Orange Claw valley. "But let us hunt this thing quickly and be done. My blooded younger brother prepares himself even now for his first full-claw hunt of a Two-Legs. His fourth hunting will be against the claw of Furlip, of the Two Rivers lair."

"Haiii!" It moved around the pool, unbidden salute to the name of Furlip.

"Furlip's Two-Legs have been hunted for a judging before this," Girta half crooned, the storytelling rhythm still on him. "Came this one to this council pool the summer Ruhoor went against Furlip's hunters on DiTenka's marches . . ."

"Furlip is known to us all," the Aland growled. "Full eight have I made the stalking pass well-sung among his blinds, and a full claw of missed strikes from lesser hunters at his side. He is a hunter."

"His claw is death." DiTenka.

A pebble smashed into the pool, destroying the dark images lurking there, shocking the hunters to rigid attention.

"Be still!" Sunto ordered. "*Evil* is the hunter, and its claw is the ending of our Way."

"That challenge has been thrown before!" Turso, laughing. "Two-Legs before this have fouled the wind with their dreams of changing, or ending, our Way. Where are they now? Gone! Gone back to the Lake of Light in their Bright Boulders light as thistle, and their stomachs much the better for their going!"

Rough laughter growled around the pool.

"Full strange, then," Sunto said coldly. "This old belly must be dim and strangled with the gas of bad eating, for it sees a Two-Legs which dens unchased within the Permanent Lairs."

Voina bristled instantly. "Thou accuse Aland somehow in this thing?"

Sunto turned his full attention upon the younger. Their stomachs locked. A moment stretched. Voina slowly smoothed his fur and sank back.

"I accuse no hahn nor hunter. Thou know full well this strange long Two-Legs dens in the Permanent Lairs, and ignores every hunting challenge from hunters who seek him out. Of late, he has denned side by side with an aging beast he believes damaged from the hunt. . . ."

"Thou . . . ?" breathed Voina.

"The ruins are my home. I have studied this strange Two-Legs."

"Are we, beneath whose bellies the herds do move, unable now to chase one simple Two-Legs to places better suited to his digestion than here?" A growl from Turso.

"Know, Arnic, last living of the Orange Claw and Only shared a hunting just this dayfire gone with the strange long Two-Legs. Orange Claw fed fear into his digestion, yet failed to chase him. Does Arnic wish a sample of the feeding he ignored?"

"A new and dangerous breed, then." Begrudgingly.

"Is this odd Two-Legs the evil?" Girta.

"Only a part of the evil; not the most dangerous part. His stomach sends me dreams of a Bright Boulder light as thistle, like and yet unlike all others ever known. It is like a hunting blind—and yet too small for the smallest Two-Legs. In some way past my actual knowing, this strange long Two-Legs is its hahn-mate. They link somehow, and hunt together. But they are only harriers for another hunter whose belly lies beyond my digestion, somewhere beyond the Lake of Light. . . .

"Since I have dreamed this evil, my belly is ill past help of warm fresh blood to soothe it. The long Two-Legs dens in the valley of my fathers, his stomach calls this strange Bright Boulder closer, and the evil that I smell drives them both. In some manner past all digestion, this evil means to end the hunt with Two-Legs and remove them from our marches."

"End our Way!" Turso.

"That is my dream."

The hunters considered the shadows of their spirit brothers in the pool. None doubted the power of Sunto's dreaming, but they could not digest that the dream could come to pass. Two-Legs fit too perfectly now into the ordering of things. His loss would be past all digesting. Therefore, if the thing that threatened their digestion was made of flesh and blood, why then—

Voina raised his head and voiced the thought that formed solid as a fanged mouth in the gloom:

"Oldest of the Orange Claw and Only, show us the spoor, and we will hunt this evil in its turn."

9

THE CAR LOST AIRSPEED AND NOSED OVER. NOW THE CROWNS OF THE BIG *coli* trees that dotted the plain were higher than the cockpit. The airspeed indicator read forty km. As I watched, the needle drifted down. Thirty-eight, thirty-three.

LaChoy concentrated on his driving. He banked around a stand of thorncane and eased between two huge *colis*. Past the trees, the land fell away in undulating waves. Maybe a kilometer away, black in the dim morning light, solid timber marked a watercourse. We angled left across the falling ground. A stretch of smaller trees straggled up from the watercourse. My mouth was dry. Here it came.

"Got yourself located?" LaChoy said without turning.

"Yes." The word sounded scratchy in my dry throat. Only the third day of this, and the tension was beginning to get to me. "Yes," I said again. That was better.

"Right. Sorry about the melodramatics, but this fella begs 'em. I've had hell's own time trying to get a client a fair shot at him. No one's squeezed a shot on him yet. This fellow's a shrewdie, all right."

"How many have tried him before me?"

"Three. Three good men, too. One a vacationing Rim Patrol type. Scouter, you know. Civil Service and all that, but damned tough job. Seen any amount of nastiness out on the Rim. He was First-In on Carbonal. Jacks, that was. Claimed hunting greer relaxes him! Then a high-finance type from Inside, and one world president. Jacks came closest. Got one glimpse of him, moving the wrong way in heavy brush. Refused the shot. Didn't want to wound."

"Three," I said. "Then he knows he's wanted."

"He knows. They catch on damn quick. But this is his urine holding, and nobody has bothered him enough to hie his bladder off elsewhere. He likes it here. I sometimes get the strange notion he likes our little dance as well as we do. Never changes his habits enough to duck me completely—just enough, you know, to keep me hot behind him, but luckless. Almost decided to take a crack at him myself."

"What stopped you?"

"Voice-post from a guy named Ramsey. Heard of him? Wanted to come out and pot a greer. Decided I'd give one more client a go. Big name in literature and all, you know. Needed to impress this Ramsey chappie a bit. Can't have bad media, or they'll all start spending their money somewhere else."

As he spoke he maneuvered the boat in a silent drift, clearing the arm of brush, dropping back at an angle toward the watercourse.

"Drop in ten minutes," Nail's voice said over the com.

"Righto," LaChoy said. He glanced across. "Ready?"

I nodded, not trusting my alkaline vocal cords. My hands were sweaty on the rifle between my knees. I caught myself leaning forward, tight. Today was it. I wasn't in a pleasure bubble or virtual palace anymore. No mind-expanding technicolored clouds, no blood-heating alcohol. No phony talk or phonier sex. I had got away from civilization, all right. All the way away. I had asked for it, and here it was.

The doors on both sides of the car slipped back out of the way and cold air burst in. LaChoy spoke, keying the robopilot, and the trim of the car changed minutely as it took over. He gathered his big frontier blaster and a little kit sack.

"Just land light and jog right on toward that brush just ahead," LaChoy said. "Take up whatever momentum you need that way. You'll see a little break in the branches dead on. Steer in there and you'll see the blind. Go straight on in with a minimum of fuss. I'll be just behind."

The car slipped gears, and now we were coasting. "Now," said LaChoy, and pivoted his seat, swung his legs overboard, and stepped out.

I was moving in a hurry, afraid to be left behind, and stumbled when I hit. A couple of quick strides and a hop pulled me out of it and into a jog, the ground pounding up through my legs and knocking the tension out of them. LaChoy was pacing me in that peculiar crabbed stride of a fit man matching his stride to somebody who wasn't. I opened up a little, my breath easy, and it was okay now, as if I could go on up the sloping ground and clear back to camp if I needed to. It wasn't true, after all the soft years, but it felt good, and then the break in the branches was there, and the blind, and I was in, dropping into a dry, springy mass of *coli* leaves, LaChoy hitting his knees right beside me.

He was grinning, breathing evenly. He laid his kit sack down in the corner of the blind and carefully twisted to rest his back against the trunk that formed the rear wall of the blind. He stretched his legs out and cradled the short, heavy stopper on his lap. I leaned the seven gun forward against the notched shooting stick and wormed around until I was close enough to kneel up behind it in one slow motion when the time came. LaChoy made a thumbs-up and pointed with his chin.

Nail's car was ghosting in from the direction of camp with the two plains bison slung beneath it, dangling loosely, legs free. They were still unconscious. The car settled deftly until their legs touched, halted, then it eased lower until they were down completely. One end of each sling dropped free, and the winches quickly reeled them under the bodies and up. The car jinked around, and first sun glittered on a silver barrel at the driver's window. Nail was supplying the restorative. Then the car was gone.

It took the bison a while to come around and finally regain their feet. They checked each other out first, sniffing and grumbling like a couple of Mickey Finned senior citizens. Then they backed off and banged heads an experimental time or two, but gave up without cows to give it sexual impetus. Finally the larger one lowered its head to browse. The other one kept moving about fretfully, testing the wind, and couldn't seem to settle down.

I wiped my hands carefully on a small dun-colored towel LaChoy had provided. The younger bull's fidgets were giving me the fidgets, too. I figured an hour had drifted by since Nail had dropped them in. The sun was clear of the timber now, cutting the chill somewhat. It looked like another of those limpid, absolutely windless and almost warm days LaChoy said we were almost out of for the season. The satellites already were tracking polar storm systems. He said the equinox would hit almost overnight. First with wind that would try to blow the tents down, and sometimes succeed, and then with driving rain or snow, depending on elevation, and we would have maybe two weeks before the real cold hit and the herds moved south, and most of the greer with them.

The cold-birthing of their young would be coming, and the season would be over.

Eliot, the other hunter in LaChoy's camp, intended to stick it out until the end for a first-class trophy, or go home without. I could feel the tension of the deadline working inside my nervousness about the hunt itself.

I looked at my watch. Time had slowed to a crawl. The waiting, and my growing nervousness, had fooled me. If I had come here straight from Acme in my youth, I wouldn't have been fooled. It took an awful lot of patience to outwait an Acme *fragle,* and you never even saw a mature one if time could trick you into thinking it was passing faster than it was. If you let the time fool you, or work on your nerves, it would finally seem to take forever for even an hour to pass, and maybe the movement of checking the time had spooked off the doe you never saw, and the buck wouldn't be coming that day, after all.

That was the way it was hunting on Acme, and I grew up with it, and learned to wait, and wait what seemed an hour longer, and then count backward from one hundred, and then forward, and *then* check the time. Anybody who doubted time was relative should have hunted Acme *fragle.*

I killed my first young buck when I was eighteen, after four solid years of teaching myself how to wait. Finally I could just sit motionless while a jarnbug spun one of those three-dimensional cone webs from the barrel of my rifle to my boots and back again, until it was completely satisfied with its construction and hid

to wait for those big, fat, stupid honeybees to be
lured by the *jarnice* it secreted on the web. I could
wait while the first honeybees began to drone around
and around the web, trying to find the nectar that just
had to be there somewhere.

The jarns were my luck and my teachers, though
sometimes I rooted for the bees to get away. They
never did, not all of them, and one jarn took three of
them once while I waited near a swamp for the herds
to feed into range. The *fragle* never came that day.
But the day I killed the imperial stag I wrote into my
first book, there was a jarn building a cone off the bill
of my cap, and almost done when I took the shot. I
had put all that in the book, too. I found myself wish-
ing for a jarn now, to build a lucky trap in a thorn
blind six hundred light-years from Acme.

LaChoy touched my shoulder. I controlled a spasm
of released nerves by main force, and eased pressure
on the seven gun's safety where my thumb had
landed before I could control it. I had gone so far into
my memory of the jarns I had forgot LaChoy and why
I was here. If a *fragle* had appeared in front of the
blind, I would have killed it cleanly and without conscious thought, I had been so lost in memory. If a
greer had shown at that precise moment, I would
have been so surprised I would have refused the shot,
because greers didn't stalk the Acme highlands of my
mind.

I turned my head slowly. He was watching me
intently. Slowly his lips shaped the individual letters
G-R-E-E-R. He was listening so hard his ears seemed
to curve forward under his hat. He gestured minutely
with his chin at the bison.

They knew it, too.

They both were standing four-square, nostrils

flared, reading the breeze that came up through the timber. A ridge of muscle in the young bull's shoulder was quivering uncontrollably.

That was the first time I recognized the fear.

It had been gnawing around the edges of my mind, and here it was outright. I was scared as hell. I was afraid with a crawling nasty little fear that turns your insides cold and your bowels to jelly, and cramps your hands like frost.

I stared at the young bull in fascination, my eyes fixed on that jerking writhe of muscle. The old bull just stood his ground, horns up, waiting. His eyes were a little walled, but that was all. The old bull knew it was coming, and knew there wasn't a damn thing he could do to stop it.

I looked back at LaChoy. The cold killer's eyes still were vacant, looking at nothing, the ears still cocked. His face had the look of someone listening to something far off. The moan of a tornado funnel, maybe, or the distant growl of an enemy armored column. Something just on the verge of audibility, but capable of being on him before he could think what to do. He still was outwardly relaxed, like a cat that comes out of sleep with an alien noise in its lair.

My palms weren't damp anymore. They were as dry as my throat and lungs, and my fingers were cold. They were so cold it was hard to resist an urge to blow on my trigger finger to ease the numbness.

The old bull remained at full ready, and so did LaChoy. The younger *askari* bull didn't want any of this, not any of it. Now, way too late, I wasn't sure I did. I hadn't expected this cold awful fear of something unavoidable that was coming out of the timber to get me. Death and taxes kept running through my brain. Nothing's certain but death and taxes. And this, whatever this was. This was just as certain.

The bulls knew they were on unfamiliar ground and couldn't run. If they ran, it would come on faster and they would never see it come, nor have any chance to strike a futile blow against it. They knew it as surely in their instinct-centers as man learns it every generation. Running wasn't the answer.

It was close now, an almost audible shock wave of fear rolling up out of the watercourse. Say three hundred meters. Close enough range for anything but this. This was the old way, the real old way. You had to be sure, and then be twenty meters closer. You did not half-shoot a greer, or they came and tore you. You didn't reveal your position by any nervous twitch, or they vanished like bog mist.

My seven gun seemed like a futile toy against the awful push of my fear. The greer-mock had been nothing compared to this. That had been reflex; target practice. This was something else entirely. I knew now beyond all doubt why greer came so high, and why this one had escaped three of the better guns. They didn't cough, or roar, or bugle when they came for you. They just brought the fear, like a cello note, strummed once and dying, and all your courage dying with it.

LaChoy was intent on the tree line, eyes almost glazed with the effort of trying to materialize the beast. The younger bull pawed the ground nervously.

It was taking too long. LaChoy was looking the wrong way.

If the greer had been coming from that direction, the bulls would have winded him and known which way to turn, or to run. If he was stalking through the brush along the watercourse, they would have turned on him like compass needles as he moved, trying to keep him in front of them because he would have been too close to run from. They might even have heard something moving.

I *had* heard something moving.

Behind me.

That's when I got it. I knew LaChoy was fooled, but I wasn't. The bulls were fooled, too. They were waiting for something in the timber to show itself, but nothing was going to. The action was going to come from the one specific place we had arranged for it to be impossible to come from. From directly behind us, down our spoor that appeared out of nowhere where the car had put us down, and straight into the blind, moving like a ghost with steel, steam-driven claws.

Not quite a ghost. That had been a pebble scraping on rock, starting to roll and chafing to a stop, as it would beneath a soft-soled hunting moccasin. I had caught pebbles like that myself, under my feet, stopping the sound. If I did it well, I still had a chance to get into position on the *fragle*, but if I failed, they were gone, and the day's chance with it.

So: a pebble grating, not under a moccasin, but beneath a leathery paw, almost not a sound, the mistake sensed by the stalking beast and corrected quickly. My kidneys felt like they were suddenly trying to shrink into walnuts under my rib cage. My buttocks were clenched as if, by force of sphincter, I could keep a muscled, claw-tipped piledriver from ripping my bowels out.

My hands were on the seven gun, but a weird kind of lassitude settled over me.

It had been coming and coming and now here it was. My ears were strained to popping for the first faint rustle of breath or heavy smash of a charge. I would get one shot. One shot, and it would have to be the hardest one, the brain shot. I wished I could magically swap the hollow-point in the chamber for one of the pencil-bombs. We were completely outflanked, as neatly as by a Zion guerrilla, and nearly out of it entirely.

I drew my legs ever so slowly under me. Blood marched like snare drums in my ears. I wouldn't be able to hear anything for the pounding of my blood. Low survival characteristic; how had I survived this long, for Christ's sake? LaChoy glanced slowly at me, and pointed again with his chin toward the worried bison. He was almost grinning in his glee that his ambush had worked. He didn't have a clue, and I couldn't believe it. It had worked, all right. It had almost put us out of work entirely. But it was too close now to worry about that. To think about that would mean I would be too slow. It was here.

I don't know what I was waiting for. I *knew* it was here, right behind us, and I knew LaChoy was completely fooled, but still I was afraid to react and be ridiculously wrong. A lot of things had changed since Acme. Too many. I never would have considered deferring to another about a hunting question back then, no matter how much the fat cats paid him for his ability. I was no longer the hunter I was then, and that was likely to get me eaten before this sun went down today on this misbegotten plateau.

That one image—of being torn limb from limb without even getting off a shot—broke my paralysis, and I came up in a lurch, like an old-fashioned jack-in-the-box, with the rifle gluing to my cheek as I spun with only the most fleeting side glance of LaChoy's shocked, angry face. He thought my nerve had broken.

The greer was in the air. He was in the air, it was that close, a huge shape hurtling down the path we had taken into the blind.

He had found us, searching carefully and thoughtfully, and allowing for the aircar, and selected his best line of attack, and he was in the middle of a leap that would have matched the best effort of a Bengal tiger when I shoved the rifle through the blind and blew the top of his head off at point-blank range.

His leap carried him right past, slamming the rifle out of my hands and brushing me to the ground like a runaway truck.

The ear-busting smack of the seven-millimeter in close quarters, the impact of my landing, and the crash of the greer's fall, seemed to occur at the same moment. The next moment I was digging frantically for my rifle and LaChoy was out of the blind, crabbing sidewise, the big Colt-DuPont flamer rammed nearly against the vast thrashing bulk in its death throes. My sleeves were soaked in steaming, stinking wetness, and the blind was drenched. By the time I came upright with my rifle, the greer had finished its unplanned dying.

LaChoy straightened. I had a death grip on the stock of the seven gun, which was coated and slippery from the near passage of that ruined head.

The fear was gone, obliterated by the violent action of the kill. The older bison bull still was standing his ground. The younger one was making long tracks to somewhere far away. I took a deep breath, trying to steady down. LaChoy hunkered by the steaming carcass, fumbling in his bush jacket for his pipe. I noticed a slight tremor in his hands.

"Well," I said.

"Sweet Saint Ernie!" LaChoy said. "I told you he

was prime. Didn't I tell you he was prime? I told you all right. I must say I didn't realize quite *how* prime myself. You seem to have reversed the tables a bit, old man. Shot the beastie off my back instead of the usual and approved manner. How in hell did you know he was doing that? Just how in hell did you know that, when I didn't even have a clue? He certainly has never even thought of doing that before."

"I didn't really know. Not really. Not until it was too late."

"Almost too late," LaChoy said. "There's the world of difference, chappie, between too late and almost too late."

I had not seen him this talkative before. It was a sign, I supposed, of the degree to which he had been affected by the kill. By the time he put fire to his pipe tobacco, his hands were steady again. Well, he was used to this.

"Old Bwana One-Shot," he said, puffing aromatic clouds of tobacco around. "Last of the hairy-chested. Sweet Karamojo and Ernie, just sweet all but forgotten Jesus Christ! I supposed I truly am born to be flamed after all. But didn't I tell you, though, how prime he was?"

I still was having trouble with my vocal equipment, so I walked over and looked down at the beast that almost got me. Got LaChoy, rather; I would just have been a bonus. The fur on the huge carcass was luxurious and fine, but befouled with dark blood and brain tissue. That would clean up. The huge head was a bombed-out ruin. He was as dead as he was ever going to get. His brains and blood on my sleeves and gun were cooling now, and really beginning to reek.

I still was trying to process the awful fear that had come out of nowhere and almost paralyzed me.

Almost like something outside of myself. Did that always happen? Was this what that crazy tramp, Python, had been raving about in camp?

I had reached inside myself to a place I didn't even know was there, and come up with the shot of my life against the damnedest thing that ever tried to kill me, and I just couldn't grasp it. Maybe later the memory would settle sharply into place, but it just wasn't real to me now.

I didn't see, after this, how anything ever was going to seem completely real again.

10

"BWANA ONE-SHOT," LACKOY TOASTED ME, AND SLUGGED BACK ENOUGH Earth scotch to drown a dipsomaniac. "You old son."

"One shot, by God," said Nail, in high good humor. "Only four days in camp, too. Only three days of actual hunting. Lucky, I guess!" He knocked back some of that smoky Pondoro brew with the taste of steel and honey in it.

"Damned good luck," Eliot said. He was something to do with banks in a system in the Tau Ceti, and he was trying hard to play the part of the good sport, for my sake. He had been in camp off and on for two months now, and had almost no time until the equinox, and then his trip of a lifetime would be over. He already was facing the grim idea of going home empty-handed.

"Damned good luck," he said again.

He was almost choking on it. He had passed up a cubless female and refused the shot on two different immature males that had made nuisances of themselves around his blinds. He said maybe the greer had decreed him unworthy of a chance at a true trophy, and he was only half joking. He looked like he wanted to cry, but he kept slugging the liquor back and grinning and offering congratulations.

"You'll get a shot," I said. "Hell, you have to get one. You'll probably get a shot tomorrow before I even roll out of the sack from all this drinking. Then we'll birdshoot till shiptime." I waved my arm at the robobar, and it floated over and squirted my glass full. "Hell, you'll get a shot, easy. You deserve it, you really do."

Anybody who has ever hunted with luck knows how easy it is to be generous to those who haven't.

"Let's just not talk about it too much, okay?" he said.

He looked ready to cry. I wondered what his board of directors would think if they could see how he was bearing up. I hoped they knew he was a good one.

"Let's just talk about your guy," he said. "God, what a beauty. The oldest male taken this season, too. Tell it again, LaChoy, that's the best thing. Tell how it went again, and maybe some of the luck will rub off."

I knew right now Eliot would swap all the trophies he had ever taken, all the finances he had ever finagled, to be the one sitting there with dried blood and brains on his sleeves, having a fuss made by the hired help. So would I, for that matter, but I didn't have to. I had paid for it in that blind today, and now I had it for all time, or at least until something luckier than my greer collected me. Some kind of internal rot from all the soft years had been burned out of me in those few seconds, and something I once was had been returned to me.

Ball was in our tent, sulking because he had wanted to record my emotions and the small party around the campfire in my honor, for future creation. He didn't seem prepared to believe I had managed on my own before he came along. I had the irrational notion that a bunch of bipeds drinking around the campfire aroused some kind of shape-envy. Ball seemed to despise every bipedal pleasure in which he could not partake, which covers quite a few of our very favorite ones and often left him, with the quality of his sensors, in a positive dither.

"Drink up!" LaChoy said, and set an example. "More liquor for the Sahib One-Shot, the Acme Hawkeye, the twenty-fifth-century Robert Ruark. Karamojo and Ernie, I almost knocked you flat when you bounced up like that! Thought a bug had chewed your tender inner-planet arse and put you orbit-bound. Can you just picture the outcome if I had done? Can't you just?"

"That would have gotten pretty involved in the hell of a hurry," Nail said, laughing.

LaChoy looked at him blearily when everybody else laughed, but I saw Nail look away. He was embarrassed by what he saw in the older hunter's face.

"Tomorrow we'll try for that big lop-eared male about two hundred klicks from here," LaChoy told Eliot. "You and I, young man. We will let Bwana Ramsey sleep the sleep of the lucky. Perhaps we should kiss his royal arse for luck. His mightiness, the greatest greer-slayer of modern times, though you deserve to be, based on good hard hunting effort."

"I'll try anything," Eliot said.

He didn't really believe tomorrow would be different. He looked like a kid who heard his birthday had been canceled for lack of interest. He had it so badly he hadn't noticed LaChoy was beginning to question himself about his lapse in judgment.

The conversation went on without me, about plans for tomorrow and when to get up and how much detoxifier to take with morning billy to ensure a clear head and good reflexes. I could hear LaChoy's own silences inside the general conversation. He was feeling carefully inside of himself to inventory what he had left to take out against the greer tomorrow.

He needed to have that straight before sunup, because this decent and trusting client was too unseasoned to realize something else had happened out there besides my getting the greer that should by rights have been his. LaChoy was past the congratulating-me part and into the doubting-himself part, and the scotch was taking a hell of a beating.

I had been where LaChoy was too recently not to read the signs. He had to decide whether he still could impose himself between his client and the greer, as he always had. If the answer was no, he had to level with the paying customer. Either that or go out and get collected by the greer, and maybe Eliot, too, beyond the power of the Medfac to save either of them. It was a decision I was glad I didn't have to face.

Ball materialized out of the darkness.

"There you are," I said. "Have a shot of ten-weight on the Sergeant Major."

For once in our association, he ignored the jibe. "Ramsey, there's trouble."

"What?" I was bemused by the fire and drink and the emotions of the day.

"Trouble, bad trouble," Ball said quietly. His voice sliced through the cobwebs without being loud. "Snap out of it, Ramsey."

"What kind of trouble?"

"Watch the Rongor rustbucket."

As he spoke, the Rongor glided into the fireglow and growled something to LaChoy. Nail uncoiled from his camp chair and faded into the night. LaChoy stood unsteadily and told the robobar to punch him up a full detox. Everybody else was leaving the camp-fire at varying rates of speed.

"You heard?" Ball said.

"No."

"The Rongor says something's coming in. Gives off a signature like Python, but not like Python. The rust-bucket is confused."

"Is it Python?"

"Yes. But more dead than alive. And tracked by greer. You might arm yourself."

"All right. You have detox if I need it?"

"Of course."

I was lead-footed across the uneven ground. The long day, the heavy bison-chop meal, and the whiskey dragged me down like extra gravity. I found my rifle and cartridges in the tent and remembered to slip on my *fragle* stalkers and *twon*-down jacket. Before trouble starts is the time to prepare for how long it can last. I learned that the hard way on Zion.

"Close, now," Ball said when I rejoined him in the clearing.

"Where is everybody?"

"Behind the Rongor on the west perimeter—where Python is coming in."

"What about the flanks, the rear?"

"Relax, Ramsey." The cyborg was imperturbable. "This is Pondoro, remember? It's not an enemy assault, it's a hunting pack."

"You're right," I said.

I was going to say something else, but lurid light-ning cracked on the western edge of the camp, strik-ing twice in quick succession. The night came apart with the rumble of discharged energy. Before the rolling thunder had died, a new howl zoomed throat-ily up to full cry: a Rongor battle siren.

11

DEATH, TERRIBLE AND UTTERLY SILENT, CAME AND FASTENED WHITE-HOT claws in his flesh. When drilled Palikar reflex saved his life from ending in that moment, Python's warm shocked life poured thickly, horrifyingly, almost eagerly out. The reflex that saved him culminated in a punishing counterstroke that arrived on the strength of blood already lost. A single heartbeat to control the outflow of his life before it all was pumped away, and then he must dodge again, all that was left of his life force unequally divided between fending off inrushing death and stanching the outpour of blood that welled into the back of his throat, to strangle him.

Python vomited abruptly, with great violence, directly onto the unseen earth before his slitted eyes, and knew tasting it, though he could no longer see it, that there was more blood this time.

"Was ever self so rent, so frayed?"

The squeaky, upper-register voice trembled with self pity. It was his own voice, unrecognizable, gibbering against a hurt so severe it could not be eased by all the training he owned, or all the effort of the desperate sybil. He reached for a shard of will to pin down that frightened squeak lest some bold night rodent come a-hunting in the dark—some rodent or far worse.

The effort cost him some of the precision that

guided battered nerve nets away from registry of his bite-crushed extremities. He sprawled in the dust, quivering. The residual warmth of the alien land was the sole friend left him in the friendless dark. He dozed. . . .

Death sprang (soundless) for his throat like formless smoke on a hurricane wind. But though the creature was Death Incarnate, and had been silent and swift and merciless as Death ought to be, what served it for lungs now labored sickly because what served it for ribs had smashed through their heaving membrane, shattered by the nastri movement that slew Iron Fennec ages—was it ages?—ago.

"I hunt not. Yet am hunted. Slay not. Yet am slain . . ."

The self-pitying litany repeated itself until the awareness that it was his whimper, his self-pity, his dead giveaway in the hostile dark, forced him back to a semblance of consciousness.

He had to be near the camp by now. He had been crawling for at least a thousand years across the veldt from the ruins where death had caught him unprepared. It was vaguely puzzling that he had fought death to a standstill but could not crawl these few kilometers of easy veldt with a thousand years to accomplish it. . . .

Death was formless no longer in his decreasing flashes of lucidity, but a raving single-minded beast that would not fall to the best martial strikes of all mankind's unarmed combat history, reinforced by the inhuman power of the sybil. It attacked and attacked, and mauled his too-fragile frame until he now resembled (in his waning lucid flashes) a chewed and castoff toy which leaked dark liquid sawdust.

Python subsided back into the ground while the

sybil symbiote fought desperately to hold his decaying body together to shield his life spark. Grass muttered in his hearing, tough stems thuttering in a night wind that wracked his ruined body with chills and touched molten fire to his coagulating wounds. Dead and decaying and alive to crawl for a thousand years like a stepped-on ant across those few kilometers, forever far from help. The sybil did not want to relapse into insensate stasis, awaiting the carrion eaters. He shuddered. If the sybil sensed a suitable host, it would not hesitate to flush its seals from the ruptured arteries and shattered nerve trunks, and let in death.

Death had come spraying the froth of its own dying and fell back from impacts that tore through panishatri, through sybil, and screamed on the grating ends of severed bones. It tore him even as his final desperate strength battered its fangs to bloody fragments, crushed a jaw hinge, tore its neck tendons asunder in a spray of blood and pain.

Python rallied again.

He said quite clearly into the night: "I sought no advantage; my blood is clean."

The old winner's ritual he had once and many times mouthed in solemn perjury while the sybil purred hidden throughout his cellular integrity. In that same unfogged moment, he realized he was closer to the hunters' camp than he had dared to hope, but that it no longer mattered.

The greer had puzzled out his neural spore, and now coursed the neural drag of his pain as surely as they might follow a blood trail he had burned up precious strength to avoid leaving. He felt emptied, deflated, and yet too aware of the feverish weight of his remaining blood upon his wounds, impatient of further captivity, aching to burst into the warm earth and freedom.

The greer were coming eagerly now. They had the scent he had been at horrific pain not to leave.

The scent? Of what? Is there an odor to my pain?

His fading consciousness struggled with the problem, and he sensed a tectonic shift in the core of his being. The sybil had become resigned to its fate. One more convulsion and the greer would find carrion—and more than carrion.

"No!" he mumbled brokenly. "I will not release you upon these beasts."

A deadly interior chill flushed through him. The sybil's answer. No—the fear came from outside, *from the greer.*

"You killed me and now you steal my courage. It is not mete to die cringing thus. . . ." His voice trailed off.

"I will rest now in the Earth," his mind dredged out of his rapidly darkening memory. "The Earth is my home."

The hypnotic force of those loaded phrases reached out of his inner darkness and washed the alien fear from his dying carcass.

The fear was back in an instant, redoubled, running down the darkness toward him like wildfire.

The sybil waited.

"I will rest now. . . ."

The fear poured over him, and the locks quivered and broke free. The pain from the eager blood forcing itself between the lips of his wounds blazed up and then fell below awareness.

The last thing he heard was a faraway rumble, like artillery on a distant front, and then a sullen buzzing as of a furious fly. Before his emptied brain could wonder at those sounds, the last vital linkage breached, the sybil gibbering in sudden terror, and there was nothing.

12

WHEN THE SERGEANT MAJOR WENT INTO ACTION ON THE OTHER SIDE OF the camp, Ball wasted no time waiting for Ramsey. He was at Python's side before the Rongor finished its lightning recon of the vicinity, and came back to verify the bubbling ruins of two prime greer.

"Medfac!" Ball snapped. "Now! Move, rustbucket—he's already clinical and his brain is packing up for keeps."

The Rongor didn't quibble. It just scooped up the broken body and ran, nearly bowling over some of the humans coming up in a tight skirmish screen.

"It's finished," Ball rapped out. "Don't get trigger happy! The only greer in miles is barbecue."

The hunters relaxed visibly, accepting Ball's assuredness with the same readiness as had the Rongor. Ramsey came up puffing hard.

Ball dropped his command voice. "Well well, the cavalry," he said.

"Go to hell. What happened?"

"It was Python," LaChoy said. "A couple of greer must have caught him coming into camp; they breached the security perim and the S-M did them." He surveyed the smoldering remains. "Sweet Spirit of Charity, this will cost me a season's net to square with the Hunt Commission. I'll be lucky if they don't order the S-M scrapped."

"Trot out Asimovian law," Ball said. "He was protecting a human."

"Where is Python?" Ramsey said.

"Medfac," Ball said. "He was clinical when I got here. No human is to touch him until he is clinically restored. I detected extremely hot viral contaminants in his body. Source unknown, but deadly. I have nothing to juice him with that'll bring back a clinical. You need to get him to Central Receiving, right now. Full quarantine drill."

"Clinical!" LaChoy shook his head. "Alien virus." He still looked hung over. "Oh, God." He headed for the Medfac.

"Greer killed him?" said Ramsey.

"Greer, yes, but not, I think, these two," Ball told him. "They were unmarked before the Rongor fired, and Python's wounds are hours old. The infection is fully evolved."

"How can you tell they were unmarked?" Eliot spoke up.

"If Ball says they were unmarked, they were unmarked," Ramsey said.

"Christ," the banker said. "I wish I could have got a shot."

"The Rongor was hasty; you had time," Ball said. "Perhaps you should sue for a return of your fees if this hunter persists in using third-rate hardware."

"Don't start," Ramsey said. "Why shouldn't the greer that attacked Python be unmarked? He went unarmed, remember?"

"The man who killed Iron Fennec in single combat before the referees could interfere is never unarmed," Ball said.

Ramsey got it first, then the others.

"Python?" Nail said. "*Python* is Baka Martin?"

"More precisely, Baka Martin is Python."

"I missed it that first night," Ramsey said. "It was

right there in front of me and I missed it. I'm getting old."

"It comes to all bipeds."

"There's suddenly a lot of things I don't understand," Nail said quietly. "Baka Martin on Pondoro? Why? He was a member of the Terran Service before he did Fennec. Did he want to try a greer unarmed? Then why all the hocus-pocus about storytelling? He's always avoided confrontations with the greer. They never go near those ruins. Isn't that why he camped there?"

"All good questions," Ball said.

"I'll set up a perimeter until the S-M comes back on duty," Nail said. "LaChoy will have the battlefreeze ready, and the S-M can handle Python to minimize risk."

As the humans scattered, Ball saw he was being forgotten in the rush, and took advantage of it. His sphere took on a mottled pattern superior to the Rongor camouflage, and he allowed himself to fade into the gloom before he powered up, aiming away from camp. No one saw him go, and the Rongor didn't care.

He negotiated a slope into a thick stand of trees, took a bearing from the fireglow, and made a cast for Python's blood trail.

There wasn't one.

Ball considered the age and severity of the wounds, and upped his estimation of the survival skills of Palikar-trained bipeds.

It would be more difficult to locate the route the injured Python had taken by snapped twig or disturbed soil alone. Stored in his data was considerable information on the ancient art of woodcraft. Ball reviewed his information and decided it could be done. Trailing was first and foremost careful observation, and he admitted no equal as an observer.

It took him ten minutes to find where Martin had forded the narrower of the two streams that flanked the camp. The water sluiced from his hide like clear oil as he crossed. Next he found a pressed-down area of forest compost beneath dense brush where Python had lain in his own vomit. There was dried blood in the depression—not only human blood. Ball congratulated himself; he had known the Palikar reflex would draw blood in a mortal confrontation.

While not exactly at the top of a hereditary pyramid aimed at trailblazing, Ball's physique did not hamper him unduly. With the feedback of his first discoveries, he moved along the back trail more swiftly.

As he traveled he developed postulations. The two greer had followed Python from the scene of his battle. They had taken pains to fox their own back trail as they came. Was Python then considered such a deadly opponent they feared he would turn on them, or did they fear reprisals from the camp?

Fear reprisals? Ball ruminated on that as he worked out their movements in pitch-blackness. Python had implied greer were more than men imagined. How much more?

One of the creatures had worked out Python's almost nonexistent trail, while the other had paralleled him at a distance. A picket against possible ambush, that was plain—but such behavior in a predator argued some rudimentary intelligence.

Python had depleted precious reserves to hide his trace, and the greer had come straight on without a single false cast to show they had been fooled. Had they tracked him by scent alone? By sound? Not by sight, in this darkness. Ball knew they didn't have the ocular range he did.

Another puzzle. They clearly had the ability to close and finish their crippled quarry, yet they had not. Why not? Fear? Or curiosity about his destination? Again—intelligence at work?

Daybreak was imminent when he backtracked the three into the scattered, roofless ruins beside the river. Ball stopped cold, replaying Nail's earlier offhand remark: "*They never go near those ruins.*"

Ruins of an alien and rudimentary civilization on a Freehold world. Their genuine character, and comparative newness on the galactic scale, were glaringly evident to one of Ball's resources. Yet the ruins matched nothing in his library of stored Pondoro data. Nor had there been a single reference to an indigenous culture here since his arrival on Pondoro.

Nevertheless, here stood the ruins, roofless and desolate, and scarred by the stigmata of beam weaponry.

And here led the back trail of Python and his shadowers.

Ball weighed the risks momentarily, then beamed a call to Planetary Information Central. He secured the central library reference number and called the library.

Deep in the control console of his multifaceted sensory array, a pinhole monitor showed him what a human viewphone would; a tiny transmitter showed the librarian an ersatz Keith Ramsey asking the questions. The librarian was a humanoid robot in a blond wig. Ball was relieved to find the local human phobia that produced the absurd false hair also left the 'round-the-clock tedium of a reference department to a machine.

"Questions, please?"

Ball considered. Ramsey might ask if the synthetic mammaries flowed ten-weight oil for little tin soldiers, but Ramsey was a throwback. Instead, Ball recited an authorization code in Ramsey's voice, and the librarian accepted it with perfect equanimity.

He put a camera to work scanning the ruins. His exoskelton revolved like a turret, leaving his brain completely immobile, encysted among its support and propulsion systems.

"These views are located on Planet Pondoro, B Continent," Ball said.

"Yes," agreed the librarian. "Questions, please."

Ball noticed a vegetable garden, identified the plants, and extrapolated their probable planter before showing them to the librarian.

"Is this find on public record?"

"Yes."

"What indigenous culture does it represent?"

"It represents no indigenous culture."

Ball found Python's shelter a moment later, his meager belongings still in place.

"These structures are not the work of a space-faring culture," he said.

"Is that a question?"

"No. How many other ruins of this type are situated on B Continent?"

"None."

"How many on the planet as a whole?"

"None."

"Wait. You mean this find is *unique*, the only find of its kind planetwide?"

"Yes."

Ball let the camera see Python's garden and living quarters.

"You are *camping* in the ruins?" The librarian seemed humanly startled for a moment.

"Is that forbidden?"

"I do not understand your question."

"Is this find off limits to humans? If so, under what authority?".

"The find is under the authority of the Freehold of Pondoro. Hunting rights reside in LaChoy Enterprises. No other rights are let. Are you a poacher?"

"Are you a policeman or a librarian?"

The librarian was silent for a moment. "Questions, please."

"Is it forbidden for humans to come here?"

"No. But no trespass rights are recorded as sublet by LaChoy Enterprises. None has been requested for decades."

"Explain."

"Records indicate both humans and the continent's dominant predator share a strong aversion for the find. A single aged greer nests there occasionally, and then leaves. Its choice of den was sufficiently unusual to merit a footnote in the Hunt Commission annual report."

Daylight was coming on swiftly now. Heavy clouds clung to the flanks of the taller mountains, and there was new snow on the peaks. While Ball assimilated the librarian's answers, he found the battered carcass of a greer between Python's hovel and where the story-teller had dug a simple latrine.

There was no doubt here was Python's erstwhile antagonist. Ball examined it, and showed it to the librarian.

"It doesn't look that old to me, but its denning days are done."

"Slain by a poacher?"

"There is no poacher!" Irritably. "Now, why do greer always avoid this place?"

"Not of record."

And not true, Ball added to himself as he surveyed the field of Python's fight. After Python had crawled away, four greer had come out of the woods and left their spoor around the dead one, and then departed—two on Python's trail, two into the ruins. He scanned the ruins for body heat and nervous-system energy signals. There they were. Moving toward him.

"Questions, please," said the librarian.

"I haven't even begun to ask questions," Ball said.

A huge greer materialized beside a sagging heap of stones that might once have been a wall. In a finite wisp of time, Ball recorded this monster was in its prime, deeper-hued and thicker-coated even than Ramsey's trophy.

Then the beast, with a growl like an oath, came for him.

13

BALL POWERED FORWARD IN A JINKING DODGE. THE GREER FLASHED BY, trying to reverse itself in midair. Ball shut off the exterior camera. No need to exercise the dim circuits of the bogus sexpot.

He blasted toward the recovering greer, leaves and pebbles cascading in all directions. The greer, undaunted, charged to meet him with admirable swiftness.

It attempted to wrap Ball up as a kitten might a tennis ball.

And spun off, flung across the clearing.

"Question," Ball said to the librarian. "What is the extent of your data on this find?"

"Searching."

The greer shook itself like a huge dog and came again. As it swarmed through the space that had contained Ball a microsecond previous, the librarian spoke.

"First Survey records, complete and annotated. The Hunt Commission footnote on the crippled greer. A study done for Algonquin University by Professor R. Allen based on six field trips to the find. Transcript of a court case, Allen v. Algonquin, which involved the find. News accounts of the court case."

The greer landed a roundhouse swipe studded with razor death. Its paw skidded harmlessly off, trailing blood.

"Give me the full First Survey record," Ball said.

"Transmission begins."

Ball rocketed forward and caught the bemused greer in what would have been a human's solar plexus. Its rib cage creaked but held as it went down. Tough animal.

Ball reviewed the First Survey data. One hundred ten years ago government survey crews had concluded no identifiable trace of an indigenous culture existed. Existence of weapon burns in the ruins, and evidence of a nuclear explosion in the nearby mountains, permitted postulation that some off-course vessel had crashed here with survivors, and the survivors built the ruins. No alien skeletons were ever found, but a handful of metal fragments and artifacts were on display in the spaceport museum. Metallurgy identified the fragments within decimal approximation to ship-building techniques two centuries old. Dating of the decaying radioactivity and weapons stigmata were approximately contemporary to the age of the mud that glued the stones together. . . .

As he studied the data, Ball maneuvered the beast back and forth across the clearing, in order to study its reflex time, observe how it handled each new frustration. Its actions already had revealed much; no mere predator, confronted with something not of its food chain, in a place habitually shunned by its kind, would press an attack with such single-mindedness.

"Questions, please," reminded the librarian.

"Give me the Allen study."

"Transmitting."

Allen had been a maverick. He had attempted to secure funding for in-depth research of the find, and been turned down without comment. On his own, during sabbaticals from his teaching position, he made six expeditions to the find before the government denied him access on personal-safety grounds. The draft report of his findings suggested a startling conclusion: pre-Survey genocide of a primitive tool-using culture by human or humans unknown, with an eye on profitable Freehold status following Survey. The report had been suppressed, but not for researchers with the code Ball had supplied the library.

The end of the greer's battle with Ball came abruptly. Ball hung whirling in the air right before its nose, daring it to come again. In a heartbeat the greer pounced. Clung momentarily. Was launched full-face into the outcrop of stone Ball's bulk had masked. The impact was ferocious. The greer went down and stayed down. Ball quickly injected a transmission chip into its blood stream. This creature warranted in-depth study.

"Give me the court case and news accounts," Ball told the librarian.

"Transmitting."

Allen actually had tried, through the courts, to compel the local government to investigate his claims. He advanced the argument that the simple existence of the unique find, marred by weapons stigmata, should be sufficient cause to compel ongoing study. Argument found wanting, case dismissed. Allen left the planet not long after his final appeal was rejected.

"Questions?" asked the librarian.

"One of these news accounts suggests the Hunt Commission forced Professor Allen out of his tenure. Was there any media follow-up? Any Terran Service investigation?"

"Not of record."

"This final news account is odd," Ball said.

Ball watched the interview spin out in his pinhole monitor. Allen was a lanky, quick-moving individual with a nervous tic. The news hen was ruthless when Allen said he feared a nervous breakdown if he persisted. She wanted a definition for the "free-floating anxieties" he said he experienced every moment he had been at the find. He had refused to sleep there and insisted on an armed guard while he worked—which had helped clean out his personal funds even more quickly, since he was in greer country.

"You can laugh if you want," Allen finally said with a bitter twist. "But those ruins are haunted. Something unimaginable happened there. I *know* it did. And will again, mark my words."

Fade to black.

"Questions, please?" said the librarian.

And two more greer emerged from the ruins to stand over their fallen brother.

Ball braced for the onslaught, but they made no move to attack. They just stood there, balanced easily on their hindquarters, front paws lightly touching the ground, and looked from the unconscious beast to Ball and back again. Their eyes glittered. At that moment, they resembled neither gigantic wolverines, nor terrestrial bears, nor any other predator in Ball's comprehensive library.

"That does it," Ball said. "First, unremitting attack. Now, observing attack is futile, a brazen study. Intelligence without a doubt."

"Is that a question?" the librarian asked.

"No."

He simultaneously launched two more microscopic chips on squirts of compressed gas. One of the beasts yelped; the other flinched and then crouched as if to attack. Ball waited tensely. It would be long minutes before the chips homed in on their central nervous systems. . . .

The greer faded from sight.

Taken by surprise, Ball raced after them. They melted through the ruins like shadows, half glimpsed. He reached for altitude—and they vanished beneath the forest canopy. His sensors tracked their body heat and the electrical signature of their nervous systems. Still nothing on the empathometer. They couldn't elude him; he wanted to follow so badly he imagined he could have tasted it if he had a sense of taste. The chips would lock in soon now.

But he would be missed in camp. He had to return, or arouse suspicion about his independent sortie. Study of the greer would have to wait. Frustration flared.

"Damn!"

"Is that a question?" the librarian asked.

"No, mild profanity. Disconnect."

With a last long look at the greer, both the sleeping and the dead, he powered back toward camp.

14

BIG FEAR CAME THROUGH THE WOODS WHERE THE DAM-BUILDER HAD gnawed down saplings at first light to repair the leak in his mud-and-stick dam. The dam-builder ignored the fear's insistent, invisible push as he did the chilling wind, and continued to worry at the spot where his home pool bled water into the sluggish stream below. Mud and wood, *slop-slop*. Mud, *slop!* His deft tail was a muddy blur.

There was a crash from the forest as of a sapling falling. But no dam-builder worked there now. They had quit their tree-falling and moved into the pond of one accord when the Big Fear first breathed through the trees. All were safe in their burrows but the busy sentinel. The crash was from something running, many somethings, careless of sound, running before the terror.

The clearing was suddenly aswarm with bounding hilldeer, pouring toward the safety of the water ahead of the terror. One more low frieze of shore-hugging underbrush to negotiate . . .

The underbrush changed shape and rose, wide pairs of thick-furred, sharp-clawed arms, wet purple mouths laughing at the trick of it.

If the deer had kept their speed, most would have won through to the water, to outswim their fate. But they flinched back, snorting and bleating, from the certain death before them, and tried to run against

the Big Fear at their back. They could not. Hunters
and hunted merged in one vast rolling, thrashing,
bleating tangle; the water sprayed, darkened. . . .
The dam-builder kept his post no longer.

With a single convulsive lunge he plunged deep,
breasting the wavering shadows, heading for his burrow, heart pumping madly. So close had the stalkers
crept with no betraying sound or scent! He would
have been fair game if he had been their target. . . .
The dam would have to wait.

One of the half-grown cubs who had closed the
trap laughed up hotly with warm blood in his throat
as their elders ghosted out of the trees.

"Good hunting, uncle," he greeted the first adult to
the water's edge. "Sweet reward. The flesh is warm
and sweet. . . ."

"Then fill thy belly, cubling, but leave it room for
heavy thinking, for that will need digestion, too."

As was proper, the adults crouched at the feeding
site, impassive, while the cubs quenched their ferocious evening hunger. As was proper, the cublings
gulped their portion while trying to demonstrate
respect for their fare, ever conscious they must leave
their bellies unsatisfied to defer to their seniors. As
was proper—and almost unknown except among the
Hahn Aland—all cubs quit almost in the same swallow, such was the force of Voina's brooding presence, aloof from all.

The adults ate sparingly, for the hunt had been
easy, and few deer had slipped the nets of fear
they cast along the trail. These were no half-belly
predators, but full-bellied hunters of the Way, conscious of the need for stomach room for the
thoughts of their leader, who ate last—and least—
of all, scarce two claws of mouthfuls. He ate medi-

tatively, his belly heavy already with his leader's burden.

"Times are good," he gave his formal greeting then, and the hahn responded with a rolling growl whose rumble transmitted through the water to the fearful colony of dam-builders. Such a gathering of the hunters was rare enough to charge the air with dread nervousness which worked on all lesser creatures equally, robbing their mindless ease and spilling frozen fear across their instinct centers, though the hahn had fed and yet had food before it.

"Times are good among the Aland," said the eldest male hunter, trainer of the cubs. "Thou saw the cublings spread this feast."

"This one saw the hunting," the leader replied. "They spread an Aland feast."

Again the rolling grumble, as of thunder. A pregnant dam-builder chittered nervously in her burrow and was still. A prowling carrion eater, following the fresh blood scent upwind, paused to listen, and left the spoor, long snout wrinkled back in fear and hate.

"Two-Legs walks at White Rock once again," reported another of the older males. "This dayfire since he has coursed big Varko's range, and Varko denning with his new-won mate!"

Another roar—this of rough laughter—Varko bristling up, then subsiding, too embarrassed to throw a challenge. His mate hid her eyes with demure paws.

"I do not see my blooded brother at the feast," Voina said across the dying laughter.

"Half a claw of dayfires since, he went out to hunt old Furlip," the eldest hunter said. "There was a hunting this one would sing."

"Thy sing must wait. My brother's name is known

to all the hahns, as is the name of Furlip. It was Furlip's time. But Furlip lives, and my brother hunts no more. It is the Way."

"By Furlip?" asked the elder. "By that old rascal Furlip?"

"Not by Furlip," Voina said. "By one of Furlip's lesser companions. It will be sung in time. But there is other hunting now to sing."

They waited.

"All here know I heeded a calling to the council. I have been at the council pool deep in mountains; I have seen my spirit brother in the spirit pool frown at me with worry. I have held counsel with the old Orange Claw Dreamer, and have heard his dream."

He raised his paw, coated with the orange clay that once had named this valley's vanished hahn.

"Hear me: last living of the Orange Claw and Only has dreamed tomorrow, and tomorrow has evil in it. The dream is real, the spoor is fresh, endingness its claw. Ending of our Game with Two-Legs—that is tomorrow's hunt, and we are the prey."

"This one would speak." It was the larger of Voina's late arriving coursers.

Voina inclined his head.

"The evil thou named hunts even now within this valley," the courser said. "Hunts, and has slain, within the Permanent Lairs. Thy courser who was selected to hunt the long Two-Legs hunts no more."

"Slain by the long Two-Legs?"

"Nor used any fireclaw in that killing," said the courser.

"No Two-Legs without a fireclaw can stand against a hunter—"

"And was slain in turn," the courser went on.

"This one sent a full claw of prime males out to

witness the hunt of the long Two-Legs," Voina said. "Less than half a claw returns to sing the hunt. Where dawdle thy companions, and on what errands of their own?"

"Upon the final errand of us all, when all our hunts are run," said the second courser. "On that trail hunt half thy coursers. And far from here, to hide an awful shame, there sulks the third, bested in single combat by no other than this smoothly shining boulder which burns like dayfire and hunts like nothing ever known."

"Two gone?" Voina barked. "Two?"

"A hunting boulder?" the eldest hunter said. "What madness is this? A Two-Legs blind that hunts of its own? For always their hunting blinds have been Bright Boulders light as thistle that float up in the dayfire against the wind."

"Not madness," Voina said grimly. "The Orange Claw's dream, coming now to pass among the Permanent Lairs. This is the tomorrow his belly tasted off the breath of the future." He looked at his coursers. "If there is more, sing it!"

"Two coursers followed the long Two-Legs when he tried to carry his death as far as the Furlip camp," one said. "His death was growing too heavy for him to carry it away."

"How died those two?"

"In a twinkling, and if there was a hunting, we will never hear its song. They dropped from our ken as the last bright drop out on the Lake of Light when dayfire climbs the mountains. And when they died, this shining boulder like a smaller brother of the dayfire came hunting us along their back trail to the Permanent Lairs. Then did Voora hunt it, to his shame."

"But was not slain?"

"Was left to sleep upon the matter after closing

with the boulder several times and being bested each," the courser said. "Awakening, he would not heed our calling, nor come away with us."

"This is the Orange Claw dream," Voina said. "There is no doubting left. Thou who survived to sing this tale, go now into the higher mountains and seek out the old one, Sunto, where he ranges with the mountain ram. Sing him all of this, and one thing more."

He surveyed the waiting hahn, saw them struggling to assimilate all that had been revealed, struggling and failing, and waiting for his lead. He felt decision heavy in his belly.

"Tell the Orange Claw that Aland has been hunted by the evil that he dreamed," he said finally. "Now Aland will hunt the evil."

15

THIS NEW WORLD TO WHICH HIS SPIRIT WOKE WAS WITHOUT STRIFE. THERE was gentle dusk always, like the dusk that always quivered between the end of the day and night in the troubled vale he left behind, and had always been his best-loved time there.

Peace held him motionless, utterly content. Motion is strife. The only motion his newly liberated spirit would forgive was that of the tiny silent firefly that periodically shared his dusk with him. Coming into his awareness without a sound, it would pause and study him, then move about its business in a steady rhythm.

He sensed in some way that the firefly was charged with his well-being, and at least shared in the responsibility for this blessed immobile quietude.

After an indeterminate time of living in the gentle dusk with the solicitous firefly, it occurred to him to wonder briefly if all the ancient monotheistic religions had been near the mark after all, and if this tiny bright sentinel was their God.

He decided he would be quite content to offer what remained of his weary soul if that were so.

The dusk endured, and the firefly came and went upon its rounds, and his new spirit doted on its travels while trying to suppress a tiny node of worry because the patterns never varied.

Would God never vary His habits?

The question would not be still.

The firefly returned, and this time it altered its pattern. His lurking question fled unmourned into the dark. *That* to heresy. He felt a great joy. But when the firefly left, the dusk was not as complete as it had been, and now more nearly resembled false dawn. The change was subtle but undeniable. His spirit yearned with all its strength for the former condition, and Python thought that if he was a baby being born for the first time, this is when he would begin to squall.

When the firefly came again, its holy glow diminished in the dawn of his rebirth, it spoke for the first time, softly and with pity.

"Isn't it awful about the sybil, though?" it said.

Some heavier, authoritarian voice, which had absolutely no reason to exist in his fading dusky paradise, answered.

"The creche is simply medicine, not magic. We can sew 'em back together and heat up their boilers for them, but we can't undo what some of these bums do to themselves."

"But the sybil . . ."

"Owns him. This one's neural linkages are married to little sybil till death do them part. Lucky, too, or somebody else around here might be on an unholy honeymoon right now. The creche isn't programmed for that kind of surgery; it can't carve out a neurological parasite."

"I still think it's awful," the night nurse said.

She switched off her penlight as the room's illumination grew. "Will you see Mr. Donlevy next, Doctor?"

Python groaned aloud when they were gone, and the creche instantly performed a blazingly swift multitude of exact studies of the outsized body in its care and reached the correct conclusion.

"Good morning, Mr. Martin," it said.

"All right, I'm alive," the patient said peevishly. "But is it worth losing my religion?"

"Sir?"

"I am in a hospital, I presume?"

"Yes, sir. Central Receiving, Firstport."

"How long have I been here?"

"Thirty-seven hours, ten minutes, twelve seconds and counting."

"Who's paying?"

"Checking with bookkeeping." Then: "Admission secured by LaChoy Enterprises, sir. Cosigner Keith Ramsey, individual. Full health benefits coverage by the Commonwealth of Terra, self-insured."

"*What?*"

The creche read too much confusion for a reborn body and promptly doused his consciousness. But the machine's act could not stem the teeming images evoked by its final announcement. Earth in winter twilight, its single natural satellite full and sallow above the training fields. The School. Blazing lights and sweat-stink of the arenas. The training gym. And always, always, the death of Iron Fennec . . .

Dutifully alarmed by the cerebral fulminations of its patient, the creche sought to short-circuit that processional—and reeled back, its circuit breakers smoking, stung shrewdly by . . . *something* . . . hidden in the reborn brain. The creche analyzed the malfunction in order to prescribe adequate sedation. Succeeded in the analysis. And held an urgent consultation with the human resident, interrupting his rounds.

"Leave him alone," the resident instructed.

"The patient needs his rest," the creche insisted.

"The patient's own resident demon, in this case, will decide that," the resident said.

"Rest is mandatory!"

"Look—the disturbance was occasioned by reference to the Commonwealth of Terra, correct?"

"That is my inference. But the patient—"

"Needs his rest, yes, thank you, I know that," the resident snarled. "All right, then—erase his short-term memory of your reference. The sybil should permit that much. His disturbance should then ease, and the patient should rest."

"That is logical."

"Thank you so much," the resident said, and a few other things under his breath about nonhumanoid robots. It was a Pondoro prejudice he was acquiring readily during his residency here.

The creche erased the short-term memory, and the sybil remained quiet. The patient's mental agitation eased at once, but accelerated brain activity that had accompanied it continued to register. Atypical impulses generated a wholly indecipherable pattern of activity that deeply troubled the creche. Whatever the patient was now doing, he was certainly not resting.

The body's increased demands for service were routinely noted and accommodated. The patient attempted to develop a fever—patent absurdity in the creche—and when he could not, that atypical pattern of neural expenditure was boosted again. The creche recorded the cycle and began to extrapolate.

The interior passage of impulses through the vast labyrinth of the brain appeared to be in an arithmetic stage of progression. The ravaged and repaired body appeared to be little more than a conduit, its healing merely the mechanism for transmuting vast reserves of life-giving energy supplied by the creche into fuel for that insatiable brain.

The brain now was operating at a level that would have been injurious to the healthy organism in an unsupported environment. Possibly fatal.

The creche interfaced with the hospital's main energy source in order to assure that the enormously expanded regenerative needs would continue to be met. Effectively, it now was working to prevent the patient's self-destruction by sheer cerebration.

That It was being manipulated by the symbiotic awareness under its care never occurred to the creche; it wasn't programmed to analyze data that way. It was evident the unpolluted brain could never have reached that intensity of function, equally evident that any attempt to exorcise the parasite would prove terminal to the host. If the livelihood of the parasite was necessary to survival of the host, and suddenly seemed to demand that vast drain of energy, then the creche would supply it. A new kind of fever, that was all, no more startling, once the demand was calibrated, than any other.

Hours bled past. A kind of crisis occurred later, when the questing brain of Python finally perceived, far off across the sluggish seas and halfway around the planetary curve, the origin of the neural impulses that first had drawn him to the continent of the greers.

Was right! The thought formed as in a dream. He locked on those faraway impulses and tried to read their meaning. *Was right!*

With something like joy, he probed those faraway flickers of intelligence, hardly distinguishable at that distance from those of human brains. Distinguishable only because they were so hard to read . . .

Halfway around the world a neural conflagration burned, burned with a scalding fury that diminished all else. It provoked his curiosity, and drew his full attention. He nearly yelped aloud when his probe rendered up a vivid and familiar image: soft, wide dun-colored mushrooms in a river meadow. The hunting tents of LaChoy.

But why? Why the camp, why the hate, why so vivid?

Quickly now, sporadic images surrendered themselves to him—of the ruins, but queerly seen; of creatures lolling near them in the sun, cubs at play—of mountains exploding in titanic fury, a mushroom cloud towering into the skies—of a flashing, twirling ball of fire that tangled and tumbled with one of the curious beasts. . . .

Greer? Are those greer among the ruins, their image of themselves at rest and play?

Excitedly, impatiently, he tried to probe more deeply, but the images blurred and altered as in a dream: now there was the strange flaming ball, and an odd, elongated stick figure that stomped and capered in a fool's jerky parody of the dance of the Palikar.

Myself! As seen by them: awkward, graceless stick man, capering like a fool!

The shock was profound. The creche found it necessary to make yet another adjustment.

As others see us! flashed like heat lightning in his mind. *As others see us. Stick man, mushroom tent and mushroom cloud—but when was there nuclear war here?—and a greer that fights the sun among the ruins. No, fights against a ball of fire.*

Ball. It was Ball, that curious cyborg owned by the writer Ramsey, which had become the focus of that primeval hatred.

Ball—and stick man. Over and over now, ball and stick man. And the mushroom cloud of doom.

He could probe no further. The effort had been too much. With a groan, he let it all go, and his mind snapped shut like stretched elastic. He crawled deeper into unconsciousness and forgot the greer.

The creche congratulated itself on pulling its charge through such a serious crisis. Hospital emergency services programmed themselves offline one by one until the creche alone maintained its solicitous watch. The creche, and the cold-eyed dean of the hospital, who studied Python's brain wave activity recorded at the height of the episode and reached a decision.

"Discharge him."

"But, Doctor—" It was the turn of the creche-wing resident to react protectively.

"Discharge him! His body is repaired. His brain, if it is damaged, is beyond our power to repair—or control. He has used enormous amounts of our reserves, virtually suiciding in order to keep the restoratives coming so his brain could function at that preposterous level. He is a quasitelepath in symbiosis with a sybil, and about that combination there is absolutely nothing known."

"Is the infected brain a separate entity from the host?" the creche put in.

"It very well may consider itself to be," the dean said. "Sybil symbiosis is a mystery. The Terran Service embargo on Blocked Worlds data is absolute."

"Then free the brain, and save the body," the creche suggested.

"Logical, but quite illegal, I'm afraid." The dean was smiling. "No, simply do as I say. Discharge him

Body, brain—and sybil. I won't have him depleting this institution's reserves for his private ends. I hope the Commonwealth of Terra (self-insured) is solvent. By all that's holy, they'd better be!"

16

I LEFT BALL SULKING IN THE SLEEP TENT. HE CALLED IT MAKING LIKE A computer, but it looked like sulking to me. He had been doing it ever since we got back yesterday from those odd ruins by the river after seeing what he'd found there. I had raised hell with him for sneaking off alone in the first place. He had, as usual, ignored me.

LaChoy and Nail were in the port city with both camp mechanics and the Sergeant Major to face an inquiry into the burning of two prime greer by the war robot. Eliot and the other guide were off hunting.

I dragged a camp chair from the kitchen tent out into the open, where I could watch the morning's building weather. Clouds marched down off the polar ice cap, and in from the sea, and the temperature had been dropping since dawn. The equinox had begun, and Worldnet was warning the fishing fleets off the seas. There already were a couple of trawlers reported in distress not four hundred klicks from where I parked my butt to drink coffee and try to enjoy the weather.

Normally, the first serious autumn weather of any terrestrial world upon which I happen to find myself is like a health cure for me. My blood starts to race, my eyes get brighter, and whatever aches and pains I might have complained about get lost in a hurry. An ancient professor of English who also was a quail hunter on Earth's northern hemisphere said it best long ago: my health is better in November.

But this storm was six light-centuries from Acme. A lot farther from Earth's Novembers. The image of my greer kept superimposing itself over my nostalgia, laced with the awful fear that had come up in me when he made his subtle stalk. The fear was so powerful I could not be sure I wasn't reliving it, in the middle of camp.

I activated my old Associated News pocket 'corder and tried to recount the way it had been there in the blind, with the greer coming but us not knowing it yet. The words wouldn't form. My coffee went stone cold during the effort. The 'corder hummed and the wind chill tried to sneak inside my old *twon*-down parka.

When it was clear I wasn't getting anywhere, I asked the robochef for a warmup and batted out a ten-thousand worder about the death struggle in the ruins between Baka Martin, alias Python, and the crippled greer. The first abortive attempt had been to create something new and unexplainable, but this was journalism. I had done journalism before when I was word-dry and under pressure. This time the words went down into the machine smoothly.

While I keyed it back for a read and a listen, I wondered how LaChoy was doing with the Hunt Commission. There had been no mechanical aberration; the Rongor was programmed for camp security, and he had secured it. With two off-world hunters in camp, one a heavy-money type and the other a minor—emphasis on the *minor*—celebrity, the insurance lobby would be sure to weigh in on his side. Some believed the insurance combines ran the known universe.

LaChoy's difficulty would be Python. It was LaChoy's lease-hold, so he would be held accountable for permitting someone to camp unarmed in greer country. The reasoning would be that if Python had not been permitted to hang around so long, he would not have finally teased the greer into taking a whack at him. It would be of record that LaChoy had knowingly permitted the storyteller to loiter on his lease-hold. He could have ordered him off, and had the law lug him if he refused to go. But he had liked Python's weird chanting ritual, liked the added atmosphere it gave his camp; cashed in on it, in fact, because some hunters booked with him because of the added element of the mystical storyteller. Too, it helped instill proper respect for the greer.

"They all loved him, and *something* generates that damned fear," LaChoy told me before he left. "Python got them to think about it before they went out. To admit they were afraid and deal with it before the moment of truth. The inner-world types just seemed to be able to handle it better when a soothsayer type made it all part of the hunt's mystique, instead of something too personal, too secret and shameful, to admit. He was worth money to me. The regulars out across the rich worlds were getting word about him and wanting to book again just for the show. Besides, I liked the color, dammit!"

I clicked the 'corder back to that quote and listened to it against the scrolling words on the screen. It sounded right, and like LaChoy. Good enough. I keyed in a query, with my old A.N. code, to the local Associated News bureau and ordered more coffee.

My own goddamned unease just seemed to keep growing with the weather. I wished the Sergeant Major was around. The camp felt naked without him.

I would have liked to ask him how the wind smelled. I had an uneasy notion it was a greer wind on Pondoro.

The Python piece was a good yarn all right. Given the time lapse for sector-wide transmission, the local A.N. bureau response was speedy. They beamed back a sector-desk acceptance by the time I'd had a cold bison sandwich, usual rates and residuals. The sector desk already was transmitting a digest alert about a news break on Baka Martin, my byline, across Commonwealth space. The bidding war was on.

These days, the major advertisers employ professional bidding companies, staffed by news analysts and pollsters, to screen agency digests minute by minute for stories attractive to readers likely to buy their products. In the ancient tradition of information-distribution, advertisers pay the freight, but editorial content drives the train. My story would be sponsored across civilized space by the successful bidders, and my final percentage would be based on the number of times a consumer called the file up. Interest from the bidders was brisk, because the digest already had stimulated an almost instant burst of orders from consumers. I closed the deal and signed off. Just straight reporting, so far. More to come, in the immortal lingo of the trade.

I should have been smug. Based on preliminary returns, the residuals would start rolling in. It would probably pay for my hunt and then some, and the spacefare here would become deductible from taxes.

If Python died, I stood the chance to be rich again. My story would become the basis for one of the classic riddles of the age: why had Baka Martin, after dropping out of the known galaxy, shown up killing in single combat perhaps the only other creature between the stars besides Iron Fennec who could have given Martin pause? It would smell like some kind of epic golden fleece of killing that would sell like fury on the hot-eyed, soft-bellied inner worlds.

But my basic training was in journalism, and I wanted the facts of the story, not speculation. I wanted Baka Martin back alive enough to tell his own story. I could write off his hospital expenses against taxes, too, if LaChoy needed help.

What had drawn Python to the ruins in the first place? No one seemed to know, or care. What had compelled him to set up camp there? And just what the devil *were* those ruins, anyway? Per Ball, the local library said they predated First Survey and no evidence of their builders had survived. They were just an anomalous bit of scenery. Pretty dreary scenery at that. Ball had it all in a file for my use if needed. The story about a professor who had interested himself in the ruins before he left Pondoro, a victim of "free-floating anxieties," sounded a lot like greer-fear to me.

I felt better with that much of the story in recorded words on the regional data squirt toward civilization. But the remembered greer-fear just kept gnawing at the edges of my mind. I finally got my rifle out where I could see it, and checked the loads. Then I put one of LaChoy's frontier Pacifiers over by the toilet tent where I could reach it in a jump, and watched the weather and my own nervousness build together.

The strongest thing was memory of that unnerving fear.

When I permitted myself to think about it directly, it was difficult to keep my stomach quiet. I wished Ball would quit sulking and come talk to me.

The wind settled into a steady whine in the safari

grass. I had the robochef build me another bison sandwich and a bourbon, but the remembered fear seemed to rise in my throat and clog it. I forgot the sandwich and tossed off the bourbon. Maybe it helped, because the fear eased again. I tried to snap out of it entirely by contemplating my future plans. That was rough going, because I didn't have any.

LaChoy said he could get me a ticket as first gun for his alternate camp, where he guided for goats and hilldeer. He was so impressed he was still alive, after my greer decided it was time for him to die, that he thought I had the makings of a professional hunter. He said the high camp would break me in until I was ready to guide for greer, and my name would do his business good.

But Pondoro already looked like another dead end to me. I still wasn't sure what I wanted, or if I wanted any of it here. If I took him up on his offer, word would go out along those circuits from which it had taken me so long to unplug, and I would suddenly be good news again. Some of them would even buy the course to come and see me perform in what they would take for my native habitat, complete with snarling beasts for me to kill for them while Ball and Python swapped insults around the campfire.

The very image was enough to make me shudder.

But that was what LaChoy was asking, even if he didn't realize it fully. The profit part of it was luring him. He could not know how bad it could actually get. He only knew the good ones from the fat worlds, like Eliot, out there in the equinoxial storm, still hunting his greer, or the old man whose stories had brought me here, or Haro, whose mortal remains had blended with this bloody soil.

LaChoy knew only those who stayed lean inside of

themselves always. But he did not know the fat birds of prey who stay fat by feeding on that kind of leanness until it either bloats into something like them or is gone for good, and then spit out the pulp and go in search of the next sensation.

If I could have legally erased my presence from the planet, so I was just Old Joe Hunter at the Singing Cliff camp, I might have been willing. But LaChoy would think I was short-changing him somehow by not remaining Keith Ramsey, a commodity that seemed to have stopped belonging to me a long time ago. He saw it as simple business sense to use my name, and would resent it if I called it simple greed. The only thing wrong with good healthy greed is that something a lot like equal and opposite reaction, which seems to govern this universe, usually sets in. I didn't want to risk being ruined that way again. I didn't want LaChoy or Pondoro to be ruined, either.

When Ball finally drifted out of the sleep tent, I jumped and half lifted the seven gun.

"What are you afraid of?" Never one to hedge around.

"Who says I'm afraid?"

"You know the range of my sensory equipment."

"Yeah. Your empatho's supposed to know when I'm ready to create. I was ready a while ago, and I had to use my beat-up old 'corder. You never said a word. Not a peep."

"I was preoccupied. You were not really in creative mode. Your creative centers were as blocked as your bowels are loose. You were just going through the journalistic motions to persuade yourself you really are pukka sahib Ramsey, great outdoorsman and writer, though your bowels are loose with fear. Why are you so afraid?"

"You wouldn't know a bowel if it kissed you," I said. "Cyborg."

"A marked improvement in situations where a nervous lower tract might impede survival skills." He used his reasonable voice.

"How can you be too occupied to work for me? I own you."

"You employ me. I am a cyborg, as you say."

"Do cyborgs have suffrage?"

"On the more enlightened worlds. Why are you so afraid you can't seem to put your rifle aside?"

"I was just checking to make sure it's loaded." I put it down, though.

"A sensible precaution, and a foolish flourish to put it aside. Low survival characteristic."

My scalp crawled. "What?"

"I ask you again: of what are you so afraid?"

"The greer," I said.

"Just so. But why?"

"Because, by God, they are dangerous as hell!"

"Yes, to bipeds." Ball adopted the patient voice of an adult dealing with a balky child. "Now please listen to my question: why are you specifically afraid—*right now*—of a greer attack? This is very, very important: are you telepathic? Nothing in our records indicates you ever displayed extrasensory potential."

"As far as I know, no records anywhere indicate *anyone* has displayed—"

"We are wasting time! How do you know a pack of greer are at this moment surrounding this camp with every evidence of a coordinated attack?"

My rifle was back in my hands before he got it all out. I was trying to look everywhere at once.

"*Are you serious?*"

"Very serious. The outlying sensors were keyed by

Nail so any untoward activity would be beamed right to me. It was the only way their insurance company would allow us to remain here alone. Not that I need the independent verification. Several subjects I am studying are among the skulkers."

"Wait a minute. You said 'our records,' didn't you? What do you mean 'our records'? *Whose* records say I'm not telepathic? Who keeps that kind of record?"

"The delay in that line of questions is proof you are under strain," Ball said. "Without the greer-fear, that would have been a news hawk's instant response."

Power of suggestion, perhaps. It seemed, on that instant, my fear redoubled into outright terror. I thought I was at least going to lose control of my bladder, damn him for saying anything about bodily functions at a time like—

"Oh, of course," Ball said. "Of course! *That's* how it works. That fits! That makes it all fit perfectly!" He actually sounded excited.

"You're making like a computer again, right?" I asked him. "When does the Hatter show up with the tea?"

I was trembling so bad I was afraid I'd drop my rifle.

"Bravely said, in your condition," Ball applauded. "Actually, I believe my computations are complete for the moment. What a marvelous by-road of evolution! This will be worth a great deal of study."

"If my bowels can hold out."

"Very well said! You were chosen well for this! The real Keith Ramsey, stepping to the fore, the primitive man unspoiled by too much civilization. And just in time, too."

Then he vanished. Or almost. He went by me like a

spaceship up a gravity well, accelerating for the Big Jump. He moved so fast the air whooped into the space he'd vacated.

Behind me the camp Sentinel bonged, followed instantly by a terrific thud and an animal yowl of pain. By the time I turned, Ball was a silver meteor, blazing a new tangent. A large, furry shape was twitching on the grass. A greer.

Ball's tangent intersected a fair-size piece of brush. Another heavy thud, and a second greer tumbled limply out the far side.

Ball sizzled back to me, and I heard that almost subliminal sound that meant he was messing with gravity again.

"Why just in time?" I said.

"Because computations are complete, and the battle to save your hide has begun."

17

I KILLED ONE GREER WITH THE SEVEN GUN, EMPTYING THE MAGAZINE AS he crawled on his last gasp to my feet.

I fried two others with the Colt-Vickers I had left by the toilet tent.

They didn't come in a concerted rush, as would have seemed logical if it were a concerted attack; they came individually. It was like some macabre pinball machine: the Sentinel would go off, always from the direction I had just looked and wasn't looking now. And a greer would be there. Trying to kill me.

The fourth came over the breakfast tent in a ghost-silent pounce, already through the Sentinel unannounced.

Ball rammed him ten meters sideways in midair.

The animal didn't stir as Ball coasted back.

"Dead?" I asked him.

"Worse for wear. I narco'ed him enough to rest awhile. Like the others."

"The full 360 degrees is a lot to try to scan at once—" I began.

And Ball zipped away. A booming thud, like some gigantic prizefighter hooking to the body, told me he had scored before I could turn around.

The Sentinel went again. This time I saw the greer coming.

Because I was about as scared as a man can be

and still function, I blasted it with a hose of heat that wasted a half-kilometer path behind him and snatched a huge puff of steam where it interdicted the watercourse.

Ball was back at my side.

"Why no alarm on those two you slapped down?" I tried to keep my voice from cracking under that humiliating terror.

"They came through at the same instant as the ones you killed, but at different cardinal points. Pinpoint timing. They spotted the trick of the Sentinel from their first penetration, but had to hustle to adjust for it. . . ."

He squirted off again. The greer coming around Eliot's tent sidestepped his rush neatly and launched at me.

My first charge was low, and dumped it. Its second effort—with hindquarters in cinders—swept the Colt-Vickers out of my hands and drew fiery streaks across my forearms, tattering my sleeves. Ball landed on its skull with a melon-hitting-stone sound. The impact threw it into violent convulsions. A flailing forepaw swept me down like a broom and slapped my lungs empty. Fear roared in my ears like jets taking off.

Faraway, I heard the Sentinel's gong. I was trying to breathe with every ounce of strength I had. A convulsion not unlike the dead greer's got me over on my belly. My left arm screamed when I tried to push up. The skull-crushed greer still was thrashing, still was too close. Through a mist of pain and fear I heard the Sentinel again. How many times since I went down? In my panic it seemed far too many.

A glancing blow flattened me back into the ground. I came up spitting dirt and blood, gagging, still trying to make my lungs work. No needle stabs of broken ribs. I crawled toward the Colt-Vickers.

Lucky, I thought, and then wondered what I meant by that.

The fear pounded behind my eyeballs, a mad drumbeat that wouldn't be still. I heard the Sentinel again, twice in quick succession. Then I heard the gargling roar of a sporting beam-gun in operation. The nasal rip of another Colt-Vickers. I wondered if Ball had sprouted tentacles to wield the firepower, or just opened ports in his hull and begun blasting.

I got the C-V and my breath at just about the same moment. My left arm was numb and useless. Blind fear of dying squeezed my heart. I braced the barrel in the crook of my useless arm and thumbed spray. As soon as I looked up I opened fire—and almost got Ball. A greer blew away in charcoaled lumps. Ball went straight up, the peripheral heat of the charge spotting his globe with points of hellish fire. He vanished over one of the still-standing tents.

"Leave me the hell alone, will you?"

His voice, trailing behind, sounded offended.

All around, fires were burning in the safari grass. The wind whipped the flames higher and snatched the smoke to shreds. Sparks flew madly. I couldn't believe all this could have happened in the short space I had been out of it.

A greer with blackened stumps for paws loped through the flames, roaring lIke a fiend of hell, the first one to make any sound at all. I blasted him back into the fire. More flames licked up. The stench of scalded flesh was momentarily as strong as my fear, and then snatched away with the smoke.

Something blurred in my peripheral vision. I turned, shooting.

Ball skipped skyward again. Molten drops sparkled off him as he went.

"Who the hell's side are you *on*, Ramsey?"

I was shocked almost out of my terror. I never had pulled trigger in my life without being sure of my target.

"My God, Ball—"

"Never mind! What can you expect from bipeds? Come on!"

"Where?"

"I called Eliot and his guide back. They thought it was an opportunity for Eliot to make a kill. I did not disabuse them. Come *on*."

I followed where the smoke ran thickest and found their grounded floater.

"Did he?" I said.

"Did who what?"

"Did Eliot get his greer?"

"He got two, and his guide got one, before the greer got them. Both of them. Hurry! The Rongor's not here to carry them to the Medfac. You'll have to do. . . ."

"But the greer—"

"Have pulled back. Now hurry!"

I was on my way to the Medfac lugging Eliot when the next greer came through the smoke and Ball did the necessary.

"Still testing us," he said.

"*Testing . . . ?*"

Was it my imagination, or did he sound tired? Do Balls tire? He was the only one of his kind, so the question was foolish. I dumped Eliot into the Medfac and switched it on. It was constructed to be idiot proof under stress, and lucky, too. I was in no shape to figure out elaborate controls. I got the skull-bitten guide shoved into the gel without further incident. My adrenaline was so high I could have lugged the Rongor robot.

"Room for one more," I said.

"You'd better make it on your own, then. I can't carry you."

I reloaded my rifle and dropped shakily into a camp chair. I was sweating and seemed as hot as I have ever been, despite the freezing wind. *Twon* feathers whipped downwind from the gashes in my sleeves.

"Is it over?" I asked Ball.

"Unlikely. The greer appear to be single-minded creatures."

"Then what happens next?"

Ball hesitated. "I . . . cannot decide."

"What? I was asking for a prognosis, not a command decision!"

"I cannot decide if it is time to end this."

"You're getting delusions of grandeur, Ball. If anybody stops this, it will be the greer."

"I have a Terran Service heavy cruiser standing off Pondoro," Ball said quietly. "If I order it in to secure this area, is it delusions of grandeur to believe it to be capable of doing so?"

"A heavy . . . Ball, are you crazy? Your brains must be scattered by all the battering."

"Look: a hostile alien force has attacked a human encampment," Ball said patiently. "The prime rule of the Service Is to protect humanity against such offense, and punish the offenders."

"But these are *greer*, Ball. . . ."

Then I shut up. I was remembering the way they had coordinated their attack to disarm the Sentinel. Granted, it's not battle equipment, strictly recreation stuff. But they had coordinated their movements to get through, coming from all vectors at once. Pinpoint communication, clockwork execution. Never more than one greer under the gun at any one time. Intelligence at work?

Good old reporter's instinct took over.

"Ball, how could you know there is a Terran Service cruiser off Pondoro?"

"Because I ordered it into place when I returned from the ruins."

Which stopped good old reporter's instinct cold. I just stared at the battle-burned globe. Can cyborgs go mad under stress? It struck me suddenly just how alien a thing Ball was to be alone with on this alien, hostile world.

"Now don't *do* that," Ball said. "You don't have the local shape-prejudice. You're more stable than that."

I had forgotten his empathometer, of course. "All right, then, who are you, *cyborg*, to *order* a Terran Service cruiser anywhere?"

"I am a covert investigator for the Commonwealth of Terra. I am here to investigate a field-staff report that alien intelligences here may be deliberately concealing their existence from the Terran Service. If true, I am to determine what threat, however remote, the masquerade offers humanity."

"You are here because I brought you here," I said. "This thing with the greer has unbalanced you."

The Sentinel abruptly bonged again, and this time I got the jump on Ball, desperate to get out of the smoke and to where I could see and move. The absence of the crushing fear, and the fact Ball did not move at all, should have tipped me. But my nerves still were keyed to maximum pitch, and I just reacted.

"Relax!" Ball's voice floated after me.

"Relax, hell!"

"For the sake of whatever spirit you will, please

don't shoot my field man. He's not as tough as me, and he's already been through enough for one assignment."

There was another floater beside the one Eliot and his guide had used. The wind eased, letting the smoke billow. It obscured the arriving pilot as he strode through the camp's wreckage, but the height and the gait of him was plenty of identification.

Python, of course.

18

Python fought the controls of the stolen boat through violent headwinds and running walls of snow, flying across the face of the galloping storm front, homing in on the neural storm that already had broken in all its fury on the continent of the greer.

The elusive mental images, projected by the collective greer intelligence, were much easier to discern now that the creche-reinforced sybil had read their patterns. He wondered how he could have missed them for so long.

The images whirled in a devil's dance and would not achieve coherence.

Ball was a label he assigned the shining roundness they seemed to hate and fear; *stick man* to the caricature he took to be himself. Those were the recurring images, counterpointed by the mushroom cloud, mushroom tents, and other assorted stick figures that tottered about on two legs and hurled lightning bolts.

The unmistakable nuclear mushroom troubled him. No recorded event in Pondoro history had stirred a battle of that magnitude.

Prehistoric, then. It had to be an accident, a starship breaking up in atmosphere shoals, a system-hopper malfunction. But why so strong, why so central to their culture? Pondoro owns weather and volcanoes spectacular enough to dim any single event to insignificance. . . .

Why this then, alone, so central to their thoughts? And why, oh why, this linked hatred against the cyborg and me?

He was close now to the mental conflagration of the greer. It was centered on LaChoy's hunting camp. That jolted him. He strained his tiring brain to search for human life there. Found one, gripped by fear and fury. Two more, bare flickers, almost gone—severely injured or dying.

There was one other mind. Not exactly human, far from greer. Totally unreadable.

Shielded! was his amazed reaction. *A Terran Service shield!*

Ball, of course. But how did he know that?

He activated the boat's navigational gear, locked into LaChoy's beacon and went down in a swift falling turn. In minutes he was above the greasy, roiling smoke among the ruined tents.

What is this now? Oh what . . . ?

The besieging fury of the greer turned on him in that moment. For a single instant fear nearly paralyzed him. Palikar discipline saved him from plowing through the camp on the boat's belly at approximately seventy klicks per hour, and Palikar reflex dropped it lightly to rest.

He popped the hatch and a charnel house stench rolled in. He nearly gagged, controlled it, got out. The mental attack of the greer stormed over him, unabated.

They are paranormal! That fear! The fear all hunters know, the fear that crippled greer taught me in the ruins! Deliberate! It is deliberate—they sow that fear—and reap the hunting. . . .

Eyes smarting in the smoke, he started for the tents. Sensed danger, hesitated. Felt it lessen—and saw

Ramsey through the smoke, in the act of lowering his
rifle. The writer's extreme mental agitation beat at
him: fear and fury.

"So you lived," the writer greeted him.

"And you," Python said. "While all else dies
around us."

Ramsey looked at the government insignia on the
boat's cowl.

"I stole it," Python said simply. "I have no funds;
there was no time—"

"I know," Ramsey cut. "Your boss is in what
remains of my tent."

"My . . . boss?"

Python felt an immaterial finger probe sharply at
his flagging awareness. His tired brain lurched.

"Are you all right?" Ramsey's voice seemed to
cross a vast gulf.

Ball drifted into view. "He is reasonably intact, for
a biped recently killed with extreme violence. But he
needs extended rest."

The mind touch came again.

Python gasped. "That! That in my brain. That was
you?"

"Me," Ball agreed equably.

Python swung his head from side to side. "I came
here—I—I came because I have begun to puzzle out
the riddle of these greer. They are—"

"A mighty breed," Ball interrupted. "How mighty,
no one dead remembers, no one living knows. That's
a direct quote from our first night here. Yes, the
rumors you spread were heard, and acted upon. The
greer also appear to be primitive paranormals with a
peculiar specialization."

"The fear . . ."

"That is my hypothesis, recently formed. It makes

sense of all the fragments. Do you now confirm they are capable of generating that fear at will, and projecting it onto the nervous system of whatever they choose as prey?"

"Can't you *feel* it?"

"Ramsey can, and my equipment certainly can read the results. He could not have known these creatures were stalking us, but he was almost paralyzed with fright. The only real question is whether they create this effect by instinct, as a wolf howls, or do they employ it deliberately?"

Python began to shiver violently. "Deliberately! Oh, deliberately! They send that fear—and then they hunt!"

He sank in an exhausted slump on the ground. After the creche and the boat's cabin, the frigid wind went through him. The hospital had sealed up the tears in his jumpsuit, but its thermostat was wrecked.

"He's your bird dog and doesn't even know it?" Ramsey said to Ball.

"An elementary precaution, in light of the suspicions. And he has flushed quite a bag, to conclude your hunting analogy. The symbiotic relationship discovered here will keep the scholars happy for decades."

"The greer and humans?" Ramsey said. "Or Python and you?"

19

ARNIC, ALAND, AND THE EREN GAINO LEADERS WAITED FOR SUNTO WHERE the orange-clay valley of his vanished fathers opened to the plains. Sunto's nervousness was tight-held as he turned to his exhausted mate, who labored along behind him.

"Thou has made a march of it, little one!"

"Little!" she grunted. "When these great cublings bloat me like dead meat in high summer? Thy old eyes fail thee, Sunto." But she was pleased by his praise.

"These old eyes serve me well enough," he said. "I see my little one, with our new cubs to come, resting with thy kin in dayfire's winter home instead of in my lonely mountains."

"Hush, old dreamer! Thou love the mountains as thou love no mate nor youngling." Then she softened. "Hunt with care this strange new prey thy dream has foretold, coming now to pass."

"With greatest care," he promised her. "Here: see two fine young hunters of the Eren Gaino come like shadows in the dark. They will take thee to thy kin, where I will find thee once this hunt is run."

They parted with no physical touch.

Sunto went on toward the river, his fur stirred by the raging wind. He dipped his muzzle in the riffled surface of the water and drank sparingly. Old Winter was afoot and hunting keenly.

Others besides Old Winter were on the hunt.

Plainly to his belly came the image of Two-Legs, many Two-Legs, hiding somewhere above the dayfire in their vast hunting blind light as thistle. They were poised to strike the Furlip camp, where that strange dayfire boulder had baited Voina and his entire hahn into revealing more than Two-Legs should ever be permitted to know.

There was another belly a-hunt.

Sunto snorted in surprise. The long Two-Legs who had denned in the Permanent Lairs had died beneath the hunting of an Aland hunter. That was beyond dispute. But here was the long Two-Legs, alive again. His stomach called once more to Sunto in its strange fashion.

"First hunter ever known to return to life from beyond his final hunt," Sunto breathed. It was an ill omen.

Sunto never had imagined Voina in his pride would loose the full weight of Aland upon old Furlip's camp. It was an irrevocable act. It had not been misread, not even by the dim stomachs of those ordinary Two-Legs who lurked above the Lake of Light. The crisis Sunto had dreamed was here.

He confronted the waiting chieftains.

"This one would speak!" Voina, bristling.

"Speak, then."

"Why thy call to council in this unaccustomed place? My hahn hunts hard upon the evil thou dreamed. I should be there!"

"Rash youngster! Thy hahn has sprung the trap they baited for us all!"

"How then, when my bravest hunt full well . . ."

"And die."

Voina's fury blazed. "Death comes when it comes!

Such hunting this Orange Claw valley has never seen—"

"And will not see again," Sunto interrupted. "Thou truly cannot taste it? This Two-Legs hahn which waits above the dayfire, ready to stoop like birds of prey upon thy doomed followers?"

"Those Two-Legs in wait above the Lake of Light, then, are part of a trap?" Korlu of the Eren Gaino. "My stomach, too, has troubled me of late. . . ."

"Aiii, let them stoop!" Turso of the Arnic. "Arnic hunts with Aland!"

"They will stoop," Sunto said grimly. "Stoop with fire and fury the like unseen since mountains cursed at history's dawn. They will eat the Aland in a gulp, as those Two-Legs long ago digested Orange Claw before they killed the mountains!"

"Not hunt properly, as we have taught them . . . ?"

"You all have heard my dream. We are hunted more cleverly than you digest."

"The anger in thy belly clouds thy meaning." Eren Gaino.

"Thou name this day another Orange Claw Lesson?" Arnic.

"All this empty chatter!" Aland. "The Orange Claw Lesson was a song sung long ago, and proper for remembering. But not while Aland hunts!"

"Thou!" Sunto's own fury overtopped the other's. "Thou marshal thy hahn against the Furlip camp, as hahn fought hahn in the long-ago, before Two-Legs came. Thy hunt reveals thee to these new and cunning hunters."

"Sing thy meaning more clearly." Eren Gaino.

"The Lesson! It always was the Lesson that most of all beneath the sky, Two-Legs fears a hahn which moves with single purpose. Their greatest terror is the combined wisdom of our bellies. They fear to know that we are more than beasts. Yet Aland's attack has taught that dayfire rock a truth this day no Two-Legs ever can forget! How right they are to fear us when our stomachs turn as one to common purpose. That was the Lesson, and that was my dream. Now Two-Legs will end our Way!"

"Forsake the ritual we have taught them all this time?" Eren Gaino. "Claw the mountains down in terror once again? Fling down the huge fire that poisons the wind?"

"All hahns know the last of my kin rotted for generations beneath that poison wind. And died in the end, all but I. Before I was full-furred. I ate the wind, but lived to dream tomorrow. This is the tomorrow that I dreamed! Learning at last our ancient trick on him, Two-Legs will run away from us. Go back to the Lake of Light and hide behind the dayfire. Return no more. End the hunt, and our Way, and leave us as we were before he came. Digest that, O my brothers!"

"End the hunt?" Arnic. "Just fly away?"

"The dayfire rock and the strange long Two-Legs outhunted us all, in the end."

"How then?" Aland, bristling. "The Way always ends when Old Winter hunts. We will finish this with the Furlip camp, and regain our strength and sing our songs in dayfire's winter home. When the snows melt and the cubs are strong, and all things come back again to season, so shall our hunt with Two-Legs."

"No! This dayfire rock has hunted us all into its trap. The evil comes behind."

"Thou, hunted by this dayfire rock?" Arnic. "Thou?"

"As a hilldeer sick with winter goes almost willingly to ground."

"There is no way to change this tomorrow of thy dream?" Eren Gaino.

"One trail only, or the evil will hunt us, even as I dreamed."

"Thy meaning is too ripe for this one's belly!" Arnic. "Leave Aland to die alone, as thy Orange Claw fathers vanished? Nay! Though mountains die like leaves upon the trees in frost-time!"

"Thou speak of unity. Unity of the hahns is the gift of Two-Legs, through the hunt we built to share with him. None but a more deadly predator could turn the hahns from one another's throats. We must cry this new hunt I taste, and quickly, or fall back into the old ways where unity began—here, in the Orange Claw valley."

"Show us thy new trail, oldest of the Orange Claw—and growing older before these eyes!" Aland. "If the dayfire rock is such a fearful hunter, how shall we quit the trail, now it hunts us? Fleeing blindly, all, like hilldeer, before that hopping gleaming gob? Bashed flat in its one-rock avalanche as we flee?"

"Avalanches fall more than one way. This is a Lesson that cries teaching to this dayfire rock. If thou would hunt clear of trouble, study trouble's spoor. The dayfire rock rushed to the Permanent Lairs to avenge the death of the long Two-Legs. Now the long Two-Legs walks again, and his belly calls and calls to me. To me alone?"

"We all have heard it." Eren Gaino. "He lives."

"Then call him in his turn, and he will come, for he must cry his hunt as we cry ours. Will not the dayfire boulder once again follow its nature, as do all things? It will follow its odd hahn-mate where we lead him. Then, weary from all this hunting it has done, perhaps this dayfire rock will welcome a long sleep among its duller, heavier brothers in the mountains. . . ."

"Haiii!" The salute was spontaneous to the hunt he showed them now.

"True hunting that would be." Aland, grudgingly. "Aland with Orange Claw in this, old one, to avenge its vanished hunters."

"Eren Gaino with Orange Claw."

"None more swift on this or any other hunt than Arnic!"

Sunto broke his formal crouch. "Together, then: a hunt such as this dayfire rock has never dreamed, if such rocks dream. Send your hunters. Turn one strong herd of the plains tree-eaters into the mountains, and into the teeth of the storm. That alone is work for full-bellied hunters. This one will lay the trap. . . ."

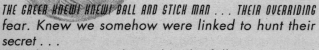

20

THE GREEN KNEW! KNEW! BALL AND STICK MAN . . . THEIR OVERRIDING fear. Knew we somehow were linked to hunt their secret . . .

Python sat cross-legged in the falling snow and drained the huge mug of soup the robochef handed him. He gazed fixedly at the red twinkle as the last lines of grass fire flickered and failed beneath the worsening snowfall.

Somehow his arrival had been a signal to break off the attack. Why? Ramsey thought they might fear flying machines, but Ramsey was in no position to know.

Yet why should they break off now, now that their two most hated foes are together, and within their reach . . .

"What?" Ball materialized out of the dark.

Python realized he had failed to maintain a tight shield. His weariness was extreme. The simple skin of Python, far-wanderer, was beginning to slough away, to reveal the constrained and ordered life beneath.

The reawakening Baka Martin mourned his lost simplicity as the reborn Python in the creche had mourned his lost limbo. But the cunning field-conditioning of the Terran Service was no longer needed, and it would be an effort to hold the Python persona in place. With a sigh he let it go.

"Good," said Ball softly, reading the change. "Ready to report now?"

Martin sighed again. "All right."

"Have you been in actual mind contact with the greer?"

"No. Surface impressions only, so far. Their latent extransensory powers are so subtle I truly did not know they had them until they turned them against me here. All I have are vague impressions: themselves as seen by themselves, clumsy stick figures which are humans from their perspective, the ruins . . ."

"No collective memory of a pitched battle fought with humans among those ruins?"

"Then you've analyzed the flamer burns there. But no. The overpowering collective memory is of a single huge mushroom cloud above the mountains. That event is somehow central to their culture."

Ramsey came into the dim light of the camp glow-globes and handed Python a too-short parka to exchange for his blanket. Python nodded gratefully and sealed himself into it, ignoring the binding of the sleeves.

"Continue," Ball said.

"Ramsey . . ." Innate caution of Terran Service training held his tongue.

"Taken care of. He already is earning a small fortune from his story about Baka Martin, killer orphan, roaming the galaxy in search of a challenge more dangerous than Iron Fennec. He also will get rights to the news break on the revocation of Freehold status, and on the true nature of the greer."

"I will?" Ramsey stared at Ball. "When did Freehold status get revoked? And who knows the true nature of the greer? I certainly don't!"

"Freehold status is revoked as of now," Ball said. "Hunting of the greer has ended for all time."

"Are you making that decision?"

"Yes."

"That's the first outright lie I've caught you in," Ramsey said. "Do you think I'm simple? No field agent in the history of bureaucracy ever wielded that much power. And don't tell me you're the Commonwealth Executive in plainclothes, because she's a broad, and a knockout, and I'm not that far gone that I can't tell the difference."

"It doesn't matter, really, what you believe. You have no need-to-know about the political details of the decision. The decision is irrevocable, no matter how much the Pondoro establishment kicks. That's news by any measure, and you're getting exclusive rights to it, on top of the Python story. His image can use a little refurbishing, anyway. It's been a long time since Fennec. The rest is irrelevant."

"There may be more than one view on what's irrelevant," Ramsey said.

Martin read the writer's flaming curiosity, and saw it deepen into suspicion. Ramsey's attention was so completely focused on the cyborg he had almost suppressed his greer-fear.

"There is only one view on need-to-know," Ball lectured. "The official one."

"So the mask comes off a little further." Ramsey sounded disgusted. "Gone is Ball the uncomplicated biped-baiter. Born is Ball the bureaucrat in charge of everything. Shit, I want my money back!"

"The money you thought was buying my services is at the moment gathering the handsomest interest available in the Commonwealth," Ball said calmly. "Nontaxable Altair IV mutuals. So is your salary, of course, since you're on active duty."

"Active . . . What salary?"

"Your salary as a Commonwealth Information Officer Six, emergency assignment Pondoro."

"I never—"

"Accepted a reserve Commonwealth commission? Sure you did. Years ago. Video records, paper documents, and witnesses to prove it. Plus the fact of your invested salary, of course. And the nature of your investment, the most telling argument of all: only civil servants are permitted to invest in Altair IV nontaxables."

"Video records are suspect in any court you can name, paper documents aren't much better, and your witnesses are liars. . . ."

Martin lost the thread of the argument.

A strange new series of images flashed hotly on his brain. A greer fought wildly against the cyborg and was beaten. A clumsy biped flung lightning bolts at a greer. Then the greer's futile swipes magically became stabs of fire from the biped, and Ball blackened and burst. . . .

The burn streaks on Ball's hide were vividly visible to his tired eyes, even in the poor lighting.

"Ball! You are burned!" Martin began to shiver. "Who burned you?"

"I did." Ramsey's voice sounded constricted. Shame and confusion warred in the writer's brain. "I have never before pulled trigger on the wrong target."

"It was no mistake! And *you* did not pull the trigger! Oh, why do the greer *hate* us so?"

Ball was suddenly attuned to Martin in a way that made his former state seem somnolent. Martin shrank from that alertness.

"You don't mean humanity at large, or even just greer hunters," Ball said. "You mean *us*: Baka Martin and Ball."

"Yes. Yes! Their most overriding hatred: Ball and stick man. Somehow they have penetrated my conditioning, and our connection to one another is known. Known, and hated with a blazing fury! They murdered me. They tried to murder you by weight of numbers. When they could not, they turned Ramsey's hand against you. Don't you *see*?"

"Wait," said Ramsey. "Wait a minute. That's a mighty tall order, even for the Pondoro wolverine."

"I am tempted to regard this as mission fatigue," Ball said slowly. "I am burned because Ramsey is a slow-reflexed biped in a tense situation. You were killed by a beast in its normal fashion. I see no connection."

"You are burned because there was no other way to *end* you!" Martin cried. "End you they must! *Must!* There is no mistake. End you, and—and me. But *why?*"

"You are dangerously tired," the cyborg cautioned. "You have been savagely killed, been reborn, regained your identity and accomplished your mission. It is enough. Your impressions on initial breakthrough to these alien minds cannot be trusted. Our job is done. A cruiser is standing off Pondoro to take us home."

"Suppose they are the super beasts you think they are," Ramsey put in. "Just suppose. Why would they reveal themselves now after playing dumb for so long?"

"Because they *know*, don't you see? They know our purpose here is to hunt their secret out into the open. They fear that above all!"

"How could they know?" Ramsey.

"It's only hypothesis," Ball said, "but these creatures appear to have some fledgling extrasensory ability. My research points to a pre-Survey contact between a star-traveling race and a single tribe of village-building greer. I've assigned high probability to a scout ship for an unauthorized entrepreneur, running ahead of official exploration. Forensics dating of the weapons stigmata on those ruins coincide with dating of a single nuclear explosion in the mountains above the ruins. Both fall well within the decade nearly two centuries ago when out-system speculators last held significant political power in the Commonwealth. Now Martin says the greer remember that blast, remember it obsessively."

"Greer don't live that long!"

"Just so. Which argues a history-telling mechanism. Which is further argument for rudimentary intelligence. Perhaps at least one colony of greer was on the first rung of the ladder to civilization, but kicked brutally off by a space-traveling race. Why? Probably with an eye toward establishing an earlier Freehold status. We may never know, because the nuclear explosion in the mountains suggests to me that the kickers did not survive the exercise. In any event, no private attempt to establish a pre-Survey Freehold is on record. My evaluation of the mountain explosion, subject to modification, is that the ship's conventional drives were destabilized in atmosphere. Why? Perhaps by a pilot trying to operate under that blind panic the greer seem to employ so effectively against humans, in which case the humans died of fright, or something like it."

"Can you prove that?"

"Perhaps. The local record says all normal greer avoid those ruins to the point of compulsive behavior. The sick animal which denned there was worth a Hunt Commission footnote for no other reason than its behavior was so atypical. Obsessive memory of a mushroom cloud, compulsive behavior toward the ruins which may have been its target: each reinforces the other, and my hypothesis."

"And now they hunt humans, while permitting humans to think they are the hunters?"

"A subtle revenge which may make sense to an alien thought-process, but seems costly from an empiric viewpoint, given Hunt Commission statistics."

"You believe all this?"

"I hypothesize. Humans believe, or not."

"So now what?"

"End to Freehold status. An end to hunting, or any other harassment, of the greer. Perhaps they can begin the long return to their pristine state, after much too long a period of abnormal adaptation to human presence. The Terran Service is not only a shield for humanity, but a shield for innocent aliens caught in humanity's toils."

"Admirable." Ramsey's tone was sarcastic. "You compose like a cub reporter at his first planetary carnival. But the stated intention is admirable."

"You really think so?" Ball sounded surprised. "Good! If Ramsey the pukka sahib can say so, that's the story we have commissioned you to write."

"Yeah. Just let that about my civil-servant status go for now. Answer me one question."

"What?"

Martin knew the cyborg's empatho gear was registering the same weary cynicism he could read plainly on the face of the writer.

"How did the Terran Service arrive at this noble purpose *before you got here* to form your hypothesis?"

"Now it's you who are hypothesizing. . . ."

"Not hardly! You're reciting a decision already made, and supplying the rationale after the fact. Typical government bull . . . "

Martin forgot them. For at that precise moment a powerful surge of alien will flowed over his tired mind and called him. Called him with the thrilling, chilling clarity of the moon yodel of Earthhome coyotes in the hills behind his training school.

At last, at last! The breakthrough! Now, now, an end to all the riddles . . .

Ball blurred in his peripheral vision, circling to intercept as he stood abruptly.

"What is it? What are they trying—"

Then the air whooped and flamed, and Ball vanished.

Half stunned by the proximity of the flamer bolt, Martin realized Ramsey had fired at the cyborg, and the cyborg was too busy trying to save its own hide to prevent his own departure.

Ball can look after himself—he's told me so a hundred times across the years. But who's to look after the greer?

He hesitated no longer, snatching an abandoned Colt-Vickers and racing out of camp. The weapon was to persuade Ball not to follow him. He fled into the night as fast as his long legs could carry him. It wouldn't have been fast enough to outdistance Ball. But Ball was busy.

21

BALL PAUSED IN RUNNING SNOW THAT BLASTED DOWN THE GULCH ON A bitter wind. He metered the windchill factor: minus ten and falling. Once more he was thankful for his advanced physique. Extremes of heat and cold meant exactly nothing to him, except as they affected conditions in which he operated.

Baka Martin was moving ahead of him up the rocky draw, well within range of his empathometer. Martin's heat signature loomed in the infrared scanner against the frigid wilderness.

It had taken Ball three minutes of touch-and-go maneuvering to get close enough to narco Ramsey without hurting the writer or getting himself cindered. He had been distracted by fear that Martin would vanish into the countryside beyond the range of his sensors. An unfounded fear. He simply pirated a fix from Pondoro's geographical-position-plotting satellites and cut cross-country to catch up.

For a long, bitter interval now Martin had trudged into the mountains, and Ball had shadowed him, marveling at his partner's resiliency. But Martin was tired, dangerously tired. When he slept, Ball knew he would move in. Ball had no illusions at all about going against a Palikar armed with a frontier-model flamer. It had been an error to leave loose beam-guns lying around. Baka Martin's grabbing the flamer on the way out of camp had frightened him deeply. His own partner!

Enhanced infrared gave Ball warm blotches on the frozen slopes above him, native small-life of the hibernating variety, tucked in for the winter.

Greer, also. Shadowing him relentlessly.

In the normal vision range, of course, there was nothing but horizontal snow drift, riding the wind. The snow made a smooth blanket, already a meter deep, smoothing out irregularities in the canyon floor.

Ball was following too close for all traces of Martin's passage to be swallowed up. There were increasing evidences of stumbling. On more than one occasion Martin had fallen. Ball's tracking library told him the pattern showed muscles no longer in even approximate coordination.

Ball remained shocked to the core of his being at his personal brush with extinction.

He never had been deliberately shot at before, not with a weapon capable of piercing all his defenses, all his insulation, and opening him like a crustacean. The Rongor battle robot didn't count, because it had been so vulnerable to his own more subtle armaments. But he wasn't emotionally geared to destroy his partner.

These frontier planets were savage places, no denying. He decided he would accept only inner-world assignments for the next half century or so, regain his equilibrium. His seniority entitled him, and those environments were where he shone, anyway. This sort of effort called for another Palikar, or at least a Survey-trained biped. Yet here he was, the perfect operative, the unsuspected, below-suspicion detective, tracking a heavily armed renegade through a blizzard on a hostile world, and tracked in his turn by hostile paranormal beasts.

Ever since his natal moment, Ball had been fully functional, and more or less convinced of his own immortality. Attendant at the deaths of scores of sentient life-forms over the years, he observed it as a remote phenomenon. That he now was virtually optic-to-eye with his own mortality, and its possible instrument his own partner, had an irony he was reluctant to appreciate. But Ball knew he was not mistaken: Martin hadn't taken the flamer to protect himself from greer. He had taken it to prevent Ball's interference with his obsessive effort to make full mind contact with the greer. Martin seemed to think he was fulfilling some holy crusade.

Ball had to interfere, of course. Such a crusade was not part of their orders.

The field man was exhausted and emotionally depleted, but he pushed on so stubbornly into the teeth of the storm, it was as if he was bent on suicide. Such stubbornness was not a tendency Ball had noted in Martin's psyche in their dozen deep-penetration missions before this one, and he was worried.

The puzzle was *why?* True, Martin was under a terrific neural strain induced by the greer, but still he was Baka Martin, partner of a thousand shared watches in some fairly incredible corners of Terranized space. Why did Martin now exhibit this obsessive need to put himself at the mercy of the greer? He already had done his fieldwork, and superbly: they had all the justification they needed for their precut orders to suspend Freehold status on Pondoro. Martin had carried out his prime mission to the letter.

Or had he?

Ball paused.

His tracking library had just extrapolated the fact that Martin was being lured, while he himself was being herded, up a box canyon.

"Box canyon," the program whispered beneath the keening of the wind. "Cul-de-sac. Dead end . . ."

Ball considered the situation.

Martin believed the greer wanted both himself and Ball dead. Now they had lured Martin—and himself, by remote control—into a trap. That the trap was meant for Ball as well was obvious to Ball by the greer shadowing him. If Martin was correct, the greer had somehow discerned that by luring Martin into jeopardy, they also would lure him.

There was an implication there: they thought they had a foolproof trap to spring, somewhere up ahead, despite his invulernability to their previous attacks. Hence the flamer in Martin's possession? Perhaps. They already had practiced the technique with Ramsey.

As he drifted forward, a new alignment of facts occurred to him.

Ramsey was a good barometer—a perfect barometer—for how easily the public at large would swallow the Terran Service story about why Freehold status here must be revoked. Yet even under the neural pressure of the greer attack, Ramsey hadn't hesitated to finger the single weak point: how could the decision have been made before the investigation was complete?

If Ramsey stayed bought—unlikely, to judge from his reputation and his reaction so far—or was eliminated, there would always be another news hawk on the make. Discovery that a sentient life-form deliberately had masqueraded as less than that to avoid detection was going to be a major media event. Perhaps the media feeding frenzy of the year. The Service *had* to come out looking good.

Nothing would look better than a couple of Service martyrs, dead in the cause of all mankind.

A pebble rattled and bounced down through the blowing snow.

Ball still was weighing his new thoughts.

Another pebble rattled past. Then a rock the size of a man's fist buried itself like a meteor right in front of him. The greer up above must be getting clumsy-footed in the cold, he thought.

There was a loud crack above, as of stone splitting. A boulder about his size clipped him spinning, and skidded finally to a halt. Ball started to power forward.

There were beasts clustered above him on both rims of the canyon. Not just greer now, but huge creatures that loomed like bonfires on the infrared. A cascade of pebbles and shale washed over him, and he sped up. More rocks crashed down, spinning his exoskeleton frantically, leaving him unspun within but increasingly bewildered. Were they throwing rocks at him now? Prying boulders out of the frozen ground argued strong leverage, and the greer had never been recorded as tool users. . . .

In seeming slow motion he reached the obvious conclusion: intelligent carnivores who can manipulate the nervous systems of other creatures don't *need* tools. They will find a whole inventory of organic tools in any ecology. Whatever flies or soars becomes aerial reconnaissance; whatever creature uses heavy muscle to survive becomes earth-moving machinery. Thus they must have built the village by the river, and thus the appearance of the huge, slow-footed creatures above him in the storm.

Came another subsonic crack, then a sustained and ragged roar. Ball took a glancing blow from something slightly smaller than a house.

The whole side of the canyon seemed to come down all at once.

He rode a torrent of stone across the floor of the canyon like a beach ball on a breaking wave. He applied antigravs. Tried to pop up through the countless fragments that tried to pin him to the far wall. Kept getting knocked off course by bounding boulders. Slammed back into the growing pile by the sheer number and weight of the missiles. Rocks began to form a ragged cairn above him. He spun and twisted, applied full power in all directions. All he accomplished was the collapse of the pocket with him in it. A full-bore avalanche was more than he had been designed to best. Beneath that awesome force, the strength of the Rongor battle robot was as nothing. A windup toy.

His optics went dark almost at once. In seconds he was wedged solid beneath a vast inert tonnage. The roaring and the banging and the settling seemed to go on for a long time, becoming muffled as the rubble piled deep.

When it finally stopped, he tried once more to move.

He became lighter than air, and tried to rise. Nothing. He applied power in a new way, linking into the gravity field of the planet itself, and attempted to repel himself skyward. He kept stepping up the power until the per-square-inch pressure on his shell approached factory test limits. There was a minuscule shifting, then a settling back. Pebbles poured in to fill air pockets, rocks shifted and dovetailed, and he was absolutely immobile again.

He ran a lightning-swift analysis of the dynamic balance and structural content of his crude prison. Then he computed the results against his battery of abilities, and extracted a raw estimate of the time it would take him to work free, using rock-shattering temperature fluctuations, sub- and supersonic vibrations, and antigravs.

He was entombed for approximately a year, if no systems failed under stress.

He remembered to check on Martin. The empathometer showed Martin's brain in an almost unreadable tumult, wild as the storm, but still fixed on that overwhelming goal of contact. Ball knew it had to be conditioning of a kind for which he had not been briefed.

Just as he hadn't been briefed on the greer village, for that matter.

That omission had cost him precious hours of investigation and analysis. In retrospect, the Service had to have known about the ruins. They would have factored the ruins into the already made decision to revoke Freehold. There would have been little knowable about Pondoro the Service did not know before they sent Martin and him in.

Ball activated a com channel.

"TS Cruiser *Forthright* from TS twelve-two-ten. Acknowledge."

There was a burst of atmosphere interference, then, ". . . *Forthright* acknowledging."

"Status on Keith Ramsey?"

"Local government indicate they will comply with your directive to hold Ramsey incommunicado, but— for the record—with utmost reluctance. They ran him; he's an A.N. Certified Correspondent—"

"We know that! You have signals traffic for me?"

"Checking. Our skipper wants to know what happened down there. The Pondoro authorities are being very hostile about injury and death of protected indigenous species. Affirmative signals traffic. Stand by for a coded directive from the Executive. Eyes only. Transmitting."

Ball unscrambled the message and was quiet for a long time.

"*Forthright*. Message received and understood?"

"TS twelve-two-ten," Ball replied. "I understand."

And, at last, he did.

22

A CRISP, MILITARY VOICE WAS SPEAKING FAR UP ABOVE ME SOMEWHERE: the Rongor Sergeant Major.

". . . Should regain consciousness any moment, sah. The Medfac has healed his wounds."

I was cold. My teeth were chattering and I couldn't stop them. The rest of me shivered in counterpoint. A needle pricked me. Some medication or other lit a flash fire along my nerves. Just that quickly, I was warm again.

"Why was he shivering so bad?" LaChoy's voice.

"Delayed reaction to exposure, sah. The narco injected by the cyborg shielded him from the worst effects of the cold, and of course the Medfac operates at human optimal—"

"Okay, fine. How long was he under Ball's narco?"

"Estimated eight hours, sah."

I opened my eyes to fluttering whiteness. Snow. The Rongor was holding me like a big baby in his ceramosteel arms. LaChoy was beside him, muffled in the snowfall and the night.

"Where the hell am I?"

"Still in camp," LaChoy said. "What's left of it now. I came as fast as I could from Firstport when you called me a couple hours ago. Damned difficult, what with all the government officials flapping about. Just what the bloody hell is going on, d'you know?"

"A lot more than I like to think about. Where's Ball?"

"Gone without a trace." LaChoy's voice was grim. "Until Ball shows up, I'm to hold you for authorities, by the way."

I tried to move. No chance, not in the Rongor's embrace.

"Let me down, for God's sake. I feel silly."

"It's all right, Sergeant Major," LaChoy said. "Let him stand. Don't let him fall."

Good advice. As soon as my legs had weight on them, they buckled. I dangled at my usual height in the grasp of the robot. I felt even sillier. The snowflakes were cold on my bare head.

"I didn't understand what you said about the authorities," I said.

"There's a Federal cruiser standing off Pondoro. The Terran Service is up to something here."

"I know about that ship. The *Forthright*. Did its captain order me held?"

"*Forthright* relayed the order. It came direct from the Commonwealth Executive. Direct, mind you. You appear to have riled some heavy personalities. Pondoro Department of Interior orders me to comply with Terran directive on this. Pain of license and so forth. They got my attention. Thought this was a bloody commonwealth, not a republic. And certainly not a dictatorship. But all out of my league. You're detained, until the powers-that-be sort out the jurisdictions."

I didn't like the sound of that one bit. But LaChoy was the wrong person to argue with. So I changed subjects.

"What makes you think I called you two hours ago?" I asked. "Didn't the S-M just say I've been under for eight?"

LaChoy nodded. "Bit curious, I admit. But it certainly was your mug on the vidscreen in Firstport, all right. Your voice, your speech patterns."

"Ball," I said.

"Gone," LaChoy repeated.

I hadn't meant that, but I let it ride. Ball must have impersonated me to get LaChoy to come dig me out of the snow. At least he'd decided not to let me freeze completely to death. I supposed the six hours in the snow were his idea of a reprimand for me trying to fry him.

My head was swimming. Had I really tried to burn Ball? Several times? It was all fuzzy. Could the greer *really* cause a man to do such a thing? Against a lifetime's conditioning in the safe handling of weapons? I closed my eyes.

"What'n hell's going on?" LaChoy said "Something bloody wrong, I can see that. All these greer dead. Can't buy it, quite. Didn't take you for a game hog."

I reopened my eyes. "A game hog! You think I *provoked* this?"

"Don't quite know, yet. Sign hard to puzzle out. Looks like there's been a goddamned *war* here . . . and then the fire and the snow covered it over." He paused. "Eliot will live, by the way. My chap won't."

I sagged against the unyielding strength of the Rongor. "I'm sorry."

He rubbed his face. "Greer never attack in droves. Never. Plus, it's the equinox now. They're all migrating south behind the herds. No reason for a pack of males to turn aside like this. Leave its females and cubs to fight the weather alone. Had to be extreme provocation. *Enormous* provocation. Hunt Commission's damn near in orbit, on top of the S-M dusting those two t'other night. I may wind up in slam for even booking your hunt. May deserve to, for the matter of that. What did you *do*?"

"Not a damn thing. I was sitting here trying to write when they attacked. You're right, it was like combat. If it hadn't been for Ball—"

"Ball." His face was stiff. "Did that goddamned cyborg do something? Kill a young'un that wandered in out of curiosity? That sometimes happens in equinox, during the migration. Whack a female with cubs, something like that? They're all very near their birthing time now. Can't believe you wouldn't recognize a pregnant female. Damn cyborg might not differentiate. Camp security! My aching arse! You were here. You have to know what happened."

"Nothing happened. Not like you mean. They just singled us out and came for us. All males—all of them I saw, anyway. No cubs, no females. Ball didn't take action until they attacked. I would have been history in under a minute if he hadn't. You're baying the wrong tree, my friend. This is Federal politics of the most putrid. We're all just bystanders."

"Federal politics. Yes. That TS cruiser, the order to have you held. All that. Even heard some growl about revocation of Freehold for Pondoro. Nonsense, of course."

"Not nonsense. She's going to try it."

"The Executive, you mean."

"Yes."

He studied me impassively. "Just what are you, Ramsey? In every sense of the word, I mean? Heard some growl you might be on the government payroll. Working for that bitch."

My legs were gaining strength. The Rongor still had me, though.

"That's bullshit," I said. "What I am—the only thing about me that matters right now—is: I'm a writer. More to the point, a Certified newsman. I have just stumbled into one of the biggest stories of my life, right here in your damn camp. Damned near got killed while I was doing it. Where's my 'corder?"

"Still there, on the camp table. Full of snow."

"That won't hurt it. I want it."

"No."

I yanked against the robot with some half-baked notion of taking it by surprise. All I did was bruise my shoulder.

"You're denying me access to my 'corder? Was that part of your instructions from the local government? Or did that come straight from the Commonwealth?"

"That's a pretty serious charge," he said.

"Which is it?"

"Neither . . ."

"But somebody asked if I had it with me, or you wouldn't have hunted for it under the snow."

His shoulders dropped a fraction. "The Feds. They just want to know. . . ."

"They want to know what I've been transmitting from here before they could get you in here to shut me up. I know what they want to know."

The flap on one of the remaining tents whipped back, and I hurt myself against the Rongor's grip again, trying to react. The greer-fear was still on me.

It was Nail, carrying a cup that steamed.

"Trail stew," he said. "Perk you right up."

"Thanks."

He looked at LaChoy. "Signal coming in. Federal cruiser says let him go."

"You sure?"

"Sure? Well, if twenty years of hard time in some plastic playpen isn't sure enough for you, it damn sure is sure enough for me!"

"Twenty years! For what?"

I savored the aroma rising off the bowl. I was on familiar ground now. "For interfering with the public's right to know." I told him.

"That's it," Nail said. "That's the language they used."

"Okay," I said. "I say again in front of this witness, I am a Certified newsman. I am on to a Federal government screwup of historic proportions. I demand free use of my 'corder."

"You don't demand a damn—"

"Uh, boss . . ." Nail interrupted. "The Feds said he'd say that. Said the Commonwealth could not even remotely appear to have a hand in interfering with a Certified newsperson. So let him go."

"But the Interior wallahs told me this was Terran Service orders!"

"This is the Commonwealth Executive, up to the usual," I said. "She's not infallible. She still puts her girdle on one leg at a time, just like you and me."

"They want to talk to him, boss," Nail said.

"Who does?"

"That Federal cruiser, *Forthright*. Private-like."

"Release him," LaChoy growled at the Rongor. "But I will have some questions of my own, by damn!"

I swayed but kept erect. The stew was cool enough to start slurping, but hot enough to groove a warm path all the way down. When I got inside the tent, it felt hot as Old Earth Africa. I finished the stew before I keyed the com unit.

"Keith Ramsey. This had better be good."

"Ball. It took them long enough to revive you."

"So it's you. Why impersonate me when you called LaChoy?"

"To get him there soonest. You were out of commission, and I need help."

"To hell with you! You left me to hypothermia!"

"And you tried to fry me. You never were in any danger. A Central Receiving ambulance would have picked you up before any lasting damage was done."

"Something might have eaten me!"

"All life has its risks. There's no time for this, Ramsey."

"Are you on board that cruiser now?"

"Actually, no. I used their recognition codes and signal personnel voices and images to leave the proper misdirection on Pondoro government recorders. As a matter of fact, I'm jamming local Federal frequencies just now."

"Is there anything you can't do?"

"Two things. I can't extract myself from my present situation. I can't help Baka Martin—Python. I believe he's dead for keeps this time."

"Where are you?"

"Classified," Ball said crisply. "Will you try to help Martin?"

"What's in it for me?"

"Well, I will continue to keep you free, for one thing. Every Federal official in this sector is trying to contact Pondoro authorities by now. They want them to raise LaChoy and countermand my release order. Keep you or kill you, not necessarily in that order. Eventually they'll figure out I'm jamming them and send someone down from *Forthright* in person. When they do that, you won't be able to help yourself. Let alone Martin. You're his last hope."

"You've shut down planetary communications?"

"Just enough to ensure the continent upon which we find ourselves is out of touch with the cosmos."

"You're a ball of many talents. Where are you?"

"I said it once: classified. Forget where I am. Now, do you help? Or do I let them take you?"

"You won't do that. Not if I'm your last hope. What's in it for me?"

"I will not grovel. I offer you a fair trade for your best effort to save my partner."

"What have you got that I could possibly want?"

"The story, of course. The whole story, nothing held back."

23

I HAD AN EDITOR ONCE WHO LECTURED THAT, EVER SINCE SOME ANCIENT guy named Gutenberg developed the notion of type, there have been two basic requirements for a news hawk. Neither one had to do with the ability to compose limpid prose or snoop out iniquity. Those are helpful but not crucial.

The first fundamental is never, under the most extreme deadline pressure, appear to be working. An early twentieth century novel preserved this for all time when the protagonist, caught at his typewriter on cable deadline by one of his rummy Lost Generation friends, invited the friend down the street for a drink. Then he excused himself, rather than simply admit he had work to do.

The second fundamental is the one I now employed in LaChoy's camp: never be caught off guard by anything. The cynical lip twist and flippant remark must be instantly ready in the face of suns going nova and galaxies falling out of orbit.

I give myself passing marks for the casualness with which I took over LaChoy's camp on the strength of the mythical communication from the Federal cruiser *Forthright*. I grabbed up my winter gear and commandeered the best vehicle in camp as no more than my due. I even cadged one of those Colt-Vickers frontier models, on the grounds I would be flying over greer territory without a guide, and his insurance companies wouldn't like what Associated News did to them if anything went wrong. I assured one and sundry my destination was none, say again absolutely none, of their affair. It was child's play: I've spent too many years sweeping through mysteriously opened doors in far more sophisticated company than LaChoy's to bobble anything as simple as that.

I climbed out of camp until my altimeter gave a sea-level reading of 4,800 meters. The snow-covered hills beyond LaChoy's plateau reached within forty to five hundred meters beneath my feet. It was time to find out what kind of pilot I was, and maintain my newsman's facade, all at the same time. It wouldn't have been as much of a challenge if the storm hadn't kept trying to paste me to the landscape.

I plotted the course Ball dictated to intercept Python's line of march, checked airspeed, then curled my lip and reminded Ball of our deal.

"You haven't effectuated a rescue yet," he replied. "You probably won't be successful, anyway."

That got me right back in the groove; bureaucratic quibbling always does.

"Cut the crap and tell me the story," I said.

"You're free of captivity. Isn't that enough for now?"

"I can handle the Feds."

It took a vicious stab of the stabilizers to hopscotch over a sudden peak that reached 4,850. I told the car's pilot to look for higher, calmer air. This time I wasn't even bluffing. I didn't know if I was beyond empathometer range or not, but Ball knew I wasn't bluffing. He gave in instantly.

"Recording?" he said. "Yes? All right: our assignment here—Martin unknowingly, following memory-wipe—was to develop a logical excuse to halt greer hunting and abort Freehold status."

"Wait. Assigned by whom?"

"Directly of course by our superior officers. But the initiating order was from the Executive. It was her specific order hunting be halted, and Freehold revoked, in favor of Commonwealth protectorate status."

"Jesus Christ!"

I could see and hear headlines across the breadth of humanized space on this one. Commonwealth complicity in revoking a planet's independence: every conspiracy kook between the stars would feel validated.

"Our assignment, as your reaction suggests, was deliberate interference with local autonomy. Absolutely illegal, of course." He was a beauty when he started spilling quotes.

I prayed my old 'corder wouldn't take this of all moments to craze its chips. I tried to memorize his every word, just in case. Meanwhile, of course, trying to stay airborne. My hands were cramped to the controls as I flew the instrument cluster. It would have taken a hell of a jolt to knock them loose. I was getting into the rhythm of the wind gusts now, flying the storm, not just piloting a strange craft through pitch-dark turbulence. Ever since man left horse behind, he has experienced this marriage of flesh and machine, in each of the devices he's fashioned to replace ol' Dobbin. Ball perhaps was the ultimate expression of the union.

"Why so eager to revoke Freehold out here in the provinces?" I said.

"I'll get to that. From the time the decision was taken, every avenue of approach was under consideration. Martin's entry was easy; it always is. His Python cover is near perfection. My entry would be a little more difficult, given the local shape prejudice.

When your visa application popped up, Service tacticians formulated the rest of the plan. You served two purposes: to introduce me, and to be the scenario control. If you failed to accept the cover story or lend your reputation to it, we would abandon it before it was issued. What one news hawk suspects, others will suspect. . . ."

I surfed the tumultuous womb of the storm, while Ball's emotionless drone recited state secrets. It was almost lulling.

"Why?" I said again. "*Why* did the Executive move against Pondoro?"

He hesitated, while I rode the storm serenely. It was almost cozy up there in the wrack and roar. Vast empty spaces plied by lighted ships full of the agents of interstellar political skulduggery seemed the sheerest science fiction against the reality of the storm.

"I was given one reason before insertion," Ball said. "I now have been given another, through coded orders issued me just before I called you."

"A cover story within a cover story?"

"Not precisely. Initially I was told certain individuals have come to Pondoro to hunt the greer. Powerful or wealthy or both, since the planet is near no commercial main line, and the fare and the hunting itself do not come cheaply. Within that rather elite number, inevitably, were individuals who are important to the Executive's party and political interests."

"Don't tell me," I said, "she's got a bleeding heart for the beasties—not *her*. Although she might consider it politically advisable to cater to some group . . ."

"Nothing so simple. Individuals vital to the Executive's schemes are in their positions because of one overriding virtue: predictability. They can predictably be pushed into some desired course of action—or they can predictably be immune to the pushing of opposing factions. They are fearful or fearsome, in their individual ways, but most of all *predictable*. Their psychological triggers are known to perfection, and the Executive can lead them like an orchestra. Yet the ones who hunted the greer changed. . . ."

A savage thrill coursed my nerves—residue of the greer-fear.

The storm almost got me then, catching me on the forward quarter with renewed violence. I concentrated on the controls and dove down a long valley, almost invisible in the falling snow. As I lost airspeed, snow began to stick to the superchilled skin of the car. I put on the windscreen wipers.

"That's the correct valley," Ball said. "It narrows into a canyon up ahead. Be careful to avoid a fresh landslide seventeen kilometers in. Go over it, and continue up the canyon. Martin is there. And the greer. Careful . . ."

I negotiated the landslide as directed, and pushed the car almost to the deck. Beneath the canyon walls, I was out of the worst of the storm. The snowy walls of the canyon glowed eerily through the night-view overlay on the windscreen.

"Very near . . ." Ball said.

Any moment now the greer would sense me coming, and turn and unleash that awful fear at me. At the thought, my pulse began to thud.

"The big shots hunted the greer—and changed," I muttered. "No damn wonder! I bet they went back to their fat planets unrecognizable, after the greer. The old harness probably didn't exactly fit. . . ."

"Certainties can become a horrible miscalculation," Ball said, "when a spineless world leader abruptly develops courage. Worse, a dependable tyrant may become shaky, unsure of himself. Or, worst of all, develop empathy for the tyrannized. Or any of several possible combinations. All unpredictable. Therefore unacceptable."

"Why not just develop an antihunting philosophy for her party, and order them not to come to Pondoro?"

"You still are naive, in some ways." Ball sounded surprised. "Had the Executive forbidden her people alone to hunt here, it would be a clear signal there is something here she either feared or could not control. To even imply weakness is to alert those who prey upon weakness—her opposition. . . ."

"So you've turned her political fate into my hands."

"Just so. To do with as you will."

"Why?"

"That doesn't matter, for the story. Since when did a news hawk care about the motives of a disgruntled employee?"

"It matters to me."

"You realize, of course, Baka Martin is a sybil symbiote?"

"You confirm that, then?" My God, the story kept getting bigger and bigger. "You confirm Old Earth has loosed the sybil parasite outside the Blocked Worlds?"

"About the only ones who don't know that are the great unwashed." It was almost a sneer.

"Which includes most of humanity! That's a whole different story."

"Indeed. The Executive likes to experiment with super beings for her personal agents. Super beings who can—for instance—be molded into champions for the games. More importantly, to ensure the preeminence of the Service in all those little skirmishes across the stars which serve us now for war."

"She sent him here to take on a greer—as a test of his abilities?"

"So I was told at the beginning. I was not advised until today he had been implanted with an irreversible compulsion toward repeated close contact with the greer. Given the nature of these beasts, and their abilities, such programming can only prove fatal. I was given no instructions—until just before I called you—that we were to have a martyr."

"She *ordered* him to die?"

"He was programmed for it. I was not informed until now. I have been ordered not to intervene. It amounts to the same thing."

"How can you not intervene? He's your partner!"

"So of course she did not ask me to collude in plotting his death. But now the programming is running as planned. I am directed to avoid intervention in his ultimate mission."

"He's already shown he can whip a greer! *What* mission?"

"The only one left: to die, and transmit the sybil to the greer. The Service will have a martyr, to reinforce its decision to place Pondoro off limits. The Executive will have a new super being with which to experiment: a paranormal predator, bonded to the sybil. And a continent, rendered off limits through revocation of Freehold status, for a laboratory."

"I can't take all this in: she *wants* the sybil loose among the greer?"

"Martin's death beneath the claws of a greer will break the sybil-stasis. The parasite will save itself any way it can. Its traditional survival technique is transfer to the victor. That's how it dominates the Blocked Worlds."

"You know that for sure?"

"Of course. Almost everyone—"

"But the great unwashed knows that. Yeah, right. Suppose Martin surprises her and outfights the greer? He did it once."

"Baka Martin died for the final time," Ball said grimly, "seven minutes ago. You are too late to save him, but not too late to stop his killer. A killer which, even now, will be looking upon this environment through the perspective of the most dangerous alien humankind has ever subverted to its purpose."

24

for Python. I nosed the car up the narrowing floor of
the canyon. The snow seemed to let up a bit, and I
could see farther ahead. The colors the night vision
screen's software assigned to the lightless canyon
weren't exactly right. I was no more than twenty
meters above the canyon floor.

Something was moving up there. The proportions
of the creature were wrong for Baka Martin. I could
see that at first glimpse, even on the night screen. It
waddled, low to the ground, like a badger. Something like a tail dragged behind it in the snow,
adding to the badger image.

I cut airspeed and dropped, silent as a hunting
owl.

Abruptly, the creature broke into an awkward gait
that resembled a run. I nudged the car off to one side
to get a profile view. What I saw raised my hackles in
primitive horror.

What had seemed one creature was really two,
one riding the other piggyback fashion. The rider's
head flopped back loosely to the pounding stride of
his mount. The ravaged, dead face of Baka Martin,
the rider, stared at me upside down from an impossi-
bly angled neck.

The queer coloring of the night screen made it
more awful. His eyes were sunken and lifeless. But his

face billowed obscenely, like a pilot under g force. His long arms, and one of his legs, were clenched tightly around the huge greer he rode. His other leg trailed limply through the snow; that was what had looked like a tail.

The greer didn't appear to be wounded. But its progress was a gruesome caricature of their usual terrifying grace. Its entire body hunched and humped beneath its burden, as if its muscles were out of control of its central nervous system. Python's torn and bloody carcass jiggled and slapped against its back in a horrifying pantomime of mixed-species pornography.

"What have you found?" Ball's voice seemed as remote from this hell-pit canyon as the planet of my birth. "Your abrupt intake of breath was clear through the com. Your breathing is altered and shallow. Your pulse is elevated. Your blood pressure is dangerously elevated. Your thinking is muddled, freighted with fear and loathing. *What have you found?*"

"Python . . . Martin. He's dead, all right. But—"

"Quickly! He's *what*?"

The grotesque couple turned with jerking slowness that was painful to watch. The greer was trying to spot me. But there came none of that cloying fear when he fastened his attention on the car. I hovered. The beast twisted away and shambled up the canyon. Faster now. Running away. I felt the killing urge boil up hotly; whether my own emotion or the greer's, I couldn't tell. But I knew it had to die.

"Speak to me!" Ball's command voice filled the cabin.

"Martin—a greer—they're . . . *stuck together* is the best way I can put it. Martin's finished, all right, but the greer looks mighty sick. It's trying to run away. . . ."

"Kill it!"

"Is it—are they . . . ?"

"*Kill it!*" The cyborg's voice throbbed with what sounded like genuine rage—and perhaps fear. "Kill it *now!* The sybil is trying to escape its own death the same way it has escaped all the eons of its existence. Kill it, Ramsey, you're the great white hunter—*kill it now!*"

There are times to argue and times to act. This was the latter. I thumbed on all the lights, grounded the car hard, and thrust out into the shockingly cold air. My rifle was in my hands.

The greer went mad when the car's battery of floodlights hit it.

It dashed against the far side of the canyon, gobbling in an awful mixture of shriek and pitiful mew.

I blinked repeatedly, dazzled by the blaze of light on snowbank and snowfall. Tried to find the beast in the crosshairs.

The greer clawed upward. Lost its purchase and fell. Bounded up and scrambled clumsily back up the rock wall. Python's corpse hampered it, clinging like death itself. It climbed higher than seemed possible before gravity and the weight of the dead man dragged it to a halt. At the hesitation, before it had time to plunge back, I set the crosshairs on its reaching shoulder and squeezed the trigger.

They came down in a shower of snow and rock. The canyon was a well of thundering echoes. Where they came to rest, I shot again, but saw the bullet waste itself in a splatter of stone and ice.

The greer kept screaming. It attempted the wall again, with incomprehensible strength. It seemed it would climb up and out by sheer brute vitality. When its climb finally faltered once more, the crosshairs settled on its rib cage beneath the reaching, straining forepaw.

The smack of the bullet was lost in reawakened echoes.

They came down again, dragging a minor avalanche of snow and stone that glittered in the car's lights.

When they hit, they separated. What was left of Martin was a raw smear pressed deep in fresh whiteness; the greer continued its roll toward cover. My fourth shot sprayed ice chips behind it.

I pulled the rifle down out of recoil, slammed the fifth round home.

The greer vanished.

Literally vanished.

There was nothing to see but a sparkle of snow crystals hanging in the car's floods. A wisp of errant steam from Python's flattened corpse. And the steadily falling snow.

I got my back planted against the car and tried to watch everywhere at once. LaChoy's voice seemed to drone in my buzzing ears: *if you try to break them down to stop them, they will come and kill you. . . .* I tried to tell myself it was dying over there. The rib-cage shot had been the telling one. But I didn't believe it. I had one round left, and was afraid to open the action to feed more. Time stretched . . .

Gradually I realized the distant staccato I had somehow associated with LaChoy's shooting instructions was not entirely in my mind, but was rattling out of the car's open hatch. It began to form identifiable words as my deafened ears regained some use; it was Ball, shouting.

"The beam-gun, you moron! The beam-gun! You can't kill sybil with a bullet! It'll collect you when you walk up to collect your trophy! Burn it! Flame it into nothing. Sear it out of existence . . ."

I fell into the car and slammed the hatch shut. Despite the cold, there was sweat burning the corners of my eyes. The cabin felt as overheated as a sauna. I reloaded my rifle anyway before I swapped it for the big Colt-Vickers.

"You should have mentioned that before," I said.

"Idiot! How was I to know you were so entirely brain-dead as to wave that sport toy at a symbiote?" He was silent a moment. "You're alive, at least. What happened?"

"Gone. It got away. I hit it twice, but it got away. Martin's body dropped off—"

"Beam it!"

My skin crawled all over. "What did you say?"

"Beam Martin's remains. Utterly. The sybil will have left a colony on the off chance this new predator form will fail it. This way, it can start all over again, working up the food chain through the carrion eaters. Destroy the body, and everything within a radius of thirty meters, down to bare rock. I don't know how fast Pondoro bacteria move!"

"Shouldn't we inform the authorities . . . ?"

"In this situation, I *am* the authorities! Now burn that body, or I'll order this canyon nuked!"

"You can't . . ."

"Don't bet on it. You'll still be in the canyon, remember?"

"But—"

"*Do it!*"

I did it. Martin's face was buried in the snow when the first wide-nozzle burst hit, but my mind's eye replayed those awful contortions it had worn as the sybil changed hosts. I got a grip on myself and got to work, sketching a rough circle of molten rock on fine beam and then gradually painting it in. Snow hissed and steamed. Rivulets of water ran off the canyon walls. The local temperature went up appreciably.

When there was nothing left but a blackened crater pouring steam up through the snowfall, it somehow seemed better. Cleaner. Wasn't there some ancient adventuring human ancestor who sent their heroes out in flame and smoke? A fitting end for a modern-day Palikari. I sat still for a bit, trying to think of a fitting epitaph. Me, the big word man. A word for any occasion, twenty if you'd rather, fifty if you'd pay for them.

"Is it done?" Ball's insistent tones.

"It's done."

"What's wrong with your voice?"

"Nothing. Damn you!"

"I'm just surprised by your emotion. He wasn't *your* partner, after all."

"It's done, damn you! Be satisfied."

"I will be. When your thoroughness can be verified by *Forthright*'s landing party."

I knew somewhere inside that ball, the protoplasm that organized its activities was, after all, mostly human. The voice Ball chose just then didn't reveal it. I wondered if that was his way of holding private his grief for his lost partner. I hoped so. I hoped all that passed for Ball's personality had not just been a clever program designed by some fancy word-and-image smith like me, working in a different medium. I didn't want to pry if I was right. And I didn't want to know if I wasn't. So I said nothing.

Ball broke in on my thoughts. A gentler tone.

"I respect your moment of silence. But we must move on. Can you still track the greer?"

"Maybe. I'm pretty sure I hit it hard, twice. It may bleed out."

"Not if the sybil was successful. Will you try?"

"I can use the car's landing lights. The car may have some locally adaptive tracking instrumentation for cripples. That wouldn't violate fair chase."

"My data on tracking suggest permitting a wounded prey's wounds time to stiffen and slow it."

"I doubt your data was developed on Pondoro. Plus, there's the sybil, as you say."

"Just so. If you wait to track it until sybil has established successful symbiosis, you will, in your turn, be tracked. By a greer that now is more than any greer could ever hope to be, in the natural course of things."

"A greer all by itself is pretty damn amazing."

"Yes. I wish I could call in a landing party, properly equipped for combat and sterilization. But the crew still is aspace, with political blockades still in place. They would have to double-check such an order to wipe out indigenous beings. If they check, the Executive's staff will know what I'm trying to kill. *Forthright* will be told, instead, to arrest me for a traitor."

"A traitor? Can they declare you a traitor for this?"

"They can, and will, and may already have. Freehold status remains in effect because I dropped off the board. No one else in this cluster has the authority to revoke it. It won't take long for suspicion to follow. If I stay missing, we are at impasse on that account, until a backup for me arrives."

"What about this were-greer?"

"That is the urgent thing. The sybil will not be confined to one host for long. Which leaves you, or we lose the scent, and perhaps Pondoro. It will not take long. One, and then several, soon many, and then all greer would share their pelts with a parasite. Perhaps before the Executive can move to eliminate Freehold. Humans will be at risk. It is not too extreme to say the sector could be at risk! The sybil will be raging to proliferate, after all the years in stasis."

I thought about it, but not for long. "I'm starting now," I said.

25

THE SPOOR OF THE GREER FILLED RAPIDLY WITH SNOW. THE BLOOD TRAIL had stopped showing long before. Ball said that would mean the sybil already was at work, buttressing its shaky beachhead on Pondoro.

I didn't really need to rely upon the washed-out colors of the night vision screen. LaChoy's car was programmed to track wounded beasts, and had locked on the greer's unique electrochemical signature. The sybil hadn't learned to conceal its presence in its new host yet. The car insisted on informing me the greer was infected with a strange, possibly off-world virus. I had to issue a flat order not to notify the Hunt Commission. The car settled for recording the evidence. Good enough; I could use that, too.

I was a passenger in a continent-spanning vehicle that operated at the speed of a brisk stroll, and read trail like a bloodhound. Despite my comment to Ball, I was uneasy about taking advantage of the technology; fair chase has ruled out use of a vehicle in the hunt for five hundred years.

Too, I was burning with impatience. I carried devastating news inside my fragile skull. News that powerful forces would suppress at all costs. Every minute I spent on this trail was one closer to being caught in a trap I would not escape with my story. Story, hell. Blockbuster.

Your first instinct, if you have ever worked news, is

to get the story out. Send the smoke signal, tap the drum, release the homing pigeon, stroke the telegraph key, key the mike—do something! The confirmed fact that Baka Martin had been a sybil symbiote would make every sports flimsy and newsread in civilized space. Organized sports interests at all levels would raise a howl that would rock governments.

The big story, though, was the second one: the Executive's abortive experiment with greer and sybil. It would unite preservationists and the blood-sports advocates in their age-old love-hate alliance against the spoilers. The political motive alleged by Ball for her shenanigans would have political machines from here to the Coalsack cluster humming at high speed. Every bigwig who ever had booked a greer hunt would have instant talk-show value.

Then there was my old alma mater, the Associated News, and the various network owners and the pompous journalism societies. They'd raise very public hell about the Service's bald attempt to write a Certified news hawk into a government coverup through out-and-out falsification of public records. Yours truly would be a cause célèbre once more . . .

The car beeped at me.

"What?"

"The quarry has turned. . . ."

"Lights!"

The floodlights lit up the empty canyon. Snowflakes glittered and spun in their beams. Nothing.

"You're sure?"

"The quarry is backtracking."

"Ball?" I said.

No answer. My 'corder's telltale blinked at me: no contact.

"Signal from Firstport," the car said. "Planetwide alert: all craft to respond immediately with call sign, registration, and location."

"Ignore it!"

"I have no choice but to ignore it; something has disabled my transmitter."

Ball, of course. If the authorities were beginning to search for him, he would be lying doggo to avoid detection. That's why no contact.

Out of the corner of my eye a shadow seemed to form in the periphery of the landing lights. When I jerked my gaze that way, it was gone. My eyelid twitched with reaction, and I realized what had happened: the were-greer out there had made its first pass at me. The quarry had turned, indeed.

"Where is it now?" I asked the car.

"The quarry has stopped."

I could almost *feel* the raw fury of the beast out there in the snow. Rage because it had not been able to shake me while it completed its transition. Hardening now into fatal resolve. But how did it expect to get at me in the car?

Maybe I was wrong. Maybe my shots had damaged the greer beyond the sybil's ability to salvage. What would the sybil do then? What else could it do but play dead and hope the triumphant hunter would walk right up to claim his prize. If Ball was right, the sybil out there was not about to go out meekly, slowly dying inside a frozen carcass that would feed no sufficiently mobile vermin until spring. Perhaps it couldn't last that long, on carrion. Perhaps it needed the electro-chemical reaction of a living nervous system to feed.

I had used the rifle before. Maybe that blasted alien virus, or whatever it was, had miscalculated. Maybe, still learning a whole alien nervous system, it had not yet mastered the reasoning centers of the host brain. If it still thought mostly as a greer, then I would be just another hunter, following up his shot. In which case the plan would be to sacrifice the greer to my rifle, and wait for me to begin the skinning and caping of the trophy.

A heavy shiver got loose along my spine.

"Distance to quarry, two hundred meters," the car said.

"Take us to eighty and stop."

"Acknowledged."

I thought maybe I should pity the poor dollop of goo, kidnapped who knew how long ago from the Blocked Worlds by the Terran Service microbiologists and imprisoned in some kind of metabolic girdle. It probably just wanted to get home with its amazing tale of far wandering, and bring the news that its kind could be coopted to the use of a somewhat larger, but equally ruthless, organism. . . .

"Count down by meters," I said.

"One three seven," the car said. "One three six . . ."

Martin had been a human sensitive with near-telepathic powers. If Ball was to be believed, his powers had been shaped and sharpened by the sybil. Ball had not said, or even hinted, how the sybil, unrestrained, might marshal the eerie extrasensory potential of the greer.

But now I thought I knew. No more simple and simply terrifying burst of fear to motivate its intended prey; instead, a much more subtle enticement to come, come on a little closer.

"One zero nine," the car said. "One zero eight, one zero . . ."

The rock outcrop loomed out of the snow in that moment.

I snatched the manual override full back and stabbed the accelerator. The car stalled. A moment of weightlessness, then the nose skid kicked a blinding sheet of snow over the windscreen. The jolt of impact with the canyon floor knocked me out of the pilot's berth into the footwell. The nose skid buckled on the second bounce. The starboard skid must have started to go then, because the car yawed hard over.

The starboard fan kicked back on and righted us. We slid to a halt.

"Nose skid inoperable," the car said. "Starboard skid severely damaged. Still able to fly. Override error by human pilot."

Every time I drew a breath, pinpoints of fire stabbed my chest. Cracked ribs.

I managed to get up out of the footwell. My head was throbbing where I had kissed the console on the way down. No safety harness in place; I had wanted to be able to bail out shooting at a moment's notice.

"Didn't you *see* that outcrop, for God's sake?"

"What outcrop?"

"That solid damn wall of stone, dammit! If I hadn't intervened—"

"The solid walls of stone are to port and starboard," the car said.

"The outcrop came right out into the center. It came right out in front of your nose!"

"There was no outcrop," the car said. "Quarry charging. Seventy-five and closing. Seventy. Sixty-five . . ."

The starboard door was slightly sprung. Just enough for something with the awesome strength of a greer, driven by the cunning of a sybil, to pry it loose and peel me out.

Out of the corner of my eye pulsing dots drifted across the thermal monitors. Closing *fast*.

I kicked open the door and fired a burst from the Colt-Vickers. The white gloom came apart with cold violet flame as I hosed a wide arc.

The greer came through the periphery of the arc, a gore-clotted, pelt-matted nightmare. It flinched as the beam burned it, but did not turn. Before I could adjust my aim, something smashed my left shoulder and hooked me irresistibly out of the car into smothering snow. My mouth clogged with shocking cold. I flipped over on my back and thumbed a blind burst. Snow, rocks, and steam exploded across the canyon. My left arm gave way and the flamer *brr-pped!* into the ground. An eruption of grit blinded me. I tried to squirm away through the thick snow, but a massive weight descended on my gun arm, pinning it beneath the weapon.

The greer was a huge crouching horror with fetid breath. I couldn't move. Its fierce jubilation welled over me, so powerful it was almost audible. Its eyes glittered in the glare from the car's lights. I knew I was eye-to-eye with the sybil. So this was where and how it ended . . .

Out in the darkness something began to chant a basso profundo dirge.

I thought of angels.

The greer woofed softly, as if in surprise. It shifted its weight, grinding the Colt-Vickers into my flesh, and looked away. Like a cat playing with a mouse, I thought.

The chant changed, hoarse and primitive and challenging. In the echo chamber of the canyon it could have been one voice, or twenty. The sound fell somewhere between the coughing of an African lion and the ghost chants of the *za-Dunni*. In some small ridiculous corner of my fading awareness, I hoped my 'corder was getting it all. It would make a fine dirge for a lost news hawk who had chosen to make news, rather than report it, once too often.

The chant rode a tidal wave of neural fury, directed not at me, but at the greer. I must be hallucinating, I thought. I had no illusions of extrasensory ability. But I was somehow eavesdropping on a telepathic assault by one alien upon another. Hallucinating, all right; ready to die. Next stop, white lights and benevolent figures in robes.

The greer crouched above me reared his head back and gave voice.

There was something in his cry like the snarl of a rabid dog, if a dog's throat resonated like a male chorale solo. The sound cascaded over me, dominating and then blending with that other singing.

I tried minutely to shift my gun arm. The song faltered. The beast's eyes lost their hooded look and burned down on me with an awful hunger. The greer wanted to meet the challenge; the sybil was fighting the distraction.

That other chant rose, deeper, more compelling. No human, as far as I knew, had ever known the greer to give tongue. Maybe this was part of what had lured Martin to his death—his knowledge of how much we didn't know about the greer. I had the half delirious thought it was almost worth dying just to hear this. . . .

My attacker's weight lifted, lightly as a songbird leaves a limb. He was gone in an eye-blink. The sybil had lost the contest for now.

The were-greer and its challenger came together out there in the gloom, just beyond the reach of the car's lights. The ground actually seemed to roll and shake beneath their combined fury. Once the battle was joined, they sang no more. There was one despairing, strangling shriek that nearly killed me with the finality of it.

After that I just lay there and tried to decide whether it was too much trouble to die, long after something else had died out there in the dark.

The victor of that titanic clash trudged toward me down the canyon. It shuffled and groaned in agony. I found strength to prop myself against the car with the flamer in my lap. The effort caused dark blobs to dance in my vision. When my hearing cleared, the thing was plodding upcanyon. Still grunting and mewling. The sound set my teeth on edge. It was very like the sound the were-greer made when it tried to shake Python's corpse.

It really didn't matter which beast had won. To the victor belonged the sybil. Or vice versa.

And the sybil remembered me.

The changing beast thrashed around out there on the edge of hearing for some time before all sound was lost. At length I was able to hear the slow, steady hissing of the snow again. The metamorphosis was complete. What I wasn't able to understand was why the sybil had not come back to finish me.

Once I thought I had a chance to get back inside the car without being clawed down from behind, I managed to crawl inside and activate its field medkit.

26

ORANGE CLAW AND DITENKA BORE WITNESS TO VOINA'S FINAL HUNT OF the long Two-Legs in the snow-choked canyon where they had trapped the dayfire ball.

As soon as the avalanche ceased, Sunto sent the other hunters down the falling ground to rejoin the season's migration to dayfire's winter home. They drove the slow-footed tree-eaters which had sprung the trap before them. Some of the tree-eaters would fall, hunted by the cold, and the hunters would have fresh hot meat to fuel their own journey down the mountains and away.

Unseen by hunter and hunted, their presence known only to Voina, Girta and Sunto stood the proper witness interval. Saw the Aland leader so trick the long Two-Legs he never raised his fireclaw before the living claw of Voina stole his life. They waited then for the Aland leader to rejoin them. Girta already was fashioning in his belly the first strong stanza of Voina's hunt to sing it down among the hahns, a fine addition to the trapping of the dayfire rock.

But Voina stayed in the canyon, locked to his prey.

The evil Sunto first had dreamed uncoiled from the ebbing life force of the Two-Legs.

And passed into the stomach of the Aland chieftain.

"What is this now?" Girta said uneasily.

"It is the evil that I dreamed." Sunto's hackles lifted,

his initial shock chased by hot quick fury. This, of all that passed, was most evil. Almost, he broke cover at once, charging down to strike the doomed Aland. But long seasons of hard living—and his fear of the evil—saved his life.

"Kill Voina?" Girta asked. "In his finest hour?"

"Voina no more," Sunto said grimly. "Canst thou not digest this?"

They crouched attentively. It was meat for the shallowest digestion that nothing beneath the Lake of Light ever had terrified Voina. Yet Voina's terror was plain now as the evil ate him from within.

"This, then, is truly evil," DiTenka crooned. "You are right, we must slay it at once. And Voina, too."

"No. This is my hunt. Mine alone. Thy hahn needs thee. My mate will need thy strong leadership when my cubs are born. You must leave the mountains. Now."

They sensed the approach of a Two-Legs blind, light as thistle. When the blind twinkled above, a bright shape against the snow and gloom, they were motionless shadows in deepest shadow. The Two-Legs stomach within the blind was refreshing to them as fresh hot blood to a parched throat. Above passed a simple Two-Legs of the breed who learned his place in the hunt without effort, a true hunter. And hot upon what-had-been Voina's spoor.

"Such a hunt unwitnessed?" DiTenka said when the blind was gone. "Not to be borne! Thou must have a witness to thy hunt."

"Then I will. A different witness for this strangest hunt of all. A witness who—should I fail—will not carry the evil down among the hahns."

"The Two-Legs?"

"None other than the slayer of Voina's blooded brother. He is a hunter!"

"Beyond this poor digestion, these new ways of thought!" DiTenka protested.

"Go now! This is Orange Claw destiny. Thine to carry the tale."

DiTenka covered his snout with both claws, surrendering. "Thy cubs will want no thing. Nor thy mate."

"Then leave me. Quickly."

And DiTenka was gone, a running shadow in the dark. Sunto turned his full attention to the piteously bleating Aland. Belly acrawl with horror, he shadowed the clumsy dead-and-living thing which was of Voina, and of the dead Two-Legs—yet neither—as it fled clumsily into the storm. At length Voina's stomach was silent. Sunto knew him dead at last, though his body breathed and moved beneath the burden of the carrion on its back. When Voina's stomach awoke once more to a semblance of awareness, it was a blind questing, as tree-eater foals touch their mothers with young trunks, unable yet to wield that appendage deftly.

The new thing that woke in Voina's belly was ruthless and unknown, but it reeked of the evil Sunto had dreamed these dayfires since. The thing that was not-Voina was a little bit afraid of its surroundings, unsure of how to drive the carcass that it rode. But Sunto could digest that its clumsiness was temporary. Soon it would stride these marches, as it had strode its home beyond the Lake of Light, undisputed master of all life. It was ready to assume dominion here as soon as it found its legs and belly. That was as plain as driven snow.

"This, then," Sunto breathed, "the evil that I dreamed. Revealed at last. The Way cannot abide this new thing along our marches. . . ."

His stomach churned with righteous anger—and this time, the thing that used Voina's belly noticed him from afar. So quickly did it learn to use its new possession . . . Voina's head rose, blindly sniffing the wind.

"Was right," Sunto grumbled. "No hahn witness to this hunt—or more hot flesh for the evil to devour. It must not flee these mountains. The nightmare of our ending was mine alone, and mine now alone to end this worse-than-nightmare come to pass."

To lecture himself thus, as if he meditated at the spirit pool, braced him. To attack the thing now, in what he knew instinctively was not its finished form, did not even occur to him. He cried this hunt as he had all others since cubhood, and would until the end: no advantage asked, none taken. The only thing worthy of regret was that Girta would not sing this hunting down among the hahns. For such a hunting lay before him as the hahns had never seen, nor ever would. There would be no returning from this hunt, either for hunter or for prey.

For the second time in that bitter canyon, Sunto witnessed a hunt, and knew it would fail, against what-had-been-Voina. When the Two-Legs carrion fell away, what-had-been-Voina fled from the big-shouting fireclaw of the second Two-Legs. Fled, where Voina would have turned and struck.

Why flee, with killing there to do?

Sunto shadowed the Two-Legs' continued stalk of what-had-been-Voina. Finally, he puzzled out the reason: the poisoned flea that roosted now in the Aland chief still was uneasy in Voina's belly. The severe wounds dealt out by the Two-Legs hot claw had frightened the flea. It fled to gain time. It would turn and come when it was ready to use its new claws. A hunter, after all.

When the blood trail played out in the snow, Sunto grunted in surprise. Thus had the long Two-Legs evaded the hunters after he was mauled at the Permanent Lairs. It seemed the poisoned flea was useful for something after all.

Not long thereafter, the quarry turned upon his Two-Legs pursuer. Sunto's belly digested the trap as clearly as the eye can see the dayfire at midsun. Here was subtle hunting! What-had-been-Voina clearly had become more-than-Voina.

Now was the proper time to hunt this poison flea!

The Two-Legs' blind lost its thistle-lightness and shook the ground when it fell. Sunto began to lope. A Two-Legs fireclaw slashed through the murk and then winked out. More-than-Voina's belly flared hot with the kill before it. . . .

And Sunto struck.

He drove the full weight of his power straight into the poisoned belly of the Aland.

The flea was stunned. Terrified. More-than-Voina reeled beneath the overriding power of Sunto's belly, last and strongest of the Orange Claw. More-than-Voina's stomach still was a ravaged battleground between what-had-been-Voina and the poisoned flea. What-had-been-Voina yearned to answer that silent challenge; the flea shrank in terror and tried to focus on its helpless prey.

But what-had-been-Voina still struggled to answer his challenge!

Sunto's triumphal song filled the canyon.

The Two-Legs in the hunting blind had pressed more-than-Voina too hard this storm-wracked night for the flea to conquer all the Aland's full-bellied pride.

Sunto's stomach locked with that of the ruined Aland. Nothing known could withstand the full fury of the Orange Claw belly. Not the long Two-Legs who had carried this poison flea down from beyond the Lake of Light. Not what-had-been-Voina. What-had-been-Voina gave voice in return. So full of rage and hate, it might have been a warrior of the ancient hahn wars who sang there in the blowing dark. Then, with a horrible, soundless shriek, what-had-been-Voina coalesced with the flea into more-than-Voina, and left its Two-Legs prey.

The ruined Aland chieftain rushed out of the gloom. For a dazed moment it seemed to Sunto that not only the Aland came against him, but the twice-dead tall Two-Legs as well.

Then a host of unimaginable phantoms, all fanged or clawed or huge or swift, seemed to ring him in a gibbering wall of death. Sunto digested at once they were the poisoned flea's trophies from beyond the Lake of Light, brought alive in more-than-Voina's belly, flung at Sunto to hunt out his fear and slow his strike. Here at last was the evil he had dreamed, flying at his throat.

"*And none to sing my hunting . . .*" was Sunto's last and sole regret as he rose, with flashing claws and teeth, to slay the fearful shadows.

27

I SLEPT FOR A LONG TIME. I DREAMED I WAS A BOY AGAIN ON OLD ACME, snug in my upstairs bunk while sleet drove out of the northern bays against the tile roof of my boyhood home. But the whine of the wind didn't sound exactly right. . . . I opened my eyes to weak gray daylight. The aircar was rocking gently in a gale force blow. The forward screens and lateral ports were rimed over with ice. Water puddled in the bay where snow forced itself through the sprung side hatch.

"Rough weather," the car said. "Strap down, please. Strap down."

I couldn't budge, because the car's crash webs had me securely horizontal. The ache of my busted ribs was only a nudge when I breathed; I must have used the medkit before I passed out. My left shoulder ached like hell, though.

"How long have I been asleep?"

"Eight and one-half local hours."

"Jesus!" I tried to jerk upright. "Leggo, dammit."

The webs released, and I sat up. The couch rearranged itself into a seat.

"Where are we?"

The car reeled off some coordinates.

"What are we doing?"

"Still tracking the new quarry you selected, sir."

"So you're finally awake," Ball's voice said out of my 'corder.

"Where the hell have *you* been?"

"Exactly where I was when last we spoke. And where I will probably remain for the foreseeable future."

"Which is classified. Still."

"Yes. We don't have much time. Now listen."

There was a burst of sound. Not static. Not speech, either. Not human speech, anyway, nor any nonhuman speech I'd ever heard. It was—reptilian— and scraped along my nerve ends like hot slime.

"What the hell was *that*?"

"A rudimentary precaution, which may or may not have worked. If it failed, you know perfectly well what that was, but have avoided betraying yourself. If it succeeded, and you don't know, then you still are one hundred percent Ramsey. Well, as close to one hundred percent as Ramsey ever was."

"I guess I'm simple; you'll have to say it plainer."

"I am prepared to gamble there is no microscopic alien riding your brainpan."

My flesh crawled all over my body. The sensation seemed to melt through my skull from scalp to gray matter, and my brain seemed to contort.

"My God, Ball!"

"Merely your partner in crime. Adulation embarrasses me."

"It was a close thing, though. That thing almost—"

"Your hunting yarn can wait"—crisply—"this can't. If you still are Keith Ramsey, and nothing else, you should know you must act quickly to avoid a news blackout on the Executive's shenanigans here. *Forthright* has planeted at Firstport. The political fences are being mended; the Service's sector administrator is en route, equipped with the same orders I had in regards to Pondoro and Freehold status. They

are attempting to monitor all channels and block anything going off planet. They are searching for me
thoroughly. So far, I have been able to evade their
best efforts, but it can't last, unless I shut down."

"What now? There's still a greer that's full of sybil
out there in the storm."

"You failed to catch it?"

"The one that killed Martin caught *me*. Almost got
me. But then another greer killed it—and inherited the
whirlwind."

"You witnessed the transference?"

"No. But you should have heard them, roaring at
each other in the storm."

"Vocalizing?"

"Yes."

"You recorded this?"

"Yes."

"Transmit the sounds to me. Right now. I still am
studying how they communicate . . ."

I keyed the 'corder and sent the squirt.

"Most interesting," Ball said. "You're following this
new sybil-host?"

"Yes."

"Acceptable. Now listen: the new cover story for
the Terran Service is that two agents—myself
included, now—have been done to death by the
greer. Either that, or assassinated by local government entities in an attempt to sabotage the Executive's
humanitarian mission to free the greer from human
meddling. The latter is a serious charge. All and
sundry in the local hierarchy are scrambling to prove
it false. If you go missing, it will be two dead agents
and a martyred truth seeker as well. A media storm,
scandalous publicity—and the Executive gets what
she wanted in the first place."

"Well, she and the greer seem to share a desire to see me disemboweled," I put in. "Common ground for two superb predators."

"My falling off the board," Ball said, "really has them in a frenzy. They know all the things I know. They finally are rethinking whether a cyborg's loyalty is automatically to the organization. There's a concern being expressed that I might have somehow been polluted by a crass human anger at the sacrifice of my partner."

"Pretty quick on the uptake, aren't they?"

"You have no idea. They will scour this world with everything they have to locate me. I can arrange for them to fail, but only if I shut up. That is why, regretfully, you will be entirely on your own from now on. *Remember:* burn every carcass you suspect of harboring the sybil; don't miss a single one, or the Executive wins. I suggest you get an Associated News outchannel secured before they invent some excuse to shut even the regional news squirts down. Good luck."

"Ball . . ."

He was gone.

The wind thumped the car, and the sleet slashed, but the cabin was warm and cozy. My brain, still fogged with sleep and pain, didn't want to get in gear.

"Storm lessening," said the car. "Lull due in seventeen minutes plus. Decision necessary: close in to afford a stalking opportunity, or open an interval to avoid alarming the quarry . . ."

"What quarry?" I said.

"The one which killed the other, at our last stop. Where you smashed the nose skid."

"Right."

The last minutes of last night began to rewind

behind my eyes. It had been tough, after mustering the strength to operate the medkit, to crawl back outside with the narcotics in me. But I found and flamed the carcass of the greer that had lost the contest in the dark. The car's sensors had confirmed my own observation before I flamed it: Baka Martin's killer had in its turn been killed. Its killer was now infected with the virus. The car was in a dither to report, but still could not; Ball, again.

I remembered that I had ordered the car into the storm behind the fast-fading spoor of the surviving greer. Why? To ensure eradication of the devil-seed? That didn't make sense now. Somewhat more rested and rational, it occurred to me my story would have more clout if a follow-up inquiry by local officialdom found widespread sybil infection among the greer to confirm the car's records.

I still didn't understand why the sybil hadn't forced its new host back to finish me off. It seemed certain that's what the sybil wanted: another human to ride home on. Was it possible the transfer hadn't taken? Or had the new host somehow been able to resist the coercion of its unwelcome guest? Unknowable.

Either way, I owed something to that creature out there in the storm.

And the story was unfinished. I could say Martin had gone to his death under Service-induced compulsion: unprovable. I could say the sybil actually had escaped stasis and transferred hosts once. Shakily provable, based on the car's records, because I had destroyed the prime evidence myself. Ball wanted revenge upon the Executive for destruction of his partner. But his vanishing act would throw doubt upon his accusations. If they couldn't paint him a martyr, they'd tar him as a deserter; anything he said would be suspect.

The first were-greer should have killed me, or infected me. But this other, unseen greer had stuck its paw in and changed things. Why? That was the last dangling thread. How had this final greer arrived just in time to pull my fat out of the fire? And why had it bothered? Coincidence? I had lost faith entirely in coincidence on this damned world. Especially when the second beast left me alone.

My 'corder paged the Associated News bureau in Firstport. I waited for a jammer to shut me down, but it didn't happen. They would be monitoring calls to all on-planet media, though, just to see who was saying what. The longer I waited to file something—anything, even speculation—the less chance I had of getting anything out at all. Including my battered person.

The A.N. robot copy editor read my ID off the 'corder's pulse, verified I was active and last reported in this sector, and patched me through directly to one of the senior correspondent's hangouts. When the 'corder's view screen lit, two faces swam into focus, extreme closeup. The woman's was half buried in a gaudy pillow, eyes closed, lips full and parted. She was murmuring something over and over that sounded like "Ah-ah-ahhh."

The man's face was youthful and intent, and as focused as a small boy trying to reach a bicuspid cavity with his tongue.

"Excuse me," I said.

The man's face opened in shocked surprise. His shoulders jerked spasmodically, as if his whole body had convulsed.

"Ah-h-h-h!" said the woman, opening her eyes wide.

A blurred, huge hand on a foreshortened arm reached across the screen and it went blank.

"Oh, don't do that!" the woman's voice snapped out of blank screen. "Don't be so old-fashioned!"

"One of you, I gather, is the A.N. correspondent here?" I said.

"Who wants to know?" The man's voice.

"I am," said the woman. "What's up?"

"Well, I *was*," the man said petulantly. She giggled softly.

"Is this terribly urgent?" she murmured, still caught up in life as usual, half a world away.

"I'm Keith Ramsey," I said.

"Oh!" And I heard the male grunt in a choked undertone. "Sorry," she whispered urgently. "Don't be mad, dear. This *is* important."

The screen lighted again. Her full face this time, down to the shoulders. Nice shoulders, nice straight neck, exceptionally molded collarbones arcing delicately out to the nice shoulders. I've always been a collarbone man.

"Would you like the full body shot now?" Her bright eyes beneath a tousled mop of hair were faintly amused.

"Sorry," I said. I focused on her eyes. "This really is important."

"Right. Recording." Her voice had gone clipped as a robot. "We've had rumors you were here for more than just big-game hunting, Mr. Ramsey. The story you filed on Baka Martin's single combat with a greer confirms that. We now hear rumors you may be involved in some classified Terran Service operation here on Pondoro. Comment?"

Perfect. I had a real news hen on the screen.

"Those last rumors are false, but they're part of one hell of a yarn," I said. "There's complications. So listen, because you'll get to hear this one time only."

"Ready."

I read off my 'corder's code, though her editor had it. I asked her to read it back. It wasn't what she expected, but she was very quick on the uptake.

"Got it. What now?"

"Notify the sector news desk. Tell them to reach Tanner, back at Central. He'll vouch. Got that? This is my byline, my story, the usual arrangements."

"Got it," she said impatiently. "Now, what's going on?"

"One more thing. Get a Certified scramble set up and call me back—we're probably being—"

And I was talking to dead air.

28

IT CAME AS AN ALMOST PHYSICAL SHOCK TO SUNTO WHEN HE FOUND THE spirit pool already coated with ice and thick snow.

All through the longest night of his long life he had struggled through the storm and the drifts to return to this, the focal point of his existence. The snow had been shoulder deep in some of the passes, but the vision he held firmly in his twisting, rebellious belly was of the pool in all its warm-weather tranquility, as it had been every council of his life.

His stomach twisted now, urgently, fearfully.

This is no refuge!

The thought hung uncalled. Whose thought? His own, or that of the poisoned flea that rode Voina to his doom and now was riding him?

Spiritual refuge the pool always had been. Yet now, through his altered perception, it was little more than a snow-covered depression in surrounding whiteness.

"No!"

He barked the word, and willed his balky body closer to the buried shrine. Here was the source of all wisdom and power among the hahns. Here the chosen watcher called the great ones of the hahns to council. . . .

In the hunting time, his traitor belly amended. *Always in the hunting time, and never in the time of heavy snow . . .*

A piercing pain ran behind his eyes so strongly he stumbled, and would have fallen. In his half-stunned condition he could feel his body's rebellious attempt to turn back down the mountains without his willing it. He tried to fashion an image of the hunter who came behind, in his bright blind, light as thistle, and was rocked by a savage, awful hunger to be off and sailing far above the snow, into the Lake of Light. . . .

Not his lust. *That* was the hunger of the thing that rode him, beating within his breast like a conflicting heartbeat to his own. The sickness he had dreamed was full upon him now.

"Here," he sang softly, "did this one call the council, and begin the hunt which now comes full circle back upon its own beginnings."

He edged toward the depression in the snow. The pressure built steadily behind his eyes as it had built and ebbed all the long night since Voina fell, bested, and all those shadowed fangs and claws, wrought by the poison flea, fled back to nothingness.

"Just so do we hunt our own meat, and Two-Legs," he told his tormentor grimly. "Just so did we lock bellies against each other in the olden times of hahn war, before the Two-Legs came to share our hunt with us. Think thou now to drive last-living of the Orange Claw, and strongest, with his own hunter's tricks?"

The thing within subsided, waiting. A hunter's patience, the old hunter knew, gathering strength to overmaster his stubborn stomach.

"Feeding on me even as I live . . ."

He was close now to the spirit pool. Where Voina's claws had raked, his fur was matted with caked blood. He could feel the cold burn against the heat of his wounds. He welcomed the familiar reality against the unreality behind his eyes.

He could not digest why the flea rode behind his eyes, unless the better to see the way. He would have thought the flea would burrow into his belly, seat of all knowledge and power. Yet it seemed capable of clouding his thoughts as readily as his vision, confusing him more and more as to which thought was his and which the product of its subtle bite.

He crouched at last at the pool and pawed away the snow. Locked in the dark clean ice of early winter, his spirit brother stared up as if surprised to see him now.

Spirit brother? Why dost thou drag me through these bitter mountains to stare at thy reflection in the ice?

With a convulsive effort of his stomach, he choked the question off. Blasphemy! While his spirit brother stared up at him!

Thy own reflection, only. The thought crept back, unwanted. *How can this place offer all thou promised?*

"Here dwells peace, and the closing of the circle," he muttered.

The flea was biting him fiercely now, turning his innermost beliefs to claw at one another. Sunto had seen hunters taken by the lowland fever in the dayfire's winter home. They would twist and tumble and claw out their own stomachs in a fatal frenzy. Just so his thoughts turned and tore at one another, though he held his frame motionless. Through it all, his spirit brother regarded him without expression.

The unflinching regard of his spirit brother was immensely reassuring. Some things endured. Panic had ridden him like an extra flea, threatening to engulf him in blind madness if he could not force his way here. Now he was where he had chosen to be, and even this vicious internal flea had not stopped him . . .

A focus for awareness, the thought came.

Explaining himself to himself. He had never questioned the meaning of the pool; there was nothing to question. Its meaning was plain for the simplest digestion.

An aid to the power of concentration, when utmost effort is required . . .

The pressure behind his eyes altered abruptly. Flowed downward through his frame like liquid dayfire. The ache of his wounds left him in a breath-catching rush. The ache of bones grown old in mountain winters dissolved in the melting heat, and the old hunter felt a lightness take him.

Young! he marveled. *I feel . . . young. And rested, though I have hunted a full bitter trail . . .*

His spirit brother read his change of mood and grinned up at him like a cub, though the teeth it showed were unquestionably as old as his.

A flea whose bite brings youth and strength to trade for this confusion . . . Strange then that Voina— and I—fought so hard against its bite. Voina perhaps because he still had youth enough of his own, and fierce single pride. Well, this one has pride enough. . . .

A fresh gust of wind sent snow running thickly across the frozen meadow. Fortified by that strange inner dayfire, Sunto welcomed the freshening of the storm as a summer breeze. Bitterly had Voina fought the flea when it abandoned the dying Two-Legs for his own hot blood. Twice bitterly, and half crazed at ending, fighting within and without, divided, in his battle against Sunto, and so slain despite the evil shadows that rose to aid his attack . . .

Those shadows. Other beings, long dead, which offered cozy nesting to the flea in their time and in their place before the long Two-Legs carried it here, across the Lake of Light . . .

His new vision awed him. His own? Or another from that thing that burrowed behind his eyes? The flea's, surely.

His blood surged strongly with excitement. Lands beyond the Lake of Light, lands without number, and creatures, many creatures, far more than just the Two-Legs. How many times had the history singers attempted to fashion songs to describe the far-off marches from which Two-Legs came to share the hunt? Here was a chance to learn, to know. . . .

Call the hahns!

In his excitement he almost sent the call. He was gathering his stomach for that mighty effort when the barren landscape came sharply back to focus. He had been far from the spirit pool just then, far out upon the Lake of Light, seeing wonders!

Call the hahns, and they will see it, too!

Sunto went rigid with shame. He first of all had dreamed this evil, he first of all had cried this hunt, and now here, in the final sanctuary, the evil hunted all the hahns through him.

The pressure behind his eyes was unyielding now. The flea was gaining strength. Sunto squinted stoically down upon his spirit brother, who returned the look unwinkingly.

So many things to learn, to know! No time to spend, herding the beasts back and forth before the elements, like mere beasts of prey. Thou art so much more. . . .

His thought, his pride in his Orange Claw heritage, but polluted for all time by that hateful flea,

whose bite clearly was far worse than lowland
fever.

"What of the hunt, and the Way?" Sunto asked the
wind. "Times are good since Two-Legs came. But
Two-Legs feared the Permanent Lairs. Even more will
Two-Legs fear hahns ridden by this flea . . ."

*This is thy final gift from Two-Legs, carried here by
one of them, with a belly strong as thine. The Way
must end before the things you dream on now can
come to pass. . . .*

"The hunt is the Way!" Sunto bared his teeth to the
storm. "So comes the hunt I dreamed full-circle. Fitting
it is that this one, who dreamed it first, should make
the final kill."

The flea behind his eyes read his purpose too late,
and struck too late, with a power that sent him reeling
in awful pain. But he was well out on the ice now,
pawing the snow away frantically, searching again
for his spirit brother in the center of the pool as the
pain squeezed his skull.

He found his spirit brother again, there below him
in the black ice, laughing up at his cry of pain. First
his spirit brother drew deeper, as Sunto rose to his full
height, then rushed up, paws outspread, to meet the
old hunter as he sprang heavily, with full force, into
the center of the thinnest ice.

29

"THE QUARRY IS DORMANT," THE CAR SAID.

"Dormant?" I said. "Dead?"

Snowdrift was running horizontally across the open ground, higher than my vantage in the pilot's chair. Occasional rents gave me fragmented glimpses of the frozen pond. The old greer had gone right through the ice near its center. Fracture lines from the jagged break ran off under the snow. His thrashing path to the pond had been rapidly smoothed over by the storm. The dark hole in the ice already had skimmed over.

"Dead?" I said again.

"Uncertain . . . There is no pulse, no respiration. Core body temperature is dropping to that of the water. But there still is trace brain activity. The virus . . ."

"Is still there?"

The beast had known what it was doing. I was as sure of that as I would ever be of anything. The violent abruptness of that final plunge would replay itself as long as I had memory.

". . . Is still there," the car confirmed. "Becoming dormant. For the record, I urgently request permission to contact the Hunt Commission!"

"Are there aquatic life-forms in the pool?"

"Unknown. I am programmed only for huntable species."

I heaved a deep breath. "So the virus is trapped under the ice."

"Unknown. It is there; it is dormant. For the record—"

My 'corder chimed. The scramble telltale was flashing. The A.N. news hen's features formed on the screen.

"Good work," I said.

"Tell me about it. The Terran Service is in my face. But they backed down when Tanner weighed in. Ready to report? You look pretty beat-up. Where *are* you?"

"The greer continent. Can you organize an ambulance?"

"Coordinates?"

"Tell her," I said to the car's autopilot.

"I cannot transmit—"

"Just read them out. My 'corder is transmitting."

"Got 'em," she said. "Wait one."

She was back in less than one. "On the way. But so is the law. The satellites have your vehicle triangulated. Your car is not acknowledging. The second I notified Central Receiving, those coordinates confirmed your location for the local authorities. They couldn't lock on your 'corder, of course."

"Of course not."

Media philosophy for two centuries has been that the public's right to know would suffer if reporter's equipment could be pinpointed: too easy to guide something nasty, like explosives, down the signal. Such assassinations had been done as early as the late twentieth century. So A.N. and some of the large media combines cribbed stealth communications technology from the Terran Service. The geeks on Ptolemy put it together in a reporter-friendly package, to the everlasting outrage of officialdom everywhere. Standard issue for holders of media-rep cartes these days.

"I am being challenged by TS Cruiser *Forthright*," the car said. "They order me to acknowledge, on pain of immediate destruction. I cannot acknowledge."

I wasn't out of the woods yet. Not by a long shot.

"Heard that," the news hen said. "My bureau already has transmitted a cease and desist to *Forthright* as we speak. If their weapons lock on your location, acquisition feedback will pick up your rep carte immunity signature. They can't claim they didn't see it. You still have it, I hope?"

"I'm out of here."

I grabbed my 'corder and bailed into waist-deep snow. The wind was brutal. I clawed my way toward the tree line. My shoulder was screaming. My lungs burned with the raw air. Halfway to the trees, the crust was frozen hard enough to hold me. I scrambled up onto the surface. My *fragle* stalkers bit, giving me purchase. Then I was between the first thick trunks, out of the wind. I was panting heavily. I sat on an exposed root and snugged my parka hood around my head. The 'corder was on my lap. My legs were shaking so bad I almost spilled it in the snow.

"You're in pain," she said.

"Damn straight. Did they launch?"

"Checking. Checking . . . no. They stood down. Good thing. I don't think those trees would protect you if they did." She looked offscreen. "Ambulance ETA twenty minutes. Can you hold?"

"How about the law?"

"Checking. For heaven's sake, catch your breath!"

"I'm trying! Get a damn ETA on the law!"

"Thirty minutes. Maybe more. It's complicated. Pondoro's arguing with *Forthright.* The Service is insisting on having observers on their first vehicles. . . ."

"Yeah. *Forthright* knows the sybil is loose down here."

"The *sybil?*" I had finally managed to startle her. "Did you say—"

"Under direct orders from the Commonwealth of Terra," I interrupted, "a Terran Service operative, Baka Martin, who was deliberately infected with the sybil parasite from the Blocked Worlds, sacrificed his life last night in order to transfer the parasite to Pondoro's dominant predatory life-form, known as the Pondoro wolverine, or greer. . . . Are you getting this?"

"Go!" she said. "Keep going! Sweet spirit of sanity, no *wonder* you've got them in such an uproar. I'm surprised now they *didn't* launch . . . "

I kept going. I didn't have it well-organized, but the paragraphs just kept coming, in no particular order.

"Sorry I haven't had time to get this organized," I said.

"Keep going! I can fill in the blanks as it goes out."

"Dates of Freehold status, background on the greer," I said. "You know the drill. Sidebar on that professor who wanted to study the ruins. You should get a co-byline. You deserve it!"

"Don't worry about that now! Report!"

I reported. She was going to make one hell of an editor one of these days. I wondered if Tanner knew about her. I'd have to remember to tell him.

The gist of the story already was on the data squirt, essentially unedited, by the time the Central Receiving ambulance touched down beside LaChoy's hunting car. Two robot stretcher bearers stepped through the ambulance's drop door and marched unerringly right toward me.

"Here come the medics," I said. "That's thirty for now."

"Why do we always say thirty?" she asked.

"Hell—I don't know. We just always have."

"Remind me to tell you sometime." And she was gone.

The lead robot—humanoid, of course, this being Pondoro—gave me a slow, searching glance. The diagnostics must operate through his humanoid eyes, I thought.

He put a hand on my neck. I felt the sting of an injection.

"Don't!" I said. "I can make it on my own. I want to look at that pool first."

Fat chance. They lifted me neatly onto the stretcher. Darkness already was gathering in my peripheral vision. "We have our instructions, Mr. Ramsey."

And that was that.

30

A HUNT COMMISSION PATROL CAR LIFTED SILENTLY FROM THE BEATEN-down snow beside the pool, and was swallowed in the night. They'd been at it all day and into the evening. The large Wildlife Research carryall still was in place. Its profile had begun to blur into the meadow after hours of snowfall. Its work lights seemed to float, disembodied, in a rushing sea of white. In their harsh glare, the skimmed-over pool had a stagy quality.

I was in the cabin of the Central Receiving ambulance. Within the cabin, I was sealed inside the field of a quarantine stass sphere. The lead medic informed me I was in quarantine for the full four weeks: the ancient meaning of the word. The decision was Pondoro's, because of feared exposure to the sybil. I found out later the Commonwealth had tried for full isolation, to include no communication with the outside world. But Pondoro officials balked at that, not wanting to alienate Associated News.

There was no way I could contest the quarantine. Pondoro was terrified into a stupor by the fact I had been in such close proximity to the sybil unleashed. Since that proximity was the keystone of my story, I had no room to argue. But I could insist the ambulance stay put in the mountain meadow. There was nothing wrong with me the medics couldn't handle—and even if there had been, there was a full Medfac forward. So I watched the activity around the pool through the eye-hurting shimmer of the stass-sphere. The field seemed to take up most of the ambulance cabin. I could use the bunk and the head and the food supply without risk of touching the field's inner circumference, but could not leave the cabin.

I keyed my 'corder to finish my fourth story since the health robots had permitted my awakening. The A.N. correspondent had bullied them into bringing me around. Another point for her.

". . . So the old greer, evidently maddened by the pain of first-stage sybil symbiosis, smashed its way beneath the ice of the mountain pool, lost to view as the blizzard threw a freezing curtain across the scene . . ." I paused, waiting for the lag to bring back the sector rewrite man's response from ninety light-years away.

"Coming a little purple toward the end of the piece here, aren't we? For hard news, I mean?" He sounded bored senseless.

"Clean it up if you want to," I said. "I've been talking too long. I'm too close to the story."

I was propped up on a bunk, bundled and doped against developing pneumonia and sundry bone breaks and ligament tears. I had talked the medics out of beginning reconstruction until I could get my work done. I was glad someone official was looking after my health just now. But the trampled snow around the lonesome little pool seemed a high price to pay for it. It somehow seemed we were mucking up some very special real estate. This place belonged by right to that scarred old suicidal greer, and nobody else.

"So the old greer saved your ass and then drowned himself?" said the rewrite man. There was a buzz of static in his words.

"I'm getting a little interference," I said. "It's not this damn sphere. I've got that interference squelched. I can't believe the Terran Service would fool with a Certified scramble this late in the game. They're already in enough trouble. But check it out, will you?"

I couldn't seem to take my eyes off the pool. The delay would be longer this time. He wouldn't waste high-priced transmission time saying he'd check; he'd just do it.

The fractured ice bulged upward with shocking suddenness. Even under sedation, my nerves twitched. Residue of the greer-fear. Bulky, spacesuited figures levitated out of the shattered ice. They streamed water that froze on them as they slanted over to solid ground. They stood with their heads together, suit lights flickering this way and that as they looked at something. Steam puffed off them as de-icers kicked in. They trudged toward an inflated pod beside the snow-covered boat: decontamination chamber.

"Some kind of spacejunk twenty-nine lights from you," the rewrite man said out of my 'corder. "By the way, the legal beagles say the Terran Service is cooking all circuits trying to get some kind of Federal court injunction against your stories. Our beagles rate the odds slim to none. This is freedom of the media here. Public's right to know. Wait one before you go, okay. Tanner's got a question."

Tanner's jaded voice came through right on the rewrite man's last word.

"Ignorant animals don't save a dumb-shit news hawk and then commit suicide to save the species, you jackoff. The Executive claims these greers or whatever they're called are intelligent. Asserts they were nuked centuries ago by the Freeholders, and were smart enough to pretend to be dumb to avoid another roasting. Says it's her sacred obligation to intervene where indigenous intelligence is threatened by commercialism. So on and so forth. Now you're describing self-sacrifice—suicide, no less—by a hoary old boar, or bull, or whatever. Don't panic—we're not going to cut it—but you may be giving her ammunition."

"I'm just reporting what I saw. You want me to go ahead or not?"

The spacesuits trudged out of the decon and up a ramp into the ship. Another, slighter figure detached itself and began to struggle toward me through the drifts. It was the local Associated News correspondent, who had come into the pool on the Hunt Commission patrol boat. Pondoro authorities were busy trying to ingratiate themselves with the interstellar media.

"Tanner says you're an idiot, but go ahead," came the rewrite man's rejoinder.

"New and final paragraph," I said.

She was tucking her 'corder into a gaudy Algonquin parka when she came through the drop door. I felt a fleeting moment of professional jealousy that she had been there to talk to the officials, mingled with irritation Ball hadn't been over there as my doppleganger. It was irritating to realize how much I missed Ball and had come to rely on him. I shrugged it off. Ball never really had been mine. And she deserved whatever stories she could dig out of this. She had got me in from the cold and kept the Commonwealth Executive off my neck. Not to mention *Forthright*'s firepower.

"So died the final unwilling host of the Blocked World parasite on Pondoro," I said, "in ice, as the first two hosts—willing human and unwilling greer—

ended in fire. And so ended the little-known parasite's brief but fierce bid to escape Pondoro into civilized space. That's thirty."

"Pretty flowery," the A.N. woman observed. Her voice sounded tinny through the sphere's field.

"You sound just like my rewrite man," I said. "Be careful—don't touch the sphere! You'd be electrocuted. Should you even be in here? I'm in goddamned quarantine!"

"Not to worry. I think you're cute anyway."

In winter garb there was rather less to notice about her than in my first viewscreen glimpse. The well-defined clavicles, for instance, were buried in a bulky sweater under the parka. The fact I even thought about what was under her parka probably meant I was going to survive.

"Why do we say thirty?" I asked.

"Remind me to tell you later." She shook snow-melt out of her mop of dark hair and took off the parka. "Well, the greer was in there, all right. Dead as a stone. A very cold stone. And it was a full-blown sybil colony, too. The biologist was excited as hell. Never thought he'd get to see the real thing."

"Tell me he didn't save any of it to play with."

"Not a chance. The observers from *Forthright* really were in charge. The sybil hadn't had time enough to adapt to its new situation, they said, but it wasn't worth taking a chance. They vaporized the carcass and sanitized the pool. Completely. There's not even a microorganism left alive. The Service guys made sure they were thorough. You want to send an add to your story?"

"No thanks. It's all yours. Plus all those local political ramifications you were telling me about earlier.

This is your beat, not mine. They definitely got all the sybil?"

"That bug scared you, did it?"

"You have no idea. Why aren't they in quarantine? Since you were over there, why aren't you?"

"They tried to explain it to me. Without any host or prospects, without even the carrion for a nest, it apparently is just so much test-tube goop as long as it's handled with care."

"I hope they're right. I hope you're you."

She gave me a strange look. "I've been kind of thinking the same thing about you."

"Well, Central Receiving says I'm clean. That's the medical opinion. This goddamned sphere is just Pondoro's peace offering to the Commonwealth Executive. Best revenge she could drum up on short notice. They didn't find any were-larvae in the water?"

"Some sort of minnow that might have been changing. They weren't sure it was complex enough for the sybil to take."

I had a quick image of a fish-eating predator, furred or winged, hunting the pond this springtime, and then traveling. A winged predator would have been preferred. Soaring far off its usual haunts, turning aside only when it had to feed. It would have been searching for human campfires, or a spaceport, without knowing why it searched. . . .

"If you're thinking what I think, forget it," she said. "They sterilized the pool absolutely. I thought the old Hunt Commission guy who ordered it was going to bawl. Said they probably had killed off the last razortail something-or-other, not to mention a couple of dozen unique—what was the word? Midgets?"

"Midges," I said.

"Midges. I've got it recorded. Pond life of some

kind. I'll look it up, maybe do a feature for one of the naturalist syndicates. The *Forthright* people said there was no alternative. Acted like they were talking about the Black Plague and the AIDS virus all at the same time."

The Black Plague I knew, but not the other one. In aid of what? An epidemic? Odd word choice. I let the question ride. Maybe she would enlighten me when she told me why we said thirty to end a story.

I thought about the biologist she had mentioned. Rendering any species extinct—even a minnow or a midge—is not what wildlife managers build their dreams on. To be required to do it because of political meddling by interstellar bureaucrats, no matter how high and mighty, would not set well. Perhaps he would be worth a sidebar.

"He was a natural for a really slap-do second 'cast lead," she said brightly. "You could probably do it better, but what the heck, I was there, and he felt like bitching. 'Joe Good Guy, game protector, sighed as he wiped out the tintail guppy'—whatever, I've got it recorded—'because, far away across the stars, the Commonwealth Executive allegedly had decreed an ill-advised biological experiment which loosed a Blocked World plague virus on Pondoro. . . .'"

"I wish you wouldn't read my mind," I said. "There's too much of that going around on Pondoro. . . ." And then bit my tongue.

For once she was too full of herself to notice the slip.

"You can't have all the glory, even if you are Bwana One-Shot, Pukka Ramsey, Starship Sahib."

"You've been talking to LaChoy, I see."

"He's as publicity hungry as the next business-man." She almost chortled. "All this publicity may stimulate hunt bookings, or ruin them, depending on which way it goes. He's betting on the former. Pretty sanctimonious about the Commonwealth Executive butting in on his tidy little slaughterhouse operation— oops!"

"Never mind," I said tiredly. "We will have been in space another umpteen thousand years, and fill it with our progeny, God forbid, before we will begin to be civilized as long as we already have been hunters, but you certainly are entitled to your opinion, ma'am. It's a shame about the clavicles, though. It's been a long time since I saw the collarbones of an ass."

She started to mottle up around the cheekbones.

"Before we fight," I said, "thank you. Thank you for being an absolute top-flight professional. I know they put you under a lot of pressure. Not only did I get my story out, you got this meat wagon here for what's left of me. I was absolutely at the end of my string."

She relaxed and grinned. A very nice grin.

"Just because we're on the outskirts out here doesn't mean we don't know the moves. So you owe me, right?"

I sighed. Too hard. My ribs bit at me through the narcotics. "I retract the collarbones of an ass. Working with Ball made me snappish. I owe you."

"Excellent!" She went forward and out of sight. She was back in under a minute. "Just hold still, okay?"

There was an almost-unheard whisper of sound. The blue flicker went away and reformed behind her. She was inside the sphere.

"What the hell . . . ?"

She laughed. "Well, you said you owe me. This is

how you pay up. I've already secured an option on a great feature story: quarantined alone with the great sahib Keith Ramsey. . . ."

Pondoro officialdom, it seemed, had no shame when it came to cultivating the media.

31

THE CANYON WAS LOCKED IN HARD WINTER. THE ONLY INDIGENOUS LIFE
left in the mountains had long since hibernated. To
outward appearance, all the world was ice and deep-
piled snow, and savage winds. For days on end the
sun never penetrated the cloud layer.

Ball was getting bored.

For the first few hours, he had meditated. Delved
into his library of stored disciplines and sampled
them all. The Greeks were interesting: sophistry, the
art of speaking well. Zen spoke to him, a little: self-
awareness; the sound of one hand clapping. He
liked that, especially. Spent some time considering
the sound of no hands clapping. Moved on.

The outward aspect of the world above his primitive tomb was one of utter desolation, where nothing
lived or stirred.

A false aspect.

The greer were keeping watch, in little squads of
four. They ghosted up the snow crust to his tomb and
settled down to wait. Tough creatures, to stand sentry
in so harsh a place. But Ball already knew that about
the greer. They didn't trust their prison to hold him; he
would have known that without the use of an empathometer. They were under discipline as severe as the
ones who had attacked LaChoy's camp. Twice now
one of his watchers had been a survivor of that battle,
each equipped with a Terran Service transmission

chip during that skirmish. They stood their watches at roughly six-hour intervals. He knew a momentary regret that he would never see that primal discipline melded to sybil in service of the Commonwealth. And then suppressed it. They deserved their hard-won independence.

The sentinels conversed. His sensory equipment was acute enough to separate out each sound from the howling wind. It would have taken a leap of imagination to call it conversation if he had not done duty on worlds far more alien than this. His empathometer gave him emotional feedback from his study subjects to compare against the speech patterns. Ball set a code-breaking program running to meld the patterns to the emotional thrust behind the phrases. Perhaps he could pass the time decoding their language. Thus far, insufficient data. He needed more transmission chips in place, but couldn't launch them from beneath the rocks. Quickly bored again, he left the program running and turned his attention elsewhere.

Immaterial probes fingered the canyon and his tomb, beamed down from the world's artificial satellites from the time they rose above the horizon until they passed around the planetary shoulder.

The Service was determined to find him.

Pondoro had altered the course of one of the weather satellites to ensure repeated passes above this quadrant. Reprogrammed its sensory array from meteorologic study to scanning for his unique life-signs. Terran Service finagling.

He had to be careful to play with extremes of temperature only when the satellites were below horizon. As soon as they were down, the steam would begin to rise. The waiting greer would come out of their crouches, hackles lifting. The steam precipitated into

ice crystals. Fell back through steam to melt again.
Just before the return of an orbital snoop, he would
reverse the process dramatically. The rocks in his
primitive cairn would become super-chilled. The greer
would prowl and curse. With their uncanny predator's perception, they seemed to know he was working his way free.

The orbital snoopers, of course, ignored the greer.
No imagination. And of course they weren't programmed to seek one spot of extreme cold in a frozen
world. Beneath his frigid camouflage he raised subtle
shields that reflected inanimate rock echoes. He had
been equipped, after all, to hide in plain sight. This
kind of hiding was even easier.

He only generated atypical sound waves when the
satellites were below horizon.

When the temperature of the nearest rock was precisely correct, Ball would apply sonics. Ear-hurting
tones thrummed through the canyon, funneled and
focused. The resulting whipcrack of fissured stone
would be loud in the canyon, echoing. The waiting
greer would bristle or cower, depending upon the
intensity. But they would not flee. More and more
impressive. Sometimes they gave voice, clearly a
challenge of some sort. The hoarse baying resembled
those Ramsey had transmitted after the two greer
fought above his weakened carcass up this very
canyon. After several such sessions, the greer sentinels settled back to watchfulness and ignored all
subsequent sounds from the pile. Quick learners.

He found it difficult to calculate just when a stone
would surrender its form into dust. As far as orbital
snoops, even if they monitored such sound waves, they
would factor them out; in such extremes of temperature
and climate, such things were random and natural.

In five days he moved half a meter toward freedom; 45.5 left to go. But he had time. The Service had no idea where to search. They knew only he had gone to ground somewhere on the continent of the greer. They probably suspected he was long gone by now, to some civilized place, where he could hide more easily. They certainly would monitor all freight off-world, in case he tried to ship himself elsewhere. His authorization codes had been suspended, of course. But they would know that posed no difficulty to one of his gifts.

He opened a games program and dealt out his favorite, five-card stud. The program was sophisticated, and allowed for bluffing. He diverted himself for three hours, amassed an ersatz fortune. His best winning hand was aces and eights. The ancient dead man's hand. He would have smiled at the irony if he had a face, or smiling muscles. The game was elegant in its simplicity. The Zen of poker. Perhaps if he escaped retribution he would consider professional gambling as a career. There were sectors where gambling was virtually a religion. A gambling cyborg would go over quite well. . . .

He was bored again.

He checked the language-breaking software. No real progress. He was aggravated. It would be instructive to learn more about the thought processes of these primitive beasts who had bested him. Unproductive: let it go. Pain is inevitable; suffering is not. So assured his philosophical treatises from Zen. He would break the language—in time. And he had time.

He turned his attention to a question he usually avoided: the question of self-awareness. Ball the cyborg, sentient and knowing since his natal day.

Equipped to last far longer than his creators. A highly organized brain, linked and bonded to the best artificial intelligence between the stars. Fed on a precise metering of glucose needed to keep his organic brain completely healthy and operational. Support systems and propulsion powered by a tiny fusion drive that could operate essentially forever. For as long as mattered. Equipped to dig sustenance out of almost any organic compound and separate out needed replenishment if his recycling system failed. And to extrude replacement elements for parts that did fail.

Finally, armed with vast libraries of data and innumerable games to play.

In theory, he could go into orbit somewhere and stay there indefinitely, fully functional, with diversions aplenty to prevent entropy from seizing his brain.

It was a theory he had no particular desire to test.

Boredom. The inner enemy.

A human trait his creators had neglected to erase from his human brain before they sealed it in.

For the first time, he wondered why.

And he wondered what other human traits might surface to annoy him if he stayed out of circulation long enough.

Grief? No question.

His grief seemed to grow out of the emotions his builders had left in to keep him loyal to the Service. To temper his deeply cherished belief he was *homo in excelcis*—superior man. Well, they had wrought too well. His loyalty to his fallen partner had metastasized to a heavy grief. When he permitted himself consideration of how Baka Martin had died, it brought a bite of something that he thought must resemble physical pain. It hurt. His poor, idealistic, martyred partner: nothing but a flesh-and-blood pawn in stellar politics.

He also knew anger, burning anger.

His grief had fired a vengeful side of his nature that he had not, with all his knowledge of himself, suspected he possessed.

Through Ramsey, his anger had struck back at those who caused his grief. He entertained a fierce hope the writer had carried through, was following his news hawk's code by pressing the story to the limits. Done properly, the revelations he handed Ramsey should cause maximum humiliation and distress to that remote Executive to whom Ball had sworn allegiance long ago.

His memory flickered there, and then was strong again. Some faint pulse of—emotion? When had he sworn that fealty? He had no memory of the oath-taking itself. Just the conviction that he had sworn it. He wondered briefly at the conundrum. Had they laundered his memory, too, as they routinely altered those of lesser beings like Martin? And what was the source of that elusive tremor of some unnamed feeling? It did not seem to belong to him—he could not see how it could belong to him—but he had felt it, however briefly. It had come when he assessed the harm he had attempted against that remote feminine personage who directed the Commonwealth. Like a final echo from some previous, different life . . .

A *previous* life?

For the first time in his excellent memory, he considered a new question: what was the origin of the donor brain that knew itself as Ball? He always had assumed—*assumed!*—his brain was taken from an artificial birthing. Late in the final trimester, perhaps. And the flesh remainder of the clone relegated to the organ-replacement banks.

But would they have taken a full-grown, life-experienced, human brain for their experiment? And discarded the body of that man as casually as they had programmed Martin to suicide?

Of course they would, if that was viewed as best engineering.

This thought diverted him for another several hours. He tried to imagine—remember?—what it would be to have hands, feet, and a fragile flesh exterior, instead of his durable sphere, to house and protect his personality. He actually made an effort to . . . *remember* . . . the taste of a lemon, heat of a sun, sensual tremor of a libido.

He couldn't.

Ramsey had amused him once by assuming he resented bipedal pleasures because he could not understand them. Drinking, copulating, the spectrum. Ball had enjoyed the whimsy, because he probably had more detailed understanding of human emotion and the appetites that drove it than any biped alive. How else could he drive an empathometer designed to discern and nourish something as abstract as a writer's creative urge? And he had used his human knowledge in other assignments before Ramsey. Just as abstract, just as complex. But his understanding always had been that of the untouched observer; never—impossible to be—that of an involved participant.

He summed up. Boredom: he had that, and knew its goad. Grief, and knew its sting. Personal anger, inflamed by grief, and understood now its hot flush could drive his mind into new turnings, and a reversal of loyalties.

Loneliness?

Where had *that* thought come from? But the truth was there: he missed the stimulating company of thinking, feeling creatures, the ebb and flow of conversation and wit, love and hate and fear. He always had shone brightest where sentient life—human and other—teemed most thickly. He checked the language-breaking program again. Still nothing. He could not communicate—yet—with the watchers.

Loneliness, then. Clearly a human emotion. Ball began to make the sound Ramsey called his true laughter. The unexamined life is not worth living: Socrates. This self-inquiry had been good for him. Already, in this enforced meditative retreat, he had learned strange new things about himself.

And from that knowledge, devised a plan to escape his prison that was far more elegant than playing with rocks.

32

PHYSICALLY, I WAS A NEW MAN.

Central Receiving had mended all my breaks and tears, and cleared my respiratory system. They had given me a clean bill of health regarding any possibility of an alien viral infection. They had toned and refreshed my adrenal and other glandular systems which had been so ill-used by the greer-fear.

The downside was that they'd found a complex transmission chip adhered cozily to my brain stem. Terran Service manufacture. They couldn't tinker with it without destroying it. But they could monitor its transmission signal to determine what kind of receiver it was keyed to: an empathometer. Which explained how Ball had always known my state of mind so well.

I wondered if he still was capable of reading me from wherever he was hiding out. Cyborg as voyeur didn't appeal to me. But I had declined the hospital's offer to expunge the chip. I could not begin to articulate my reasons. Maybe I wasn't ready to accept that I was done with Ball.

My quarantine quarters were carved into an isolated mountainside well away from Firstport. The sitting room offered floor-to-ceiling windows and a long view of snow-choked mountains dropping toward the distant sea. We could sit there and watch the storms roll in, one behind another, and marvel at the light show when the sun made its intermittent appearances between weather fronts.

Her byline was Anne Starr. She'd had it officially changed. She flatly refused to reveal the name she was born with. Said it was too long and full of consonants for a memorable byline, anyway. Clearly, the only thing that mattered. She was kicked back in a large recliner by the windows, with a pad of actual paper on her lap. I sipped a mug of strong, sweet local tea and watched her. She was chewing on the end of her writing implement. An antique pen she'd found during an off-world vacation. She said the physical act of putting words onto actual paper in the ancient way centered and calmed her, and filtered clarity into her work. There was a time when I would have sneered at the pretension, but that was before Pondoro. Now I was wondering if the technique would help me find my personal story about the hunting of the greer.

I wasn't ready to find out. At this moment, fresh from the ministrations of the medics, greer-fear was a fading nightmare I was not ready to resurrect for the sake of my writing. Not yet. Quarantine with Anne was part rest cure and partly like an old-fashioned honeymoon. I was going to enjoy it while it lasted. I touched up the tea with a tumbler of bourbon and stirred. I could just imagine what Ball might say about me writing words onto actual paper. He already thought I was a throwback. He'd probably say not even a cyborg of his acuity would be able to decipher my handwriting.

How the hell was I going to *find* Ball, if the Terran Service couldn't?

She looked up at me and smiled. "I'd *love* to interview Ball. Where is he?"

I was getting used to her virtually reading my mind. I was getting used to a lot of things with her, in just the first week of this quarantine business. Not only was I a new man, I was a well-sated one. She was a direct and passionate lover. One of the reasons I wondered again, uneasily, if Ball's empathometer still was functional. Goddamned voyeur.

"I don't know where Ball is," I said. "Unknowable, if the government can't find him."

"That doesn't sound like Keith Ramsey to me!"

"Yeah. Well, I admit I have been thinking about it." I wasn't going to tell her about the empathometer. I didn't know what her particular moral stance on that might be, and I didn't want to find out. Not for another three weeks anyway.

"He must be fascinating. A rebel Friday ball."

"You interviewed the Customs guy from when we landed here? More and more impressive. Yeah, a rebel Ball Friday, sulking out there in the winter storms. I will admit I doubted him, when he insisted I flame Martin's corpse and that first infected greer out of existence. I was eliminating the proof of my own story—if there was proof. Thank God for my car's recordings. Thank God the old greer in the water was full of sybil. Because they really set me up to ruin my media-rep credentials with those phony records about me being a reserve information officer for the Commonwealth of Terra."

"You worry too much. Your reputation would have carried the story, sybil or not."

"You do know how to sweet-talk a guy."

"I'm serious. Besides, Tanner said to tell you that PIO scam is so old it limps. It would never work on Pukka Sahib Keith . . ."

My face must have changed, because she mercifully laid off. "What are you working on?" I asked her.

"My notes: life in quarantine with Keith Ramsey." She gave me a mock-soulful look. "If they only knew . . ."

"Do I get to see this work in progress?"

"Absolutely not! Your head is swelled enough already."

"In a manner of speaking," I agreed.

"You're insufferable when you're smug," she decided. "Are you trying to distract me from my work?"

"A two-writer household," I said. "It would never work."

"Hmmmm." She was reading her words, her teeth back worrying at the pen. "Been working so far . . ."

I went over and stood behind her, resting a hand lightly on her bare shoulder. Warm, silken, and now well-known territory. "Yes, it has. Maybe I should be writing a piece myself: four weeks of bliss with Anne Starr."

She covered my hand with hers. "You'd botch it up, love. You're not a romance writer, you're an action-adventure man all the way. Wars and rumors of wars. Government corruption. Bloodsport. When are you going to write the truth about the greer?"

"The truth?"

"Why did that old greer drown himself? That truth. He went straight to that specific place—that frozen pond—on a beeline. Your car's records show that. Then he crawled in and pulled the sybil with him. He knew what he was doing, didn't he?"

"Home territory," I said. "Tanner questioned that, too. But I say the old beast tried to drown the sybil when it bit him, because its bite hurt. Probably maladaptive as a host; he went for a swim to drown the flea that bit him—well-known behavior even in Earth critters—and the water was too cold and he went into shock."

"Now you're lying like a bureaucrat," she said softly. "The sybil picked on something its own size for a change. That old greer killed it the only way he could, and be sure the infection wouldn't spread. The ultimate sacrifice for its kind . . ."

"Don't write the Executive's media bites for her, dammit."

"You trailed this one last greer because he saved your ass, and you knew he was something special. Otherwise you would have just come in with your story. You were hurt!"

"That sybil was trying for me, to get off-planet. I was luckier than I can imagine that its greer host trespassed on that old boar's range and drew the attack. That's all it was: strong sense of territory."

"Not in winter; the greer packs cooperate in winter for the cold birthing of the cubs down south. Don't try to lie to me about Pondoro fauna!"

"I didn't know it was a lie."

"This old boar collected the sybil when it tried to collect you, and then carried it straight to the pool and drowned it, as if drowning himself was a mere detail." She stared out at the vista. "I don't have much data on the Blocked Worlds. No one does. But I know the sybil must have been singing that old beast sweet, sweet songs of mastery of the greer continent, with this old boy leading the pack. It wouldn't be the first horde sybil raised against humanity. . . ."

"So the greer led his sybil to the Big Sleep and went with her just to make sure she found the way?"

"How Ramseylike." She laughed. "I love your tough talk, you know that?"

"It's so much hooey, and Tanner knows it. Self-sacrifice for the species is allegedly a mark of high social order, and of an individually developed social conscience among members of that order."

"See? I knew you knew."

"It was just an addled old animal trying to ease its pain."

"That's poetic. That sounds just like you. I may use it in my story. But *that's* hooey."

"All right." I caressed her shoulder with my fingertips and she shivered slightly. Her hand tightened.

"All right, what?" she said.

"Here it is: the greer are really the game managers here. They move humans around by mental powers beyond our wildest imagining. Guys like me are no more to them than selected fighting animals against which to test their rituals of courage. Any do-gooder who attempts to interfere is caused to have bad, bad dreams, and goes away. Any creature smart enough to grasp their secret, and too powerful to be chased away, is finished off without mercy. Whether it's Baka Martin, Ball, or sybil. They *like* the way things are."

"Stop that!" She firmly removed my hand. "I can't concentrate when you do that! And stop trying to patronize me. You're just reciting Baka Martin's myths again, campfire yarning by the hairy-chested to justify your own ritual murder. That's just feature stuff, and worse, old news."

"Then you tell me what happened out there."

"Well . . . Maybe there is something to this greer as game manager bit. I could do a think piece on it. Tanner might give me a byline. But no. That's your story. The one you'll write when you get around to it. Maybe. Someday."

"You think greer hunting will continue?"

"That's why you're not writing, isn't it? Afraid if you tell the truth it will solve the Executive's problem for her."

"No. Pondoro already is off limits to her schemes. Not even she would dare to try it again, after all this publicity. No, I'm rich again—plenty of residuals rolling in. That A.N. lawyer I talked to said we probably can get back the money I thought I spent on Ball without too much trouble, too. May even get the accrued interest in a negotiated settlement. A fat bank account makes me lazy. . . ."

She leaned her head back against my groin. "And lustful?"

"No. You do that."

"What a charmer. Drink your tea. Let me write. Go take a nap."

"A nap?"

"Well, you said you're feeling lazy, didn't you?" She rotated the back of her head gently against me. "So rest up. You're going to need all your energy in an hour or two."

She was right.

33

THE NORTHERN COAST OF THE CONTINENT OF THE GREER WAS A WORLD OF ice. Immobile ice that coated the rock-ribbed cliffs above the cove, restless ice that churned and ground together on the tidal swell of the sea.

The dome structures of the InterSystem fishing station stood like giant igloos on the strand between the moving and the unmoving ice. The fishing fleets were securely drydocked in their sheds. The vast automated processing plant was silent and still, but for the small robot maintenance crews working here and there. The season's catch already was in orbit, being loaded onto InterSystem freighters which happened by for the runs to the near worlds. All that remained was balancing the books and maintenance, until spring.

Kathryn Kinsella detested the Pondoro shape prejudice for robot help with the cold disdain of a formally trained engineer. She didn't like supervising mechanical men with limited programming who were fashioned like athletes. But the money for a station manager was too good to pass up. She lived frugally, and invested wisely. One day soon she would shed this place and find some bright orbit where only human athletes looked like them, and service machinery followed the precepts of Heinlein and of the Ptolemaic equations.

"A waldo is a goddamned *waldo*," she told the

fishing fleet's skipper in frustration. "It should look like one!"

"Yes, ma'am."

The skipper—whose physical aspect might have been suggested by a Jack London sea story—was unfailingly polite. She found herself distracted by the trim muscular line of his body. His rough-hewn face. God-*damn* Pondoro!

"Will you be down to supervise the new software inputs in crew?" he asked deferentially. A Pondoro robot couldn't be anything but deferential; it was against the damn law!

"Yes," she sighed. "Tomorrow. There's plenty of time. Have you completed the corrosion survey?"

"Yes, ma'am. Thirty percent of crew are so corroded they are prone to malfunction. Full software replacement recommended. Another ten percent will need attention before fishing season."

"Tomorrow," she said. "Go away."

She sternly did *not* avail herself of the view of his trim buttocks as he went.

As the only flesh-and-blood on the station, she wondered if she was losing her grip. The most optimistic estimate of bookkeeping and maintenance would keep her here another month. She ought to just bag it and go to town, she told herself. All the wildlife department people would be partying. And the professional hunters. As well as other lonesome fish station managers. There was plenty of time until ice-out.

But there was a handsome bonus for being first station ready to fish. Corporate policy: didn't matter if there wouldn't be any fishing for several months. She held the record: three bonus years in a row. She wasn't going to let that record slide. More capital toward her freedom. Easy money. Well, not exactly *easy* . . .

She went up to her apartment. The viewscreens showed unrelieved bleakness. The sea ice groaned and shrieked as if in agony. She sighed and keyed scenery from some tropic paradise—graceful trees bending in a trade wind, the boom of a surf that never froze, the muted strum of stringed instruments. Then she turned to her com center.

"You've got a caller," the screen told her.

"Display."

A single word superimposed itself on the sunny images: BUSY?

She felt an unaccustomed flutter at her throat. It was her new screenpal.

"No," she said. "You?"

"Bored," said the screen. "Lonesome."

She eased into her recliner. "For anybody special?" she said.

"Bored for anybody special, you mean?"

"Flirt! Lonesome for anybody special, I mean."

"Are you special?"

"Some might think so. Why?"

"Because I'm lonesome for you."

I said I wasn't going to do this anymore. If it's somebody on this planet, that's too close for comfort. If it's not, the transmission time is too damned expensive.

"Are you on Pondoro?" she asked.

"Some might say I'm *under* a good portion of Pondoro."

She stared at the words hanging there. *Under?* Her curiosity stirred.

"As in *buried* under?"

"It's a long story."

"I've got lots of time. How did you get a com unit in your coffin?"

"Segue." The word hung on the screen as a catamaran

sliced the emerald seas. Illusion. Only the bitter ice and her loneliness were real. And the goddamned humanoid robots who weren't programmed or equipped to deal with either.

"Segue?" she said.

"I was going to respond to your jape about the coffin with an ancient acronym of appreciation," the screen said. "A symbol several hundred years old. It came into use when people first began to correspond electronically, according to my research. It occurred to me you might not recognize, and therefore appreciate, the homage."

"How *did* people correspond before electronics?"

"Ah! I have aroused your curiosity."

"You have."

"A single arousal leads to all. It's a start. They wrote letters."

"You mean, as in letters of the alphabet?"

"Clever, Kathryn! They wrote words on paper, physically, by hand. Sealed the correspondence, called 'letters,' into containers called 'envelopes.' And sent the envelopes."

"Sent them? How?"

"By horseman. By horse-drawn coach. By carrier pigeon. If across a sea, by sailing ship. In time, whole services grew up whose duty it was to ensure that the mail always went through."

"That's a strange spelling of male."

"Control yourself, girl! Mail was the generic name for correspondence."

"What was the acronym?" she said.

"For mail?"

"No, silly. For appreciation!"

"LOL!" The letters hung there, larger than the previous ones.

"Which means?"

"Laughing out loud."

She couldn't help it—she did laugh out loud. "I'm LOLing," she said.

"An ancient and venerable thing to do. Historically correct."

"Are you an historian, then?"

"No. I am a terribly terribly secret agent. So secret no one can find me."

"Hah!"

"Perhaps no one *wants* to find me. Sigh . . ."

"Hence . . . lonely," she said.

"Terribly lonely."

Her throat suddenly felt a bit tight. "Maybe you don't . . . want to be found?"

The screen remained unworded so long she thought he'd logged off. Then, "That would depend upon the searcher, my dear."

"Hmmm," she said. "It would, would it?"

"It most certainly would."

"Maybe we should talk?"

"Maybe we should."

34

THE ORANGE CLAW CUBS WERE BIRTHED IN A OPEN GLADE. THEY CAME early into the light, expelled from a mother's stomach so torn with grief she could not carry them to term. The matriarch of Eren Gaino, her natal hahn, attended the grieving mother as she licked the cubs to squalling, lusty life. But when the matriarch placed them against their mother's dugs, she pushed them away and averted her eyes.

"They do not need this bitter milk!"

"Hush now, youngling!" The matriarch was stern. "Firstborn of thine, lastborn of the last of the Orange Claw. Shoved forth rudely, in thy grief. They need thy milk and no other."

The birthing glade lay far down the southernmost peninsula of the continent of the greer. From its lip, dayfire's daily birth could be observed out of the Big Wet, and the hahns could follow its entire low arc across the winter heavens until it went back again into the sea. All each short day, the dayfire flirted in and out of cloud formations that came marching down from the high cold country, trailing gilded veils of rain that dried before it reached the ground.

Beneath the tangled blood-soaked birthing moss the ground trembled continuously from the nervous roving of nearby plains game. The beasts were near panic in this proximity to the neural waves of pain that flowed unceasing from Sunto's grieving mate.

Thick dust stirred by thousands of hooves hung in a pall above the dry grass prairies. Where the fading veils of rain penetrated the rolling dust, slanting dayfire struck a riot of rainbow colors overhead.

"They enter the world surrounded by its beauty," the matriarch said. "Feed them strong."

"No strength can save them. They are doomed. Better thus to die, eyes unopened to this bitter life."

"Bitter! Thy grief blinds thee, then, like thy newborn, to all this beauty. Feed them! Come early into the light, they need this strength of thine, bitter though it be!"

"They are doomed. Marked by that old dread sickness of the Orange Claw hahn! Cannot even thou digest this plainest truth?"

"They are marked," the matriarch agreed. "Marked out for lonely destiny. The Orange Claw bred true, and as did thy own particular strength. Let them feed! All hahns will need these cubs of thine to taste the future off the wind, ere dayfire hunts its final time across the sky and all is silence. It is their destiny."

"Destiny! The destiny of their vanished father? To die alone, unsung, in bitter mountains?"

"Who can read the future? Not this one. And not thou! Orange Claw alone has this gift. Sunto could— and saved us all. And so even now can these small weak cubs, weakening as thou hug thy grief instead of them."

Upon the matriarch's words the cubs went silent. The mother felt a lurch of fear.

"They are marked," the matriarch said grimly. "See? Even just born, they read my fear for them. They know that thou reject them. They prepare themselves to die."

With a convulsive lunge the mother hugged them

to her. Then curled back upon the moss. Instantly, two small mouths were busy on her. Her milk came down in a hot, hard rush, dizzying as spilled blood. She groaned with reluctant pleasure. Sensed a strange and yet intimate penetration of her emotions . . .

"Sunto! Is it thou?"

"Hush now," crooned the matriarch. "It is the awakening stomachs of thy cubs. Their questing stomachs are as much of Sunto as remains beneath the dayfire. How strong their bellies! Yet just born! Strength bred true to strength, the Orange Claw's and thine own."

After a time, the mother slept. The cubs writhed and crawled against her, bleating impatiently. The matriarch's instant concern brought Korlu to her side.

"Her long march here, and her overwhelming grief, have dried her," the matriarch told the Eren Gaino chieftain.

Korlu's snout wrinkled in concern. "The cubs are so small!"

"Come too early to the light. Forced from her belly by a grief too large to leave them room to grow. In urgent need of sustenance her grief has stolen."

"They must live! Thou see this?"

"It is seen. Needed of all the hahns, the hahns now must serve their needs."

"I cannot ask this thing of an Eren Gaino female."

"Not your duty. Mine. Am I not matriarch? A milk-rich female of thy hahn—her own cub lost in river crossing—already has been summoned."

Korlu crouched in obeisance. "Thou are matriarch. None finer through all the hahns."

"Save thy pretty phrases for the council. It is meet a female of each hahn should feed their life's strength into these Orange Claw cubs. That strength, redoubled, shall be returned to all alike in time of future need."

"Canst thou then digest our future plain as Sunto could?"

"No . . . but plain, even to this poor digestion, is the great legacy he has left us in his get."

"The pool is locked in winter, trampled all about by meddling Two-Legs. Who may call this council, now that last-living of the Orange Claw is no more?"

"Digest this, O my leader: last-living of the Orange Claw is not dead, but lies before thee, mewling for fresh hot milk. As hahn-chief to Sunto's mate, the council is thine to call."

"Then I will." And Korlu was gone.

A long night passed in the glade. Across the grass, the council met, and heard his words, and decided. Soon, one and then another shadowy form joined the matriarch in her watch above the sleeping mother, and lay down to nurse the cubs. The exhausted mother did not stir. By dayfire's awakening the cubs had fed four times, voraciously. They slept at last, with full rounded bellies. One against Arnic, one against DiTenka breast. The matriarch was off hunting in the dawn when Sunto's mate finally awoke.

She mutely observed her cubs at peace upon her sleeping sisters. Her stomach seemed empty of all emotion, prepared. She slipped away into the growing dayfire with single purpose. The distant growl of the surf drew her to the beach where she had cavorted in her cubhood. These were home marches to Eren Gaino.

She paused where barrier dune marked the end of prairie and beginning of sand. Two silent forms awaited her upon the dune.

"Two mighty chieftains." Her tone was bitter. "To attend this lowly one?"

"Hush now!" Girta, leader of the Hahn DiTenka. "Last living mate of the Orange Claw? Never lowly!"

"DiTenka's song always the sweetest," was her weary response. "So Sunto always averred. What song then do thou fashion of his hunt unwitnessed high in bitter mountains?"

"All hahns alike know this grief of thine." Korlu. "It is a pain among us all, and never will subside, that Sunto's finest hour goes unsung."

"Finest hour!" Her teeth showed beneath her scowl of anger. "He died alone! Alone! Leave me. I would take the warm soft air along the beach of my cub-hood. Alone."

"This cannot be." DiTenka. "Poorly would we honor Orange Claw memory should we permit—"

"*Permit!*" Her instant fury flared out at them. "*Permit?* I am freeborn of the hahn. And mate of Sunto. I would take the air alone. No thing beneath the Lake of Light dares bespeak me of *permission.* . . ."

DiTenka flinched beneath her scorn. Not Korlu. "Sunto gave into my care thy birthing of thy young. What kind of faith would be kept if this one permitted them twice-orphaned?"

"So thy *honor* holds thee here, in the path of my free will?"

"Sunto—"

"Sunto's song is sung! The council will see him no more." She gazed out against the rising dayfire, haloed in rainbow rain. "This one will touch him no more. The empty bed moss chills these frail bones, down to their very core. The cubs are birthed. They belong now to all the hahns, to raise up in the Way. They do not need this bitter, inadequate milk."

"Thy cublings cry for thee, even so," Korlu said. "Thou must—"

"Thou *dare* to lecture me upon a mother's part?" Her claws were unsheathed. "Chieftain or no, I will kill you where you stand. Last living mate of the old Orange Claw will empty your stomach for you of such pretension!"

"Haii!" DiTenka's spontaneous salute, half laughing.

"Thou find in me amusement, thou . . . *singer*? Then perhaps would taste this fury that feeds upon my gut?"

"If would ease your pain, then rip my belly out," DiTenka said. "Take this poor stomach gladly. But do not drink the Big Wet while thy cubs cry in the moss for thee. Only thou can sing them their father, back alive before their eyes. Only thou. And these cubs need that singing most of all. For the Orange Claw has bred true. They will taste tomorrow off the wind, as clear as Sunto did."

"And die, unwitnessed, both? Better they stayed within me while the Big Wet drinks all three."

"All things die, in their season." Korlu. "Even that evil which thy mate dreamed, and which came to hunt us all. It was an evil so strong only Orange Claw could hunt it to its own ending. Absent the old Orange Claw, it would have been our ending, not the evil's."

"Hear me." DiTenka. "To my hahn falls the singing of all our history in the council. Sunto will have his song—or this hahn of singers will sing no song again."

"How then?"

"His hunt was witnessed, after all."

"DiTenka in a lie?" Her contempt was cutting. "Thou of all should know such a lie will not give me pause. No hunter attended Sunto's fall!"

"Not true. A hunter did. A Two-Legs hunter, following on Sunto's spoor."

"A Two-Legs! Of what is that to me? A Two-Legs! And so did the cold rocks among the mountain crags witness my mate's dying. Will thou have the *rocks* sing Sunto's final hunt?"

"It may well be," DiTenka said. "One cold rock, at least. If this could come to pass, would thou turn aside from this weakling mission of thy own? Sunto's get and thine *must* one day take their place at council. Read the future off the wind, and guide all hahns alike to proper living."

"A Two-Legs and a cold rock as witness to his hunt?"

"None other," DiTenka said. "The singing is my duty. Thine to raise thy cubs to know their heritage and place. I will say no more."

"Then leave me. I am unpersuaded." She flowed into a determined stride, straight at them.

DiTenka moved aside. Not Korlu. She rose up dangerously.

"Then slay me," said the Eren Gaino. "Feed thy cubs my hot fresh blood."

She snarled at the blasphemy. "Hahn cub feeds not on hahn flesh!"

"Not since the Orange Claw Lesson. Full true. But if thou insist upon this death of thine, what then? Who will sing thy cublings how to live? Who will save the hahns when next the evil hunts? Who then? All things die. Ours to plan death with proper ritual and awe. Without the Orange Claw, all falls again to raw blood hunger. Hahn against hahn, and hunter against hunter. This one would die before bearing witness to such a thing. I know my duty. I know thine. I will not stand away."

He extended his paws. She saw a broad, folded leaf.

"What is this now?"

With a single claw he flipped the leaf open. Wet orange clay shone in the shifting morning light. "Sunto's wish. To stain the paws of his get with clay of his hahn's home range. So when their eyes unseal, their first vision confirms them Orange Claw."

Her stomach convulsed with something like an audible scream of pain. On marches beyond earshot the nervous plains beasts stampeded into frenzied flight. Young hunters raced like shadows in the shifting light, trying to turn the herds and calm them. While holding their own stomachs tight-closed against that awful pain.

She sank upon the dune, clawing up great gouts of sand as if in grip of lowland fever. DiTenka and Eren Gaino stood over her, impassive. Nor tried to guard against her grief, which tore their entrails as she tore the sand. Dayfire stood high as it would climb this winter day before she finally was still. Her blazing pain ebbed at last, her exhausted stomach unable to feed it hot again. Slowly it drifted into an endless aching. Across the plains, the young hunters controlled the demoralized herds, and turned them toward water holes. All the mindless running had parched hunted and hunter alike.

She reached a trembling paw to her immobile hahn chief and touched the clay. Her fur was matted with damp sand. She wiped the trace of orange clay across her muzzle.

"Sunto's song will be sung?"

"Or this hahn of singers sings no more."

"Then leave me," she said once again. "I must clean and groom myself. I have my cubs to tend."

35

BALL NO LONGER WAS BORED. HE HAD BEEN VERY BUSY. HIS PLAN OF escape was complete. Though complicated, it was not complex. Each move was simple, and linked to the next.

First, a communications link undetectable to the orbital snoops. He reprogrammed his minuscule manufacturing facility to extrude a single fine wire. An old-fashioned antenna. He devised a tiny crawler for its tip, and fed it through one of his surface ports into the rocks. Worked it carefully this way and that until it probed free of the rubble through the snow and stiffened into a meter-high whip.

The commonplace electronic chatter of the planet now lay open to him.

He found his new screenpal in less than a day's monitoring, and began to court her. She was lonesome and lusty. They moved from screen words to vox almost at once. Before very long she admitted possession of an upmarket virtual boudoir, within which she could turn the sensations of her body over to his ministrations. If, she hinted demurely, he was of a mind to indulge in virtual sensuality. He downloaded the design of her boudoir and tweaked it to give her an almost mirror image—inhabited by a simulacrum of Keith Ramsey.

For lovemaking technique, he recycled Ramsey's farewell fornications during the last days before he had embarked for Pondoro. The bouts with the Inter-Galactic Cybernetics heiress had been particularly intense. Ball had injected the empath chip into Ramsey the first night of their association, and had borne witness to what he chose at the time to style the writer's incessant rutting. Ramsey of course was unaware of his observations. The miscellaneous leave-takings had provided Ball ample opportunity to calibrate and cross-check the accuracy of his empathometer. Now he had another use for the data.

Should his new screenpal begin to be bored with Ramsey, of course, he could access several centuries' history of electronic lovemaking for form and variety. He assumed he would be able to assess her boredom without the aid of an empath chip.

The emotional impact of the virtual play upon his own brain surprised him. More than once he felt that strange almost-memory of some previous existence try to form—but when he reached for it, it faded. He distanced himself from the whirl of feelings evoked by the love-play. He was manipulating the "K.R." simulacrum very effectively, that was all, using the stored data to play her body and emotions like a fine instrument. Just as he could simulate a full orchestra for her edification, if it came to that. She was indefatigable. Articulate in mid-coital retrospection about her loneliness and frustration among the waldoes on her isolated station.

"Heinlein was right all those ages ago," she said sleepily. "Robot form should follow function. Only the designers on Ptolemy seems to follow him anymore."

Ball considered her statement. She was highly intelligent, but her education was lacking. Would he antagonize her by offering historic correction? Interacting in this intimate way was not the same—even when none of it was real—as simply observing and manipulating the interactions of others, a task for which he had no peer. He was losing his objectivity here. New ground was being broken with every encounter. No chance he was going to be bored anytime soon. He hoped—*hoped!*—the same was true for her.

Because she was going to dig him out of this trap.

He decided to risk challenging her intelligence. "Boucher," he said.

"Hmmm?"

"Boucher was the ancient logician who established that robotic form should follow function. He usually wrote in a discipline almost as strict as haiku—that is to say, mystery stories. When he veered into speculative fiction, Boucher predicted that robots built in man's image, but compelled to do specialized work, would become dysfunctional. He called it going insane. Heinlein's waldoes were essentially remote-control devices for a wasted human form."

"Boucher? Never heard of him. He should have lived to see goddamned Pondoro! You think my fishing-fleet waldoes are insane?"

"I wouldn't presume to judge. The Pondoro shape-prejudice is a little out of kilter, I grant."

"So which are you, dear heart?" she said lazily.

"I beg your pardon?"

"You heard me. Are you a robot or a waldo? Or just some new goddamned commercial program, and in a month or two I'll try to reach you but I'll get a sales pitch instead? Maybe we can just cut to the chase. How much are you going to cost me? So much I'll never get off Pondoro? What the hell . . ."

Ball was as close to dumbfounded as he could ever remember being. Intimate relationships, it seemed, had unexpected pitfalls. How in the name of his creators had she sensed he wasn't exactly human?

"It's okay, love. Don't be so shocked. You can tell me. Can't you? Or do I have to talk to the sales department first? InterGalactic Cybernetics, right?"

InterGalactic Cybernetics: part of the cover story the Terran Service had fed Ramsey to get him to sign Ball on for Pondoro. The lonesome fish-station manager was a Terran Service trap. Had to be. Someone clever back at headquarters had run a projection on all the possible ways he would attempt escape, and the avenue of seduction had come up high in the probabilities. He suspected the Executive herself, for some reason.

"Speak to me, K.R.," she said sadly. "Spill it out. I can take it. I just wish . . ."

"What?" He was nearly incapable of repartee for the moment.

"I wish I wasn't so damned smart is all. I would like to have been in love—in *lust*—with you for a month or so before it all fell into place."

When in doubt, try honesty. "I am nearly speechless," Ball said. "How could you possibly conclude I am affiliated with InterGalactic Cybernetics?" If he had owned the biologic mechanisms for sighing, he would have sighed. He had gotten tricky in his bid for freedom—and the Executive had gotten trickier. Had he ever played five-card stud with his ultimate boss? Unknown. But he probably would have lost.

"It's simple, really," she said. "The initials you go by: K.R. Keith Ramsey. I follow all the women's channels out here. Got to keep current, you know. Don't want to be a hick all my life. InterGal is rumored to have rolled out a Keith Ramsey party progue. Primitive man, packaged to go. I guess I'm honored to be part of the blind market survey. Do I get a price break?"

She was telling the truth. He could hear it in the words. He knew almost dizzying relief—and almost laughed. The Executive was busy all right—already was taking punitive action against Ramsey for his part in interrupting her plans for Pondoro. Ramsey would want to die of embarrassment; he was far too prudish to enjoy the implied homage of a pirate progue in his likeness—and too much of a reactionary to even think of suing for royalties.

"I don't understand your silences," she said sadly. "Did I fail some test? Do you just log off and vanish? How can even InterGal do that to a living human being? And why? That's mean-spirited, K.R. Damn you, speak to me!"

"You," said Ball, "are wholly new to my experience. And take it from me, my experience is extensive. You are a most impressive lady."

"So where do we go from here? Do I get to keep you? *Are* you a commercial progue?"

He gave her Ramsey's embarrassed laugh. Perfectly rendered.

"I am not a progue. No more than you are. You aren't, are you? Some famous courtesan progue, all programmed by the Terran Service to trap me with your charms?"

"Right now I guess I wish I were. I wish I did have you trapped. I'd never let you go." Her sadness tore at his newly sensitized awareness. He realized he was experiencing something close to full empathy without a chip transmitting from her brain stem. Amazing. Unsettling. But definitely *not* boring.

"Well, I don't wish you were," he said. "I wish you were exactly what you purport to be."

"Why would the Terran Service want to trap you?"

"A little slow on the uptake today, dear," he said.

"No fair! I'm distracted. You love me almost to death, and all the time I'm thinking you're just a progue, and how I have no sense of shame left, and don't even care if you are. Don't you *ever* have any uncontrollable emotions? Why is the Terran Service after you?"

Ball felt—stung—by her words. Unbelievable! Distracted in his turn from his purpose of escape. But she was ready now. A tool for his using. Just as the greer manipulated whatever life-form they chose to their own ends. They used fear; he used love—beyond that, much in common . . .

"Why would the Terran Service care about a runaway progue?" she said. "I wish you weren't one, but you are. You have to be. You're too perfect. Far too perfect. I adore you. But there's this—edge—to you. Where all emotion—just stops."

"I am *not* a progue—commercial or otherwise. The truth is more complicated than that. I am beginning to grasp the reach of your intelligence. I should have told you the truth straight out. But I was afraid—for many reasons."

"If you really need to hide from the Commonwealth, of course I will help you. There—it's said, *en clair*. I've convicted myself of conspiracy against the Commonwealth."

"No you haven't," Ball said. "Our every communication has been ecrypted beyond their ability to break. Trust me on this. I would not expose you to harm."

"I trust you on anything. Unfortunately. Now tell me what you're afraid to tell me."

So he did.

36

I WAS SWIMMING IN ICY, MURKY WATERS. UP, TOWARD THE LIGHT. I couldn't breathe. I could not remember the last time I had drawn a normal breath. My pulse pounded in my ears. There was an enormous pressure in my chest. I tried to swim faster, but couldn't. My arms moved slowly, as in a dream.

A dream.

I tried to open my eyes. But my eyes *were* open. Above the surface, wavery and indistinct, dangerous shadows loomed. Their eyes burned down. Watching my struggle. The roaring in my ears . . . altered. Began to come in rolling billows. Like ocean waves—but not that. Something . . . Some other rhythm.

Chanting. They were chanting over me, their heavy voices rising in a dirge.

I was drowning. They knew it, and mourned.

I *had* to breathe—could not—*had* to awaken. Could *not*. The chanting rose, and steadied, urgently demanding some answer. I *had* to answer them. . . . I strained up toward the surface. But something had me, pulling me back, holding me down in the threshing darkness. From some forgotten corner of my brain came an ancient word. *Succubus*: night creature, straddling my chest to suck the breath from me. Feverish hands clawed at my shoulders, the heat of her loins sank into me. I tried to strike out, but my limbs were leaden, unresponsive. . . .

". . . Damn you, wake up! Wake up, wake up! Breathe, damn you!"

A woman's voice. A woman's hands, shaking me with fear and fury.

I awoke all at once, gasping like a boated fish, soaked in sweat. In the darkness of the quarantine-hut bedroom, Anne Starr crouched on me. Her eyes glittered in an eerie resemblance to the dream shadows. She was cursing a steady stream.

"The patient is awake," said the hut's diagnostic voice. "Crisis has passed. Blood pressure normalizing . . ."

She collapsed atop me, sobbing and cursing. My arms went around her.

"No infection," droned the diagnostic. "No fever. Diagnosis: simple night terror."

"Simple!" She struggled and then quieted against my grip. "You wouldn't breathe! Wouldn't!"

"I was dreaming. . . ." I said.

"Some goddamned dream! You scared me senseless! Are you okay? Really okay?"

I still was drawing deep, ragged breaths. So was she. "I think so," I said.

"Then ease off, dammit! You're making my ribs creak!"

"Sorry . . ."

She heard something in my voice. "No. Don't let go! Let 'em crack—they'll mend. Hold tight as you must, love. I won't let them have you!"

A huge shudder got loose then, but she clamped onto me like a limpet, arms and thighs gripping with convulsive strength. Maybe my own frame creaked a little.

She steadied me and gentled me like a frightened animal—which I was, just then—and when she sensed the worst was past, propped up on one arm, thighs still clamping me, and stroked my damp forehead.

"What *were* they? Some awful awful thing you lived through? Trying to kill you now, because you let down your guard here with me?"

"How could you know what was in my dream?" I said. "It was the greer. A pack of greer. They sang to me. Not to me. To that old boar in the pool."

"The pool?"

"I was underwater in the pool. Drowning, just like that old boar."

"Sweet spirit of space. The sybil—?"

"Conclusively, no," the diagnostic said. "No infection. No alien virus present."

"Just you and me—and the doc," I said. "How intimate."

"Don't you start with that tough-guy shit! Tell me about this!"

"It was the greer," I said again. "Not a pack. Some kind of gathering. Powerful beings! They were . . . mourning . . . that old boar. They wanted something from me. Not my blood. Not my life. My . . . memories? I just don't know. But I couldn't breathe, and I couldn't understand."

"The greer? You know things about them you've never told. Just how powerful *are* they? You don't mean they really spoke to you—it was just a dream, right? They can't truly invade your mind. Can they? Can they? They're thousands of kilometers from here!"

She was guessing close to the truth. "I don't know what it all meant. Just a bad dream, I guess. What time is it, anyway?"

"Past dawn." She gestured at the bedside sentinel.

The windows unshuttered on a world of morning sun, blinding on the snowpack. "You want to try to go back to sleep?"

"No!"

"Then take a shower, try to wake up. It's over. You're safe here. You want the diagnostic to analyze your dreams?"

"I don't think so. I think I want some breakfast. Coffee."

I had a brief irrational tug of fear when I stepped into the shower. Have a dream about drowning, and immediately immerse yourself in water? I shrugged it off and dialed the water hot. The spray drummed some of the tension out of my neck and shoulders. By the time I joined her in the breakfast nook the nightmare already was fading into unreality. Maybe it was just my subconscious editor telling me it was time to try to write the greer.

"You're really popular this morning," she said. "Lots of messages. What do you know about InterGal Cybby rolling out a Keith Ramsey erotic progue?"

"A *what?*"

"Tanner's fielded a dozen inquiries about it. Just a strong rumor, so far. Are you chipped? Have these past few days been just more research for a damned *progue?*"

Now was clearly not the time to tell her about Ball's empatho chip. I wondered briefly if the Terran Service had another monitor on me. If they did, and were using these days to embarrass me—and her— somebody was going to pay. Big-time.

"They couldn't be using this. How could they? It was your idea to share my quarantine, remember? I haven't authorized any such damn thing! It's got to be crap. Who'd buy such a damn thing anyway?"

"Oh, baby—they'd buy. Believe me. And Tanner says the rumors are pretty strong. Didn't InterGal design Ball?"

"So I thought at the time. Who the hell knows? Maybe they actually did—under contract to the Commonwealth. Ball is a damn Terran Service op, remember? I swear to you—"

"Hush," she said. "I'm just being possessive. Forget it. I've been using you to get an exclusive—why shouldn't it be reciprocal? Maybe I'll become famous as one of your inspirations for the progue. Hell, I might sue for royalties!"

I buried my nose in a cup of pungent Pondoro coffee. "I'm not ready for this."

"Are you ready for an audience with the consular office of a significant power?"

"What are you talking about now?"

"The sector consulate for Ptolemy is sending an official. Tanner says it's a big deal—some kind of a formal invitation to visit their world."

"Visit Ptolemy? Why, for heaven's sake?"

"We'll know when he gets here. In person. It *must* be a big deal."

"I'm still in quarantine, dammit!"

"Not if Ptolemy wants to talk to you, you're not. Even the Commonwealth Executive doesn't mess with Ptolemy! You going to take any calls from people asking about this progue?"

"No!"

"Not even your lusty female fans?"

"Fans? What are you talking about now?"

"There's some local woman who runs a fish factory here. She wants to talk to you. About the K.R. progue. Claims she was part of some market test and just *must* talk to you. I could interview her, if you like. I'm kind of a resident expert by now on the K.R. progue, wouldn't you say? I could tell if she knew what she was talking about."

"Will you stop with that? There's no such thing!"

"She seemed pretty positive you'd make time for her."

"Yeah?"

"Yes. Her exact message: 'I've just had a ball with your K.R. progue. Don't you think we should get the ball rolling again? In person?'"

"Ball!" I said. "*Goddamn* him. I should have poached that egg when I had the chance."

37

THE ORBITAL SHUTTLE FROM THE PTOLEMAIC CONSULATE'S FRIGATE WAS an impressive sight as it drifted to a halt above the isolation hut. Its bulk blocked the slanting afternoon sun. A vast golden saucer, its topside was etched with meters-high hieroglyphs. Its propulsion was absolutely silent and barely stirred the snowpack.

"Do you know what those symbols represent?" Anne was by the window, shimmering in a flame-colored formal gown which displayed her collar-bones and cleavage to best advantage.

"No," I said.

"They're from the Rosetta stone. The original Egyptian, not the Greek."

"The what stone?" My attention was divided between the spectacle of the hovering ship and her mouth-drying loveliness.

"A stone tablet found by Napoleon's troops in the city of Rosetta in the late eighteenth century. Finally decoded by a Frenchman. It turned out to be what amounted to a press release about the glories of Ptolemy the Fifth's rule in Egypt."

"A press release? Carved in stone? Give me a break."

"Where do you think we got that phrase about carved in stone, anyway?"

"The Ten Commandments?"

She made a face. "Maybe. I prefer that it was from the Rosetta stone."

"Please stay indoors," the hut's diagnostic voice chipped in. "Snow-removal commencing . . ."

On the words, a pale beam washed over the thick snow beyond the window. Steam billowed and curled away. Within seconds a precise and perfectly dry path led from beneath the disk to our door. A port dilated in the belly of the disk, and a resplendent creature dropped lightly to the path on antigravs.

"Conrad of Pirsig," Anne said.

"Pirsig?"

"A town on Ptolemy. They always use their town's name."

Tall and spare, wrapped in robes that caught and refracted Pondoro's sun in a technicolored riot, Conrad of Pirsig approached the door.

"I think his gown has yours beat," I said.

"Be quiet! Those are full ceremonial robes. This must be big!"

"Your quarantine is ended," the hut announced, and the door sighed back into the wall.

The Ptolemian inclined his head gracefully to pass within. He was nearly as tall as Baka Martin, but slender instead of rangy. His skin was dark-hued and fine, and his slightly slanting eyes glowed. He bowed first to Anne.

"Anne Starr of Firstport, Pondoro."

Damned if she didn't curtsey! "Conrad of Pirsig."

"Your journalism has given me pleasure," he said. "Precise. Evocative. Work of quality. This sector is lucky in you."

She blushed. "You say that to all the girls!"

"Only when true." He bestowed a serene smile and turned to me. "Keith Ramsey of Highlands, Acme."

"A long time ago."

He bowed. "Your work ennobles that world. Your

personal writing on blood and death is powerful and primal. Your journalism is incisive and accurate. Official iniquity trembles when you seek. Mendacity skulks away."

"Flattery," I said. "There's usually a price to be paid for hearing it."

Anne shot me a venomous look. But Conrad smiled. "Not flattery. Certainly not flattery from the perspective of the Commonwealth Executive. Whose life work is mendacity."

"A harsh pronouncement," I said. "She's got a hell of a job. I wouldn't want it. But somebody has to do it."

He bowed again. "Then you forgive her this latest transgression? The rumor of a salacious program in your likeness, openly marketed to the lonely and the sad?"

"Just a rumor," I said. "Probably nothing to it."

He smiled. "Perhaps. One thing is certain: she means to cause you grief, for your temerity here. Which indicates how important this Pondoro . . . experiment . . . was to her. Your journalism has impeded her grand design by some significant measure. Which is why I have been sent to you."

"Because of a pirate progue?"

"No—because of your work in revealing her design. Your refusal to accept the substantial bribe— that is in effect what it was—to compromise your profession. I am here to offer you a working residency on Ptolemy. To lecture on the subtle corruption which can tempt the unwary when government leaders profane the great Ptolemaic principles of rule set out in stone so long ago."

"Oh, my!" Anne breathed.

"Words are powerful things," Conrad said. "Ptolemy, as perhaps you know, is devoted to the study of words. The words of the ancient and revered wise ones of humanity. Words that free, words that enslave, words that wound, words that kill. We are known across the stars for our continuing study of personal enlightenment, and of forms of governance, proper and improper. Not as venerable as the texts of those mandarins who undertook to advise China's warring states after dissolution of a continental empire—but equally as revered on Ptolemy—is the American principle of the Fourth Estate. Known colloquially all these centuries later as freedom of the media."

"I don't see myself as a teacher."

He smiled again. "You are a storyteller. Perhaps the oldest profession, antedating even the formal practice of arms—or of lust. All that we ask is that you tell your stories. You will find rapt listeners on Ptolemy."

"I could do that."

"Of that we have no doubt. Your words are eagerly awaited. This invitation, of course, extends to your participation in our decade-celebrating Renga."

"Renga?"

"An ancient poetic form, Japanese in origin. Linked verses from several poets, designed to penetrate to the heart of things. Each poet in the competition fashions words in accord with the old discipline. Our poets are excited at what you might bring to the form."

"Tell him the rest of it," Anne said. Her voice had changed, constricted. She wasn't liking this anymore. "He doesn't know!"

He bowed to her once more. "The lady refers, I believe, to the emperor's prerogative. The authority to extinguish a poet whose work fails the form. But that is a privilege restricted to poets nativeborn."

"That's not what I've heard!" she said hotly. "Some privilege!"

He nodded solemnly. "It is true this privilege has,

upon rare occasions, been granted off-world writers. But only when they freely choose it. As Commonwealth citizens, of course, they would otherwise be immune to such local custom. The Terran Service would never permit local custom to interfere with a citizen's inalienable rights. Not even on Ptolemy. Unless the citizen formally renounces those rights. Such renunciation has occurred. In my own meager lifetime, I recall an aging poet laureate from the Llralan worlds who chose that path. He is among the most venerated of individuals on Ptolemy!"

"Big deal!" she muttered.

"Renunciation is not required, nor even expected, of honored guests."

"Good," I said. "When I go, it's going to be kicking and screaming all the way."

"Keith Ramsey," he said, "would not be who he is, should he go gently into that good night. . . . Forgive me, an obscure poetic reference. There is one other thing. . . ." He hesitated. "Your cyborg companion in these Pondoro adventures."

"Ball?"

"Just so. Our invitation extends to him, as well. We had hoped to invite Baka Martin. There was considerable excitement among our native poets when your story revealed he was alive and on Pondoro, living the life of simple storyteller. The tales he could have spun! But your subsequent dispatches revealed an unusual opportunity—a cyborg who had closely partnered with the storyteller. And who has been your constant companion here. Our research has been thorough. Those two have seen—and done—many things across the years since Martin slew Iron Fennec. Some of them questionable. And Ball is a Terran Service agent!"

"On the run now," I said. "Well, on the roll might

be more appropriate. The Commonwealth considers him a traitor."

He shrugged delicately. "A freighted word, traitor. Your dispatches seemed to infer a higher loyalty—that of friendship—than to his calling. You have written 'a Ball of many talents,' and we concur. No cyborg ever has received a Ptolemy invitation. To be host to you both at once . . ." He smiled and made an encompassing gesture.

"There's a problem," I said. "I don't know where Ball is!"

He smiled. "Of course not! Not with the Terran Service searching high and low for him. That search will stop, of course."

"It will?"

"It will. An invitee of Ptolemy is vested with full diplomatic immunity. A protection he will find most comprehensive. You, of course, do not need immunity—you are a Certified newsman. Freedom of the media!"

I was thinking about the message from the fishstation manager. "And if I could find Ball for you? Do you need to make this invitation in person?"

"It is the usual form."

"What if the Service grabbed him before you could get there?"

"The Commonwealth is on notice. They will not interfere."

"So I could bring him to you?"

"We will wait in orbit. This is most exciting. Think of it! A writer of your gifts could tell Ball's life story to the stars! Be his Boswell!"

"Boswell?"

"His chronicler. Given the disguise he chose to accompany you to Pondoro, a delicious irony, don't you think?"

38

THE FROZEN SEA WAS AN EYE-HURTING BLAZE OF REFLECTED SUNSHINE beneath the clear lavender midday sky. The vast indifferent bulk of Pondoro sprawled across the viewscreens and dwarfed my tiny craft to something slightly larger than a random molecule. Pressure ridges bulked up like the spines of dinosaurs, if dinosaur spines were made of glittering ice. There wasn't a single con trail in the sky. The rental car's autopilot said we were over the continental shelf, landfall due momentarily. But I couldn't tell where humped-up ice left off and coastline began.

It was liberating to be out under the open sky again, even one as deserted as this.

And slightly unnerving, too, after the coziness of the quarantine arrangements. Without willing it, my ears were tuned to the steady hum of the motors. The primitive centers of my brain were acutely aware of my dependence upon a manufacturer I'd never heard of and maintenance mechanics I'd never met. I was warm and physically comfortable in the cabin. But my reptile brain stem wasn't fooled for a second.

The coastline showed at last, right on schedule. I heaved a small sigh of relief and almost said something before I caught myself. There was no one to hear. Anne Starr had gone back to her day job. Probably was pounding out her quarantine piece at this very moment. She had point-blank refused to come with me, not even swayed by the prospect of an interview with Ball. She had decided I was going to get myself killed on Ptolemy, and she was cutting her losses. Said call her if I decided against Ptolemy and decided to take LaChoy up on his offer of a guide slot. I was missing her already—stupid and sentimental, but there it was.

"Two minutes to InterSystem Fishing Station Sixseven," the pilot said.

I hadn't read up on Ptolemy yet. I couldn't imagine what it would have to offer that would make a Pondoro resident believe it more fearsome than the greer.

Ptolemy was old-settlement, far out the stellar arm that led to Earth. But Anne was a careful journalist. I'd worry about it later, if I managed to dig Ball out of whatever he'd gotten into this time.

"Landing permission granted," the car told me.

We circled in over the ice-coated domes of the isolated station and homed on a finger pier where a steady column of steam rose straight into the still air. The car dropped in lightly, and I saw the steel planking still was wet from snow removal.

A single lonely figure, bundled in a parka whose coloring was conservative by local standards, waited at the edge of the cleared area. I zipped into my own new parka—a parting gift from Anne—and stepped onto the deck. The frigid air burned a track into my lungs. I saw her stiffen momentarily, and then relax as I approached.

"God!" she said, half laughing. "I thought for a minute you were a greer!"

I glanced at my sleeves. The perfectly felted greer fur shimmered deep purple in the brightness. The Firstport tailorbot had painstaking sewn the contents of my old *twon*-down coat into the new parka. Greer felt over *twon* down: I was snugly warm.

"Well, the original owner of this coat almost ate me," I said. "A friend of mine said I might as well wear it in his honor, since I was only slightly more civilized than him, in her humble opinion. I'm Keith Ramsey."

"I would have known you anywhere." She was short and sturdy, with curves her parka didn't quite hide. Her eyes were bright and assessing, but her face suddenly was a deeper pink than the cold warranted. "That is . . . well. Hi! I'm Kathryn Kinsella. I guess I'm pleased to meet you, but . . ." She hesitated. "God! I'm *so* embarrassed!"

"You?" I said. "How do you think I feel? I'd strangle that goddamned Ball if he had a neck to get hold of!"

Surprisingly, she giggled. "Well—but why? I mean"—now she was blushing furiously—"he did a *marvelous* job of being you. Believe me, you have no reason to be embarrassed. . . . Oh, shit—I promised myself I wasn't going to talk about this! Not to *you!* Maybe my analyst . . . "

"Where is he?"

"In the mountains. Buried under a few metric tons of debris." She looked guiltily at the sky, as if for eavesdroppers. "Should we be discussing this *en clair?*"

"Relax. The hunt is off. Ball has found a very powerful protector. If he's safe where he is, then he's in no danger. Buried? An avalanche?"

"Let's go inside? I'm *freezing!*" We headed up a freshly cleared path. A lean figure in a jumpsuit opened a door in the nearest dome. He looked unaffected by the cold.

"A robot?" I said.

"A goddamned waldo," she said. "Pondoro and its shape-prejudice!"

She led me into what looked like a reception area, and we shed our outerwear.

Her curvaceousness came into clearer focus in a form-fitting jumpsuit similar to the robot's. She blushed again.

"Sorry," I said.

"It's all right. In a weird way, it's kind of nice, actually. That you're actually here—and as embarrassed about this as I am. Even though it never was *you* in the first place. Do you like our local teas? Yes? One of the waldoes will bring some. I'm sorry about not taking you right up to my quarters." She paused, hearing the sound of that. "Oh, God—that's *not* what I meant. I have *no* plans to take you to my quarters. I wouldn't trust myself—and I'm amazed your girlfriend let you come out here all by yourself. . . ."

"Not girlfriend," I said. "Professional colleague. The local A.N. correspondent."

"Whatever. I know how her voice sounded when she talked about you. I think I'm envious, a little. . . ."

"Look," I said, "I have absolutely no knowledge of whatever Ball pulled here. Okay? He used my image in vain, you might say. Whatever you remember is yours—your private memories. It's more or less an accident I resemble anyone in those memories. I'm not about to intrude. If he's got a soul, Ball will have to answer for what happened between you. I'm just here to retrieve him and get him out of your life. Fair enough?"

She heaved a deep sigh. "You might as well know. I'm in love with a goddamned cyborg. There, I've said it! Even if he *was* pretending to be you. I have no shame left, it seems. I suppose you find this all amusing, in some way."

"He had no right—"

"Stop! Don't get self-righteous on me. I *gave* him the right. Even when I more than half suspected he was just a progue. Like he said, the truth was rather more complicated. I have to figure out how to live with this—and I will. He was trapped, poor baby. Trying to figure out how to escape without involving you directly. Afraid he'd get you hurt, or killed, like he did his partner. He thought he had to get me . . . bonded . . . is the term he used, to get my help. A stranger, you see—use and discard, as needed." Her voice went slightly hoarse. "Well, it worked. I *am* bonded—probably for life. The discard part is going to hurt. Bad. But that's my problem. Not yours, as you say."

"You already had plans to extract him?"

She nodded. "Simple, really. I'm an engineer, you know. And I've got plenty of idle equipment just now. Shifting rock isn't that much different than shifting heavy catches of biomass. Simpler, really, without these infernal currents I have to fight up here. My waldoes are pretty effective within their limited range."

On cue, one of the waldoes showed up with tea. The Pondoro seagoing models seemed to run to the lean and wiry look. He wore a coverall, too.

"Why coveralls?" I said as we sipped our tea.

"Two reasons: one practical, one aesthetic. Practical—the suits help shed salt corrosion and neutralize chemical reactions. I still have to do a lot of reprogramming each winter. Pondoro's seas are a ten for corrosiveness, if Earth's are a one. As for aesthetics—it would drive me crazy to see all these perfect masculine forms walking around minus male equipment. I could design some, of course—don't look so shocked; I'm an excellent engineer—but it wouldn't be right to cost off the alterations to the company. And I'm saving my own money to get the hell off this godforsaken planet. Meantime, I may have to live with it, but I don't have to live with it 'not staring' me in the face. So to speak!"

Time to change the subject. "When do we leave?"

"Whenever you're ready. I can ride up with you. The waldoes will bring up one of the big net lifters. Ball gave me the encrypted coordinates already, so he won't have to activate a beacon. He still was thinking lowest profile. Are you *sure* the hunt is off?"

"I verified that with Pondoro officialdom and the local Commonwealth office before I came. Ball is now under the protection of Ptolemy political asylum. A consular vessel is in orbit waiting for him."

"How in *space* did you arrange that?"

"I didn't. But the point is, the Terran Service hunt is called off. Shall we go?"

It was less than a half hour's flight. She drove. When she took it down among the snow-softened crags, I thought I felt the first frisson of greer-fear. But maybe it was just the location.

"I've been here before."

"Ball said you'd recognize it." She glanced up from the controls. "The canyon where his poor partner was killed by the greer. It's winter. There shouldn't be any greer up here this time of year. But Ball says there are."

She said it matter-of-factly, but my kidneys constricted. I seemed to sense a faint whisper of that deep-voiced chanting of my dreams. But I was probably only replaying the chants I'd heard in this canyon the night I thought I was going to die.

Kathryn spoke into the com, positioning the lifter. It settled like a giant praying mantis, bathing the snow-choked canyon with de-icer beams. Steam boiled hundreds of meters into the sky.

"The weather satellites will home in on that in a heartbeat," she said. "You're *sure* . . ." She seemed suddenly nervous. And so was I. The greer were there, all right—and now they knew we were.

"Nothing is absolutely sure," I said. "But that Ptolemaic consular vessel is up there, too. Watching. I don't think the Service will try anything. Capturing Ball probably isn't worth a shooting war with Ptolemy. Or even a major diplomatic set-to. I hope not anyway."

The lifter launched a slender filament above the rubble. The filament's terminal end blossomed into a vast blue-green canopy that settled like an ancient parachute. In seconds it had molded itself to every jagged contour of the slide.

"Adjust and tuck," Kathryn said tensely. "Calculate required lift."

A flat voice instantly recited a burst of figures.

"We'll get half of it off him in the first haul," she told me. "Haul away!" she told her lifter.

"Are you all right?" I said.

"Of course I'm all right!" But she wasn't: her eyes kept darting over the instruments, out the windscreen, back again. A light dew of perspiration sheened her forehead. I could feel it, too, like the onset of a headache—the beginning of greer-fear.

The lifter eased down canyon. The net line came taut. For a long moment there was no further movement—then the lumpy blue-green mass shifted slightly and began to tumble and undulate through the snowpack beneath its shimmering shroud.

"Release," she said. "Clean up."

The net retracted. A half-dozen robots spilled out of the lifter's maw, swarmed over the remaining rocks and began to heave chunks clear. They wielded smaller individual versions of the lifter's net. Lugged their "catch" away with smooth precision. She had said they were strong; they were. The rock pile dwindled swiftly. A familiar voice spoke out of my 'corder. "That's right, Ramsey. Make such a damn fuss everybody on the damn planet will know where I am."

Kathryn jerked. The car dipped slightly. She swore and caught it. "Who was *that?*"

"Ball," I said. "His real voice."

"As real as any of my voices," he said. In *my* damned voice. "I'm sorry, dear—I forgot."

"Well, forget again!" she snapped. "I'm concentrating here. It's easier if I'm talking to a stranger. Especially since I have 'K.R.' himself right here with me. In the *flesh* this time!"

"Cheap shot, Kathryn." Meekly.

"Ball," I said. "By God, you've found your match, haven't you?"

"Go to hell!" They both spoke at the same time.

I couldn't help it. I began to laugh. A release of tension. Amazingly enough, she joined in. Ball had nothing to say. I laughed harder.

"Go ahead," he said at length, in his own voice. "Live it up while you can. Kathryn! Put the car on auto! Now!"

"What?" she was still laughing. "But—"

"Do it!" A whiplash of command. "The greer—"

And then the terror struck full force.

39

UNADULTERATED TERROR TAKES DIFFERENT INDIVIDUALS IN DIFFERENT ways. Kathryn Kinsella slammed the car into full acceleration at approximately the same instant I thumbed my seat harness release and spun my chair to get at my cased rifle. The collision-avoidance buzzer went off a millisecond later. The autopilot override yanked the car into a steep climb to avoid the cliffs. I hit the rear wall of the cabin with considerable g force.

The car cleared the cliffs in a burst of displaced snow. A near thing. Leveled out and hovered. For a wonder, I didn't seem to have any broken bones this time. But the wind was half knocked out of me, and I was slow unpeeling myself from the deck and getting to my rifle. Aircars and greer-fear just didn't seem to mix very well. Kathryn's hands were locked to the controls. The tendons stood out in her wrists, and her eyes were glued to the windscreen. Shock: she still thought she was in overdrive to a safer place. If the greer-fear was hammering through her brain like it was through mine, no damned wonder. But I'd been here before. I thumbed some cartridges out of my shell belt.

"Safe to proceed," the car said—and released control to her.

The instant acceleration slammed me back against the wall and spilled cartridges rolling and skipping around the cabin.

"Auto overide!" I shouted. "Return to hover!"

"Complying." The car slowed gently. I grabbed my shell belt and scrambled up to my seat.

"Switch controls to this chair."

"Are you *crazy?*" She was coming out of it—sort of. "They'll get us, eat us—wreck us! God!"

I nosed the boat around and back into the canyon.

"Oh my God!" she choked.

Greer were among the waldoes—purple smoke and slashing speed. I saw a robot go down, its coverall ripped right away. Another was smashed headlong into the canyon wall. Each got stolidly back to its feet and took hold of its individual net to drag a boulder away. They still were following orders to dig Ball out. Not programmed for self-defense.

"Stay aloft!" Ball gritted out of my 'corder. "Do *not* put Kathryn at risk!"

I couldn't keep track of the number of greer down there. They seemed everywhere at once. Another robot went down, was slow getting up—something jarred loose. A greer tore its head half off. It went down and stayed down, legs churning slowly in the snow.

"Get them out of there!" I told her.

"Bastards!" she sobbed. "Bastards!"

"Kathryn! Get them *out of there!*"

Another of the robots was having a hard time getting its balance. Two greer flowed around it, obscuring it. It went down under their combined weight.

"Return to lifter!" she screamed. "Return to lifter . . ."

The robots turned as one and trudged toward the lifter as it settled to the canyon floor. A greer flashed toward its open hatch . . .

"Nets away!" she shouted.

There was a blue-green puff and the greer was a

rolling, twisting cocoon. The robots marching toward the gangway paused.

"New program!" She was holding her fists to her temples, rocking back and forth in her seat. "Net the life-forms! Now!"

Two more greer went down, threshing. A third bobbed and weaved with almost supernatural speed and grace. Three of the nets missed. He clobbered the end robot off its feet. Its next-in-line companion turned and netted him neatly as he tore at the supine waldo.

"There! They won't get out of *those*," Kathryn panted, triumphant. "Nothing that swims can tear that mesh . . . Oh!"

The greer-fear was back, redoubled. We were trapped in this enclosed space—they would get us! We had to get out, run, run like the wind . . . I gritted my teeth and rode it out. For the moment I forgot Kathryn. It was enough.

Eyes wide and glaring, mouth open in a silent scream, she lurched against the controls and switched off the car's engines.

In the sudden stillness I heard the angry caterwauling of her captives. . . .

The car fell. The seats flipped back to crash position. My stomach tried to crawl out my gullet. "Switch on—" was all I got out before we hit. Hard. And at an awkward angle on the uneven ground. I bit a hole in my tongue. My whole mouth went numb. I wondered distantly how many teeth were cracked. No time to worry about it. More greer would be coming. . . .

I somehow got out of the seat, found my rifle, fed a couple cartridges. I was moving as if underwater . . . and suddenly my nightmare was back, that doleful chanting as I tried to swim toward the hatch. Kathryn was twisted half off the crash pad, her neck twisted at an impossible angle. There was blood all over her face. Her eyes stared at nothing.

The car rocked—a flickering shadow on the windscreen. A greer was clawing deep gouges in the tough material. I worked a round into the chamber.

"Status?" Ball. "Dammit, Ramsey, I can't hear Kathryn's respiration!"

"She's not breathing," I said. "I think the fall broke her neck—"

"Nooooo . . ." Even hammered by the greer-fear, that awful sound tore at me.

Past the shoulder of the beast on the windscreen, the remaining rock pile . . . erupted.

Ball burst into view, cascading dust and pebbles. Flashed toward us at hallucinatory speed. The boat slammed and rocked under the impact. Dark blood sprayed the starred screen dark. The greer slid away. I dimly heard scrabbling claws. Then more of those horrific blows I had heard when Ball smacked a greer in the fight at LaChoy's camp. A single long bleat of hopeless pain. The greer-fear went away in a rush.

"It's done," Ball said. "They've stopped. They know I'm free and there's nothing they can do about it. Open up! Get her out here to me!"

I released her webbing, popped the hatch and lugged her out. Knelt and eased her into the snow. My hands were instantly numb. I was bleeding all over her. My teeth were chattering. Ball hovered above her. Chill metallic sphere touched chilling flesh.

"What the hell are you doing to her?"

"Injecting her. Chilling her down. Slowing the brain-cell decay. She's clinical."

The same term he had used when Baka Martin came crawling out of the night, savaged by greer. What seemed a lifetime ago. I knelt there bleeding on the snow and couldn't seem to make my mind work. My pulse was thudding in my ears. Then, subtly, the throb altered, began to take on the rhythms of my nightmare.

"Don't fight it!" Ball said sharply. "They're not going to attack."

I plodded back toward the car and my rifle. The chanting was clear now in my brain. They were coming again. I was surprised Ball couldn't hear it.

"I can," he said. "What's more, I can interpret for you. Partially. I've begun to decode their language."

"Language?" I paused in the hatchway. "What language? They're predators, Ball. That's *all*."

"That was *never* all," he said. "Listen to me now. For once in your sorry life. I've taken over her waldoes—they'll put her in the lifter and we'll take her back to her station. There's a Medfac there. I'll be back for you."

"You're leaving me *here*?"

"I'll be back. As soon as I have her stabilized. You have nothing more to fear from the greer."

"Easy for you to say!"

I fumbled rounds into my rifle. Pulled on my new parka. When I emerged again, the robots were taking Kathryn into the lifter. Ball hovered by the gangway.

"You look the part," he said coldly. "Brave Neolithic in the skin of his trophy. Firestick in hand. Maybe they will kill you, after all. Maybe I'll let them. You should have protected her."

He disappeared up the gangway behind the robots. The lifter went up instantly, gone from sight in a heartbeat. I sealed my parka shut and started trying to shiver myself warm. Lavender shadows were reaching across the canyon floor. The netted greer all had stopped struggling and screaming. Waiting. One of the greer Ball had zapped twitched and snuffled in his sleep. The wrecked robot's legs still crawled and marched in place. That sonorous chanting was louder, closer. I shook my head to try to clear it. Belatedly, I realized the chanting now was actual sound in the canyon. It resonated with the rhythmic pounding inside my aching skull and woke doleful echoes from this frozen hell.

Anne had been premature to worry about Ptolemy killing me. It looked like Pondoro was going to have one last crack at it.

40

"CAN YOU FLY?" I ASKED THE RENTAL CAR.

"Flight is not authorized at this time."

"What the *hell* are you talking about?"

"I am the second vehicle you have damaged on Pondoro. Your atypic robot damaged personal property of LaChoy Enterprises. The Insurance Consortium has canceled rental privileges pending a review."

The chanting grew louder, filling the canyon. Many voices, harsh and strong. I was braced in the open hatch, trying to look everywhere at once. The greer were coming for me. And making no secret of it this time. They were in my brain; the pounding there synchronized perfectly with their voices. There was no denying the compelling demand in that summons. They wanted something fiercely—wanted it *right now*—but what?

"What the hell happened," I asked the car, "to Asimovian ideals on this rotten pigsty of a planet? The prime law of robotics: not to permit a human to come to harm?"

"*Your* driving," was the prim response, "resulted in harm to a human. The passenger's death. My company is not at fault. The Travel Authority Police have been notified. A patrol unit has been dispatched. You are not to leave the immediate vicinity—"

"You've *got* to fly me out of here. Now!"

"Flight is not authorized."

"Are you *hearing* this, Ball? Goddamn you! Override this piece of junk's programming and get me *out* of here."

When I looked downcanyon, the greer were there. Seven of them. All large, full-furred, in their prime. Not attacking. Not running full-tilt. Just there, as if they had materialized on the snow. They crouched motionless in a rough semicircle maybe a hundred meters away. Their voices were almost deafening. I scrambled into the car and looked upcanyon. Not a single greer up there. But there was no way I could outrun them.

"Ball . . ."

"*Listen* to them, Ramsey!" His voice, speaking out of my 'corder. "Listen to them. Listen to me. I will interpret. *Answer* them. Hurry! The local satellites already are reporting an anomalous greer formation to the Hunt Commission. Given what happened at LaChoy's camp, the locals will be all over you. Very soon now. And of course they're still terrified at the thought of the sybil getting loose into the greer population."

I had thought I was as scared as I could get. I had been wrong.

"Is *that* what this is? The sybil is loose again?"

"Absolutely not! This is an alien indigenous intelligence, demanding what's theirs by right. I told you, I've begun to decode their language."

The seven remained motionless, their voices rising and harmonizing in a stunning clarity. That peculiar mental power of theirs, linked and focused, seemed intent on sucking my identity out of my brain. My head swam; my legs were rubbery. I couldn't take much more of this. My rifle held six rounds. A hundred meters. If I could break that smothering lethargy, I might get off two head shots before they broke formation and charged. I didn't even know if the damned car would shut the door for me! My vision seemed to blur—probably from the bashing I'd taken in the car. I snicked off the safety. If I got the pack's leader, they *might* turn tail.

"No!" Ball's voice thundered out of my 'corder, momentarily drowning out the greer.

"No, what?"

"Don't shoot. Have you forgotten my empathometer? I know you're about to try it. Do *not* shoot! *Listen* to them."

"How the hell can I *not* listen to them—"

"Moron! Throwback! They want to know how that old boar died. The one who saved your sorry ass! *They need something to tell his cubs!*"

"Tell his cubs?"

I couldn't fully comprehend his words through that awful pressure. It was all I could do to hold the central greer in the scope sight. I could see his jaws move in unison to the sounds cascading over me. It seemed we made eye contact. He knew I had him cold. His gaze didn't waver. His chant didn't falter.

"They know you trailed that old boar to his death. Tell them what happened!"

"He drowned," I said. "Far up the mountains. After you stopped talking to me. He was infected with the sybil. It hurt him. He didn't like it. So he drowned himself in a frozen pool."

"Strong emotional content!" he said. "Excellent! Kathryn fed me all your news stories. I know what you saw. But tell it now. Simple words. *See* it again—and so will they. Hold those images—hold them hard. You were his only witness to his last and finest hunt."

"The pool was frozen over. . . ."

Just like that, the image of that forlorn pool formed

behind my eyes: the scarred and wounded old beast gathering himself for the fatal plunge.

"He killed the beast that killed Martin—and became infected. . . ."

"Excellent! Excellent! I have some of them chipped now. They're getting this. *They understand.*"

The chanting stopped. Just stopped. Echoes rolled far up the canyon and back, and chased themselves to silence. I stood braced in the door, rifle down, for what seemed a long time. My brain seemed to bulge and contract within my skull to the vanished rhythm of that primal baying. With each contortion a new image formed, clear and vivid. The linked and entwined images of that long pursuit from LaChoy's camp: Baka Martin's ravaged features, his dead body sealed to the greer that killed him; my abortive attempts to kill his killer; my terror as the sybil-crazed beast had crouched above me—and the vicious unseen single combat of greer against greer.

Over and above it all, that stunning final act: the old boar's destruction of the sybil in the only way it could.

Gradually, my throbbing brain quieted and I became aware of my surroundings again.

The seven greer were gone.

The canyon was in shadow now. Much colder. My mouth still was numb. My tongue hurt like fury, but it had stopped bleeding. The damaged waldo's legs still churned uselessly where it had fallen. It had dug itself into a snowy grave. There was one dead greer sprawled on the bloodied snow in front of the car. A frozen sheen of black-purple blood coated the front of the vehicle. Where the netted greer had fallen, struggling, and then paused to watch when the chanting began, all that remained were blue-green shreds scattered on the snow. Greer evidently were a tougher catch than whatever swam Pondoro's seas.

"Ball?"

"Returning now," he said. "I've called off the Insurance Consortium and the traffic cop. Never mind how. The Hunt Commission will be along to pick up any carcasses. They won't begin to understand what happened, so don't even try to tell them. They won't believe it, after LaChoy's camp, but they'll have to accept it was just a rogue pack interfering with a human couple out for a winter picnic, when it should have been perfectly safe."

"That's not what this was! Is Kathryn . . . ?"

"On her way to Central Receiving. She will live."

"But what?"

"What do you mean?"

"I hear something in your voice. Some—emotion?"

"You are unnerved from your latest greer encounter. Which, I must say, you handled admirably. Once you steadied down to it. You gave them what they need, somehow, to hold their culture together."

"I have? What have I given them?"

"A story, storyteller. The story of that old boar's final hunt. Their whole culture appears to revolve around a ritual of facing death properly—always with a witness. An oral historian. This old boar who drowned himself will be their archetypal hero for as long as they sing."

"You call what they do *singing?*"

"Don't be homocentric. *They* call it singing. They knew somehow that Martin threatened them—we may never know how they knew. They knew we were partnered. And somehow that old boar intuited the sybil, long before it got him. That boar was—had to be—a change mutant. He somehow puzzled out our entire scheme—impossible as that is to believe—and marshaled all the greer to stop us."

The big net-lifter appeared above the canyon rim, bright in the slanting sunlight. It dropped in beside the balky rental car, and two waldoes trudged out to retrieve their fallen fellow. Ball drifted over to me.

"So," I said, "you're telling me this avalanche was no accident? And that you didn't pull it in behind you as a way to hide from your boss?"

"That old boar laid a trap here, and baited it with my partner. A singular beast. Extraordinary."

"But he's dead. How did they know I'd come here to get you?"

"Well, that's no mystery," he said. "Once I decoded simple concepts in their language, and grasped what they wanted, I managed to convey to them that you would be along. And then told Kathryn to send for you."

"Why?"

"My Terran Service oath. An oath, strangely, that I cannot even remember taking—which is immaterial. To protect humanity from harm, and to protect the helpless from humanity. Our machinations destroyed their principal leader. Sent their culture into shock. It was my duty to ensure his sacrifice accomplished his purpose."

"Noble. Your nobility got Kathryn killed."

"Unfair!" That—something—was in his voice again. "She will live. She will be perfectly fine."

"But . . . ?"

"A minor thing. Short-term memory fades first when a brain goes clinical. She probably won't remember me."

41

BLAISE LACHOY DID NOT LOSE HIS GUIDING LICENSE. PONDORO DID NOT lose Freehold status. Under color of Ptolemy's newly granted political asylum, Ball chose to testify before a Pondoro court of inquiry. His decision resulted in an economic boomlet for the off-season. Anne Starr was in a foul mood about her beat being usurped by inner-world media celebrities, but held her own. Pondoro officials were bucolic, but not dumb. They knew she still would be there to cover their activities after their brief supernova in the interstellar media. So they kept her liberally supplied with scoop material. She was the one who revealed Ball had agreed to testify.

The inquiry judge selected Pondoro Parliament chambers for the hearing, in order to seat as many as possible. Given Pondoro shape-prejudice, their architects had never thought to design ceremonial doors wide enough to permit Ball ingress. He solved the problem neatly and dramatically. It was raining hard in Firstport the morning he came to testify. At the appointed hour, a vast skylight above the speaker's dais rolled back. Rain flooded in—and puffed into steam before it touched varnished wood or leather. Quite a show—and then Ball drifted down through the hissing clouds and hung quiescent before the judge on the high dais.

The crowd, for all its collective cynicism, was momentarily silent.

It might have been some ancient tableau: alien life descends to confront humanity.

The skylight was back in place. Ventilation around the high domed ceilings whisked the steam and moisture away.

"Your Honor," Ball said in carrying tones, "I presume we can dispense with raising my right hand—since I have no hands."

The room erupted into laughter. The judge slapped a husher-button. Suddenly it was quiet again.

"Are you trying to be objectionable?" she said levelly.

"Don't have to try," he responded breezily. "It's built right in,"

"I'm inclined," she said in a dangerous voice, "to test the limits of your new diplomatic immunity for this openly contemptuous behavior."

A tall form rose gracefully in the first row of spectators. "Conrad of Pirsig," he said politely. He was in an unadorned uniform today, but no less noticeable. "I see you, Barbara of Firstport. Ptolemy of course welcomes all tests."

"My name is Your Honor," she said. "In this room."

"No." Gently. "That is your rank. Your reputation is spotless. Too fine to demonstrate regrettable annoyance at the posturings of a *cyborg*." He placed a delicate twist on the final word.

"Are you this—cyborg's—counsel?"

"Should he need such—yes."

The special prosecutor probably saw his chance to nail the Commonwealth slipping away in typical courtroom bickering. He was on his feet.

"Permission to approach, Your Honor?"

While he and Conrad muttered at the dais, Ball, for a wonder, said nothing. He had made his point—

on the record and very publicly—that he was solidly under Ptolemy's protection. Another slap at his former boss. And of course he was planning his next surprise.

Having settled whose urine-holding this was, the judge gestured for Ball's testimony to begin. The special prosecutor walked Ball through it. His status as a Terran Service op, his orders regarding Pondoro, the role Baka Martin had played. I was flattered to note the government cribbed whole lines of inquiry from my early news breaks.

Ball testified as to the fact of his partner's sybil infection—confirmed he had been a symbiote during the games when he killed Fennec—but declined to discuss any other assignments the two had shared prior to Pondoro. He verified his orders from the Executive had been to permit Martin to sacrifice himself to the greer to release the sybil on Pondoro. It was all old news after my original stories—but on the official record this time. Then the prosecutor asked why the Executive had decided to release the sybil here. The Executive must have had some use in mind for the infected predators, he said. That cover story about rescuing an intelligent but primitive race from human oppression was, of course, utter propaganda.

Some of the media types shifted in their seats. They weren't so sure it *was* propaganda. But the hotter story was the tweaking of the Executive, so they would let that go. Ah, journalism! When Ball began to speak again, they immediately forgot the smallest qualm.

"The Blocked Worlds," said Ball. "She planned to mount new expeditions into the Blocked Worlds. Using sybil-enhanced greer on point, instead of humans. Controlled by cybernetic organisms in my mold. A combination of the most primitive and the most advanced. It is a matter of record that even Survey-trained bipeds almost succumbed to the sybil, and nearly released it upon an unsuspecting humanity."

That wasn't old news. The rows of correspondents whispered heatedly into their 'corders. Anne, too. She never glanced at me the whole time of his testimony. Kathryn Kinsella, on the other hand, winked at me from the public galleries right in the middle of it. Fully recovered from her death experience, she had been making eyes at me since my return from that frozen canyon.

I wondered if Ball was telling the truth about the Blocked Worlds. Not that it mattered. He had dealt his erstwhile boss another heavy blow in front of an assembly of media whose reach encompassed civilized space. Within sidereal hours there would be opinion polls running on a thousand planets to question her audacity at daring to mount a secret expedition to the Blocked Worlds. Whether that had ever been her intent or not.

Barbara of Firstport called a half-hour recess after Ball was done. Most of the big-time media began packing up. Anything after this would be anticlimactic. They'd be chasing this new angle for weeks. A lot of the gallery hung around to watch Ball's departure. I stopped him at the dais.

"So you're going to Ptolemy?"

"I am," he said. "With Conrad. We lift in three hours. I'm done here. I will see you there?"

"Unless my ship drops into the Lost Dimension." I still didn't like space travel. "Nice trick about the Blocked Worlds."

"Always have a hole card. I thought of it while

playing endless hands of poker with my A.I. during my late inconvenience."

"A bald-faced lie, then?"

"Ramsey, clean up your language. I don't *have* a face."

"The hell you don't. You use mine just any old time you feel like it. Goddamn it, Kathryn's recent memory is all hashed up. All she remembers is luscious sex with me!"

"You made a lasting impression, then. Beyond the death of the organism, engraved upon her immortal soul. Don Juan to the galaxy."

"You are a monster."

"No. I am a cyborg, and you're a throwback. A Neanderthal with romantic pretensions."

"You're the one who launched that goddamned erotic progue, aren't you?"

"No. That was all the Executive's doing. She didn't like your taking my part in this. A subtle revenge. There will come a time when you wonder where you leave off and the progue begins—or if there is such a demarcation. And so will many, many others. Given Anne Starr's feature story about your time in quarantine, and the progue, you will find you have developed a whole new loyal fandom." He made that laughing sound. "A rest cure on Ptolemy may well be just what you need at this point."

"There's *got* to be a way to stop this!"

"I disagree. Even should the Commonwealth itself outlaw use of the progue, that would only make it more valuable. More sought-after."

"You chipped me long before we left for Pondoro, didn't you?"

"Of course."

"And supplied early data to the Terran Service."

"Just so. Unfortunate. If I had my life—call it a life—to live over, I would not do it now. I have learned too much here—or perhaps remembered too much—about the fragility of human emotion."

"Remembered?"

"A manner of speech. My brain originated somewhere. Why not scooped out of a thinking, feeling adult?"

"My God. Would they *do* that?"

"Why not? Perhaps I even volunteered. Given what I have learned here about the sting of emotion, and knowing how my brain works, I wouldn't be surprised."

Conrad of Pirsig approached with stately tread. "We should be going." He bowed to me.

"Yes," Ball said.

"What about Kathryn?" I asked him.

"Treat her with kindness," Ball said. "She will find she has her little adventure with 'K.R.' filed electronically, of course. But she doesn't remember that now. It may be that she will desire you in the flesh. I leave that decision strictly up to you."

"Thanks a whole hell of a lot!"

The skylight slid back, the rain rushed in and vaporized, and Ball left as he had come. The room seemed larger, and emptier. Anne Starr shut off her 'corder and met me at the rear of the room.

"Victory on all fronts," she said. "Pondoro has been good to you. And would continue to be, if you stayed. But you're still determined to go to Ptolemy, aren't you?"

"They've got my curiosity up. Why not come with me?"

"That's sweet. But no. Tanner says I'm next in line for a sector correspondent slot. Lots of interesting stuff going on out here. Don't get killed out there! And keep an eye out for my byline?"

"Always," I said. "You never told me why we say thirty."

She smiled and traced my chin with her fingertip. "You could look it up. Or Ball could."

"No. I'll wait for you to tell me. One of these days."

"One of these days, I may."

Kathryn was waiting in the rotunda. "Been a whirlwind few days, hasn't it? Busted waldoes, busted memories, a busted *neck*, for crying out loud."

"I'm really glad you're all right," I said.

"Hmmm. Physically intact again, yes. As to all right, I'd have to think about it. Buy a girl a drink? What were we doing on a picnic in greer country? Were you romancing me?"

"Well—what do you remember?"

She blushed, and I remembered our first meeting on her station's pier. "Some things—just vivid, vivid flashes." She linked her arm in mine. "Maybe you can fill in a few of the blank spots for me before you skip this sorry world. I *hate* to think I missed anything."

I could be Ball's chronicler, Conrad had said. I doubted this was precisely what he'd had in mind. Still . . .

"Why not?" I said. "Why the hell not?"

42

THE DAYFIRE LINGERED SLIGHTLY LONGER IN ITS ARC ACROSS THE BIG Wet. The rains had come at last to the dry southernmost peninsula on the continent of the greer.

Bright flowers bloomed among the burgeoning grasses. Plains game waxed fat and lazy, and the hunt was good.

The Orange Claw cubs, sighted now, rolled and tumbled in mock combat along the beach, their baby fur matted with sand.

"Thy cubs are strong and healthy," DiTenka said with delight.

"Too strong," their mother replied with feigned severity. "They wear me down with their constant scampers,"

"The dayfire climbs the sky a little higher each day. Not long now and the herds will be restless for the migration. Then we will see if Two-Legs returns again to share our Way with us."

"They must! Else Sunto hunted in vain."

"The song of the Two-Legs hunter who bore his final witness was strong and sure. That unkillable dayfire ball sang to us! And went away. Sunto did not hunt in vain."

"And thou," she said. "Thou fashioned a singing unlike any ever known to ease this troubled belly. The hahns will sing thou to the spirit pool this summer."

"It cannot be! This one is a singer among singers—

but not the leader Sunto was. Far better Aland—or even thy Eren Gaino chieftain."

"Thou it will be," she said calmly. "My male cub has seen it. Thou, crouching at the pool to call the hahns."

"He is too young—

"He is Orange Claw. Bred true."

"A *singer* to keep the pool?"

"Who better? Sunto always called thy song sweetest and most true. Long before the Orange Claw power grew out of the poisoned wind, our songs bound us through all the dayfires to those who hunted long ago beneath the Lake of Light. Thy new strange song gave Sunto back to me, to sing these cubs strong and worthy of their birthright."

"Thy cubs are too young to digest such things as the meaning of the pool!"

"This we shall see—if they are too young—when dayfire climbs into its summer home, and the hahns consider the question of who shall keep the pool."

"This one is not a mountain hunter!"

"Nor was this one. But learned it from old Orange Claw. And can teach. Orange Claw cubs should roam Orange Claw mountains. We will share thy lonely watches."

DiTenka stared off across the Big Wet, impassive. "Heavy thinking you feed this belly to digest."

"There is time," she said serenely. "Time now to digest many things. The evil is past."

"Not past," the singer amended. "But gone somewhere else to hunt."

WILLIAM R. BURKETT, JR., 54, is a native of Georgia who grew up in Neptune Beach, Florida, and began writing when at age fourteen he was given an ancient Smith-Corona typewriter. His first science-fiction novel, *Sleeping Planet*, was published in *ANALOG* magazine when he was 20, and subsequently published in hardcover and paperback in the U.S. and abroad.

On the strength of being a published writer, he was promoted to reporter at the *Florida Times-Union* in Jacksonville, Florida, beginning a career in journalism which led him from the Bahamas to Pennsylvania to the state of Washington. He continued to write creatively, and had some fiction and nonfiction magazine sales. But he found journalism a beguiling mistress, due to the twin incentives of a steady paycheck and seeing his byline on page one.

In 1978 he left journalism for public relations, and was a public information officer for three different state agencies in Arizona and Washington State. He edited a monthly tabloid for the Arizona Game and Fish Department, which "required" him to spend days on end out in the wilds with a gun or fishing rod, doing research. In Washington, he headed up a negotiating team which settled major litigation between the state and local Indian tribes over tribal sales of untaxed liquor. And he won a Clio, a Telly, and other writing awards for TV commercials which promoted traffic safety.

He left state service in 1993 and returned to full-time fiction writing. *Bloodsport* is his second science-fiction novel. He has two grown children, Beau and Heather. He and his wife, Wanda, live in the small logging community of Buckley, Washington with a cranky cat and a gun-shy Lab retriever.